The Price of Freedom

In Library

CAROL UMBERGER

INTEGRITY®
PUBLISHERS
Nashville

THE PRICE OF FREEDOM

Copyright © 2003 by Carol Umberger.
Published by Integrity Publishers, a division of Integrity Media, Inc.
5250 Virginia Way, Suite 110, Brentwood, TN 37027.

HELPING PEOPLE WORLDWIDE EXPERIENCE *the* MANIFEST PRESENCE *of* GOD.

Published in association with the literary agency of
Alive Communications, Inc., 7680 Goddard Street,
Suite 200, Colorado Springs, Colorado, 80920.

Cover design: David Uttley
Interior: Inside Out Design & Typesetting

Library of Congress Cataloging-in-Publication Data

Umberger, Carol
  The price of freedom / by Carol Umberger.
    p. cm. — (The Scottish crown series)
  ISBN 1-59145-006-3
  1. Scotland—History—War of Independence, 1285–1371—Fiction.
    I. Title.
PS3621.M35 P7 2002
813'.6–dc21

                                                    2002038834

Printed in Canada
03 04 05 06 07 08 TCP 9 8 7 6 5 4 3 2 1

DEDICATION

To Tom,
whose steadfast heart is my delight.

ACKNOWLEDGMENTS

So many people contribute to the success of a writer's career through their encouragement, support, and expertise. With each newly published book, my list grows. My heartfelt thanks to the following people:

Rick and the wonderful, talented staff at Alive. Thank you for seeing the potential and nurturing it. Special thanks to Linda, lunch buddy, friend, and fellow servant. And to Lee, for picking up the ball and running with it.

Joey Paul at Integrity, who I admire as a publisher and as an example of Christian faith in action. And to the rest of the hard-working, incredibly talented team at Integrity who have performed marvelous things for me and for the Lord we serve. Special thanks to Rob Birkhead and David Uttley for the gorgeous book covers.

Khrys Williams and Lori Sly for reading the manuscript and making countless helpful suggestions. And for listening to me whine. Keep writing—dreams do come true!

Lisa Tawn Bergren, a wonderful writer and editor who makes my manuscripts infinitely better with her wisdom and insight. You made my stories shine.

And always, thanks and gratitude to God for the gift, for showing me how to use it, and for putting all these special people in my life.

PROLOGUE

BRYAN MACKINTOSH TENSED as Lady Christian of Carrick approached her friend and monarch, Robert the Bruce of Scotland, warning filling her face. The brave noblewoman had brought fifteen mounted men and the promise of money and supplies to aid Scotland's beleaguered king. But along with the help clearly came dreadful news.

Tentatively, Bruce exited the cave and reached out both his hands in welcome.

Taking Bruce's hands the lady said quietly, "My king. Elizabeth and the others have been captured."

Bruce recoiled as if the woman had struck him. His family, taken! "When? How?" he demanded.

Bryan closed his eyes, listening in growing agitation as Lady Christian continued. Were they alive? Or already beheaded? "The Earl of Ross—may he and his Comyn masters rot for eternity— seized them when they sought sanctuary at St. Duthac's chapel."

Bruce raised a hand to his brow. "O, God. What have I done?"

Lady Christian laid a hand on his arm, her expression echoing Bruce's pain. "You did the only thing you could, dear friend."

After the Scottish army's defeat at the battle of Methven, no place within reach of Edward of England was safe. He had declared the

1

wives and children of all the Scottish rebels to be outlaws. No man would be punished for harming or even killing them.

Robert the Bruce had wisely taken his wife, daughter, and two sisters under his immediate protection. But when the women had nearly been captured at Dalry Pass, Bruce sent them north to his younger brother Nigel at Kildrummy Castle. They hadn't made it.

The men all listened intently as Lady Christian continued. "There is more, I fear. Kildrummy has also been captured." Looking to where Bruce's brother Edward sat, she swallowed hard and said, "Your brother Nigel died on England's gallows."

"Dear God, no," Edward cried out. He jumped up and paced before them. "No!"

Bruce put his other hand to his head, pushing back his stiff, brown hair, his face ashen. Pain radiated from him, a physical, living thing that stole the breath from Bryan's own lungs. Although their blood ties were never mentioned, the Bruce family was his own. Nigel, the king's youngest brother, had been everyone's favorite . . . he had always treated Bryan with warmth . . .

Many of the men hastily crossed themselves, but Bryan did not join them. How could they continue to believe in a God that would allow such a good man to die such a terrible death? And where had he been when Bruce's loved ones called out to him for safekeeping?

James Douglas—the youngest of Bruce's knighted men— asked, "What of the women, my lady? Surely the butcher Edward spared them?"

Lady Christian again searched Bruce's face, as if to find the least painful way to deliver her words. "The king's sisters are displayed in wooden cages, high on the battlements of Berwick and Roxborough Castles. They are to hang there indefinitely, exposed to the elements and the gazes of passersby."

Bruce roared in impotent fury, striking the air with his fists.

A tremor coursed through Bryan at Edward of England's mindless cruelty and the hatred that fueled it. Known as the Hammer of the Scots, Edward I had wrested the throne of Scotland away from its rightful owner some twelve years ago. Rebellion had ensued, and Edward used an increasingly heavy hand in his attempts to subdue his northern neighbors.

Bryan cleared his throat, fearful that in his anguish, his adolescent voice would betray him. "And what . . . what of the king's daughter, young Princess Marjory?" Bryan immediately glanced at Bruce, who dared to meet Lady Christian's eyes once more, dread in his own.

Tears dripped down the lady's face as she said, "The young princess lives in a similar cage, suspended from the walls of the Tower of London."

Someone gasped. "What sort of monster would treat a child so?"

Bruce sank to his knees and Bryan dropped down beside him, head in his hands, his despair and anger at God deepening. Even young Marjory had not been spared! His half-sister! All but twelve years of age . . . Bryan had seen comrades in arms fall on the battle-field, known fine men who were hanged for their loyalties to the Bruce, but this! Innocents, all, treated like savage animals.

"You have not told me of my wife," Bruce stated, his voice strained, eyes still on the ground. An expectant silence fell, because they all knew of Bruce's fierce devotion to Elizabeth de Burgh.

Lady Christian shook her head. "She is being held in solitary confinement somewhere in England. That is all that is known."

Beaten at last, Bruce's shoulders shook with sobs.

Lady Christian knelt and hugged Bruce fiercely. "I'm so sorry, Robert," she murmured. "I thought it best you heard this from a friend." She looked over at Bryan, imploring him with her eyes. Feeling queasy himself at the news, Bryan rose and helped the king to his feet. A knot formed in Bryan's throat, choking him as he felt a portion of Robert's pain. The women were undoubtedly in danger, suffering. Everything in him told him to go, fight for their freedom! What madness was it that kept armed men from defending their women? It was impossible!

Robert the Bruce drew away from them by a few paces, pinched the bridge of his nose and took a deep breath, struggling for control.

"Is there any other news?" Bruce asked.

"Nay, Robert," the lady said quietly.

Bruce turned and to a man, Bryan's companions strode forward to stand at the ready for him. "I thank you Lady Christian, for risking your own safety to bring me word of my family." The king stopped, still clearly struggling with his emotions. "God bless you for your bravery and speed you safely home." She hugged him, and Edward accompanied Lady Christian to her horse.

Bruce watched her leave with her escort. Bryan stepped forward to try to offer comfort but Bruce waved him off. "I need some time alone," he said. Head bowed, the king of Scotland walked into the cave where they'd been hiding for the past two weeks. Despite their recent success in capturing Turnberry Castle, Bruce and the spare remnants of his army had retreated to the glens of the wild hill country where Bruce had spent his childhood. Today's news did not bode well for the war against England.

EDWARD RETURNED and started to approach Bruce, but Bryan shook his head. "Leave him be," he said quietly. Edward surprised him by turning and sitting back down—as shocked as Bryan to see Robert in such despair. The king walked farther into the gloomy recess of the cave while Bryan and Edward sat by the fire.

As the men repeated the news among themselves, Bryan tried to absorb what he had heard. The circumstances of his birth and his service as Bruce's squire during the recent bloodshed with England had combined to mature him beyond his sixteen years. But any man, no matter his age and experience, might well break under the weight of Lady Christian's tidings.

Nigel was dead and Bruce's womenfolk were, by and large, gone. At any moment, they could all be beheaded or die from exposure to the elements. All of them just out of his reach. All of them!

In an attempt to bring his swirling emotions under control, Bryan held his shaking hands toward the flames. The fire did little to lessen the damp interior of the cave or the chill in his heart. And it did nothing to lighten Bryan's spirits as he studied the small band of knights and common soldiers gathered around the meager fire.

Would they all meet the fate of William Wallace, once the great leader of the Scottish resistance? After being dragged by horses over four miles of cobblestones, Wallace was hanged, but cut down while half-strangled and still alive. Finally, mercifully, he'd been beheaded. His body was then hacked into four pieces and dispatched to the four corners of Edward's kingdom as a warning to any who would defy him.

Edward of England's treatment of Wallace two years prior was meant to make an example of the rebellious Scot, but instead his heavy hand had created a martyr. No man deserved such a death, and Bryan's hatred of all things English intensified with the memory of William's fate. His stomach took a sickening turn as he relived that day in London. With a shudder, he brought himself back to the present, fighting for courage, fighting for the belief that ultimately, right would prevail.

THEY ALL CONTINUED TO STARE into the fire, each lost in his own thoughts. Finally Douglas put their greatest fear into words when he said, "Will Bruce surrender, then?"

"I don't know. A lesser man certainly would." Bryan wished he could offer more hope, but how could any man recover from such unthinkable horror?

"A time like this makes me glad I have no wife or kin to be used so shamefully," James Douglas said.

Bryan glanced at his companions, whose faces registered varying degrees of dismay at this admission.

"Sorry, lads." Red-faced, Douglas apologized. "I shall pray for the safety of your loved ones."

Bryan nodded. "No need for apology, James. You echo our own fears. And though I sympathize with the others, I share your sentiment." With everything in him, Bryan swore never to allow himself to be vulnerable to such matters of the heart, nor to be shaken from his devotion to king and country. Head bowed, heart shattered by his own grief and that of his king's, Bryan made a solemn vow. *I will not take a wife until Scotland is free.* Stunned by the intensity of his oath, Bryan hesitated before looking up.

"We must do something," Edward muttered. "We can't just sit here and let the lassies suffer."

A murmur of assent echoed Bryan's longing, yet he knew there was little to be done. Bruce had but a half dozen accoutered knights, little money, and few mounted troops beyond those the lady had just brought. Bryan could not foresee a time when Scotland would be able to match the heavy cavalry or siege machinery of the English forces. And this helplessness must surely be agonizing for the king.

"For now the only thing we can do is evade capture ourselves," Bryan told them. "And we'll be hard pressed to stay out of Edward of England's grasp. Our people are so cowed by his atrocities they dare not lift a hand to help us."

"Aye, and we've a price on our heads to encourage treachery," Douglas reminded them.

Bryan poked a stick at the fire. No one spoke for several minutes.

"I fear our king has lost heart," someone said. Those words echoed Bryan's trepidation, and no one spoke into the silence that followed.

AFTER A TIME, Robert walked out of the depths of the cave and joined them at the mouth, his face haggard from the time spent in solitude, no doubt wrestling with private demons. He accepted the seat Bryan offered.

The king waved aside the men's assurances and offers of sympathy with brusque words of gratitude. For a moment, Bruce's gaze held his, and Bryan saw a spark of life had returned to this incredible man's spirit. The pain was still there, but determination had settled around him like a well-worn plaid.

"We will fight," Robert said with quiet resolve.

"Of course we will," his brother said.

"We feared you would lose heart," Douglas ventured.

"Aye, I came close, very close," Robert answered. His voice grew stronger. "But an amazing sight came to me as I stared at the wall this past hour. I watched one of God's tiny creatures, a spider weaving its web, and for a while I forgot my misery."

Every man focused on the king as he continued. "The spider tried to attach its thread to a rock below the web. Seven times it launched into the air and missed, then climbed back up to begin the process again. On the eighth try, it succeeded. God seems far away at a time like this, but if we persevere, he will reward us. Just as he rewarded the spider."

Bryan wasn't so sure God was close at hand but marveled at the way this renowned warrior could captivate the attention of men as diverse as these. The sheer force of his will and his ability to articulate his vision for their future had garnered their loyalty and devotion in the first place. Now, from the ashes of his own despair, he wove a tale, no doubt strengthening his resolve as he replenished theirs.

Edward Bruce stood. "We can be ready to ride at first light."

"We must be patient, brother."

Edward scowled and Robert said, "I do not doubt your willingness to fight. And though our cause is just, the English have superior weapons and numbers. We cannot best them unless we play to our strengths. We must ambush the enemy, raid in the dark of night, raze captured fortresses."

As though to ensure his message was clear, Robert searched each man's face. "Like the spider who fits his web to the space it finds itself in, we will learn ways to fight that take advantage of terrain and circumstances. I will never give up until Scotland is free of this tyrant's rule. No matter the cost, I will pay it, until we are free men once more."

Relief flooded Bryan. He would rather die himself than give in to a man as cruel and despicable as Edward of England.

But offering one's own life was not the same as sacrificing your loved ones. Robert the Bruce had picked up the gauntlet after Wallace's death, struggling to unite the Scottish nobility and common men against the might of England. And his family had paid an unholy price. 'Twas a lesson Bryan would not soon forget. And although Bruce's reminder of God's faithfulness lightened Bryan's burden somewhat, his faith that God was on Scotland's side had been badly shaken.

The death of his brother and capture of his women might have crushed another man. But Robert the Bruce was not just any man. In his veins ran the royal blood of the Celtic House of Canmore, and he was determined to rule the land he loved. As long as their king held fast to his faith, Bryan knew he and this ragged band of loyal men would follow Bruce through the very gates of Satan's lair, if need be.

For freedom.

February 1308
The Hills of Carrick

CEALLACH KNELT BEFORE his foster brother, the king of Scotland, not on the marble of a stately palace but on the dirt floor of a small stone cottage in the hills where they'd lived together as children. No trappings of office surrounded the royal personage, for Robert's clothing was nearly as threadbare as Ceallach's own.

The months of hard travel, of hiding and fear, of physical pain, threatened to overcome Ceallach. He knew that Bruce had also known treachery, deceit, and physical deprivation this past year, and knowing that had given Ceallach hope that Robert would understand. Raising his head, he prayed his eyes would not betray his desperation. Robert was his only chance for anything resembling a normal life.

Robert rested a hand on his shoulder. "Rise, Marcus of—"

"Nay, sire." Glancing at the three men standing nearby, Ceallach pulled Bruce close to whisper, "Please, Your Majesty. I go by the name of Ceallach." It had been fifteen years since they had seen each other and just two months since Ceallach and five others had escaped from prison in France. Despite their injuries, they had made their way here through the wintry countryside. Bruce studied him a moment before saying, "I understand. Rise then, Ceallach."

Ceallach stood as the king motioned to the others. They moved to the other end of the cottage, giving the king privacy. All except a tall, black-haired youth who stood still and scowled. Despite the scowl, the boy looked familiar.

"'Tis all right, Bryan. You can go," Robert said quietly. The boy nodded and moved off, but kept himself and his sword at the ready. Ceallach stared at the boy and then at the king. Despite the difference in coloring the boy had the same straight, narrow nose, the same slanted, Celtic eyes, and the natural grace of movement that had made Bruce one of the most accomplished knights in Christendom.

Ceallach returned his gaze to his foster brother. "You are married, then?"

"Twice, but never to the boy's mother."

Ceallach found his voice. "Does he know?"

"Aye, of course. But we do not speak of it."

Ceallach glanced at the youth once again. "You are proud of him."

"I am."

Ceallach nodded.

"What, no sermon, brother? No reproof, no rebuke for my sin?"

Even if he weren't desperate for Robert's sanctuary, he would not have lectured his foster brother on sin. Ceallach's own lessons on the subject had been both painful and permanent. "We all fall short of the glory of God, Robert."

"You also? With your holy vows?"

"Even the holiest of vows can't save you from sin or suffering, Robert. Especially suffering."

Robert's expression became one of compassion. "We must talk of it."

Ceallach wasn't sure if he'd ever be able to talk about his recent ordeal. "Aye, but 'tis a long story, best saved for another day."

Robert laid his hand on Ceallach's shoulder. "All right. How can I help you?"

Ceallach managed not to flinch from the touch—he simply moved away so Robert had to remove his hand. "I think we can help each other, my laird. I have need of sanctuary. You have need of weapons and money."

"You were among those Phillip of France arrested?"

"Aye. You may as well know that my comrades and I are wanted men. No ruler in all of Europe will give us sanctuary for fear of excommunication." They had managed to evade capture thus far by staying aboard the ship that carried them from France. When they had recovered their health they'd walked for nearly ten days to Bruce's camp.

Bruce snorted. "I may be a king, but at the moment 'tis in name only. Very little of Scotland is under my dominion." He smiled ruefully. "And since the pope has seen fit to excommunicate me, you are hoping I'll ignore the bounty on your heads."

"If you can."

Though he'd known of Robert's disfavor with Rome, Ceallach had no idea the war with England proceeded so poorly. As for his own difficulties with the pontiff, Ceallach feared the reaction of the others in the room if they should realize his former occupation. He prayed no one would make the connection between Ceallach the warrior and Marcus of Kintyre, late of the now disbanded Templar Knights.

Still unsure of his welcome, he said, "There are six of us—trained in the Saracen ways of war. We have access to money and weapons in return for your protection."

Bruce grinned and it was as if the years fell away. "'Tis good to see you again, brother, after all these years. I would clasp you close in friendship if it wouldn't arouse suspicion. But it seems we both have a price on our heads and a need to conceal our whereabouts."

"Aye, we've much in common, then." Ceallach allowed a brief smile.

"I trust you, Ceallach, but I need to know how you found me."

"You have no need to fear, I've not betrayed you." Ceallach paused. "Nor will I betray those who helped me."

Robert nodded in understanding.

Ceallach had nothing to lose. Either Robert accepted him and gave him refuge, or Ceallach's life would end here in the wilds of Carrick. No sense mincing words. "I have no home, Robert. I am not safe in any country in all of Europe, save possibly for Scotland. All I held dear was stripped from me, and I'm lucky I escaped with my life."

Robert's expression became bleak, and suddenly, Ceallach feared Robert would banish him, since his presence would only increase Edward's desire to destroy Bruce. Hoping to forestall such a concern, Ceallach confessed. "I would pledge myself to your cause, Robert."

"You would fight for Scotland's freedom?"

"I am a warrior. 'Tis the only life I know."

"This is no holy war, Ceallach, fought to uphold the Church."

Ceallach laughed. "No war is holy, Robert. To think otherwise is a fool's game, and I'm done with being a fool."

"But you and your companions would fight for freedom?"

"If that is your cause, then, yes. We would do so willingly, because we have no home, no country, not even a church to pray in."

"Nowhere else to turn." A gleam came into Robert's eye. "Then join with me. We shall be free men once more."

Ceallach the Warrior, weary, desperate, at his strength's end, wiped tears from his eyes and followed his king into the night.

He would live to fight again.

For freedom.

ONE

Year of Our Lord 1312

THE PERFUME OF HER MOTHER'S ROSE GARDEN surrounded Kathryn de Lindsay as she strolled on the arm of Lord Rodney Carleton on a late summer afternoon. As they approached the secluded bench near a bubbling fountain, Rodney steered her toward the seat and Kathryn allowed it. They sat down side by side and Rodney tried to draw her into his arms. Mindful of proprieties, she held back as a proper young maid should.

"Come, Kathryn. Surely I've made my intentions clear to you by now. I mean you no harm, only good." Rodney looked at her with such longing in his gaze. He loved her, but she wasn't sure how she felt about him. Perhaps if they kissed again?

He bent his face to kiss her, and the touch was gentle, beguiling. Surely these strange fluttering feelings were a sign that she was in love, truly in love. She didn't resist when the kiss became demanding and the fluttering. . . . She pulled back in haste.

"My lord, we must stop."

"Ah, then you do feel something for me, sweeting?"

"Aye." But what did she feel? How did a woman know when she was in love? Was it the pleasure of looking at her lover's face and form? Rodney's handsome face and blue eyes were framed by deep auburn curls. And his body was that of the renowned swordsman he was—lithe and strong. A most pleasing sight.

How did one avoid the temptation promised in a man's kisses? If only her mother were still alive to guide her in this business of being courted. Sir Rodney was but one of several men, young and not so young, who had paid court recently to the Earl of Homelea's only child, the future Countess of Homelea.

She'd turned all of the others away, because most of them were more interested in becoming an earl than they were in her. But Rodney was different—attentive and charming and altogether persuasive. Kathryn found herself envisioning a life with him as a cherished wife and mother of his children.

If his eye roamed over the kitchen maids now and then, who would censor a bachelor for behaving thus? Once he was happily married to her he would stop such behavior, she was sure. *Married. To Rodney.* The idea grew of its own accord and the fluttering feeling started once more.

Rodney tugged her closer. "Tell me I may speak with your father." He kissed her again and he touched her bodice.

She jerked away from him and for a brief moment hard anger showed on his face. But the look was so fleeting she doubted she really saw it.

He drew a deep breath. "I'm sorry, Kathryn, love. Forgive me. I cannot seem to help myself."

Surely Rodney must care for her to have such strong feelings toward her. And she must love him to feel the way she did, all loose and fluttery and, dare she think it? Warm and soft. Aye, this must indeed be love.

What if he did speak sharply to the servants? And what did it matter that he didn't attend morning mass? One couldn't expect perfection in a prospective spouse. The hand of a gentle woman such as Kathryn would tame his lesser inclinations.

Rodney pulled her close again and kissed her until her knees nearly gave way.

He loves me.

"Talk to Papa, Rodney," she said breathlessly.

His face lit up with joy. Aye, she was sure it was joy and not triumph. "I'll speak with him yet tonight. Then there will be nothing to keep us from bliss."

He held her close again and murmured in her ear. "May I come to your chamber after I've received your father's blessing?"

His strong arms enfolded her and her heart pounded at the thought of Rodney's suggestion. Betrothed couples often engaged in intimacy before the actual wedding. The Church taught that she should wait, that though a betrothal was a legal contract, a betrothal could be broken. Marital relations were only sanctioned within the commitment of marriage. But since neither she nor Rodney had cause to break the agreement, what harm could there be?

They were in love. And she longed to know the secrets her body yearned to discover.

She swallowed. "Aye, come to me."

Rodney kissed her again with what seemed like reverence. "I will hasten to you, love, as soon as your father says yes to our betrothal." They stood and walked to the keep's entrance where they said good night and parted amidst promises of undying love and devotion.

LATER THAT NIGHT as the rest of the castle slept, Rodney stole into her chamber and to her bedside, stroking her long hair. "My bride," he whispered. "You will soon be my bride."

Kathryn shivered with pleasure at his touch, and thrilled at the knowledge that soon she would be a married woman. Papa had said yes! Rodney was a fine choice, and he made her feel so beautiful, so desirable.

And so it was that Kathryn gave herself to the man who would be her husband.

The pleasures of marriage were indeed a prize, and for hours, Rodney cradled her in his arms, delighting her with his tender touch. She had not known what it would be to lay beside a man, to be one with him. She had not known the joy that awaited her. Marriage would be a gift, and Rodney a fine husband . . . Just as she was dozing off, he suddenly moved away, letting cold air beneath their warm covers. Kathryn blinked rapidly, trying to focus. He pulled on his trousers and his shirt, then his boots.

"I will see you in the morning," he said over his shoulder as he walked away.

Kathryn rose to a sitting position, confused at his brusque manner. She clung to the sheet at her breast. What of the tender words he had spoken earlier? What was this chill that ran across her bare shoulders? Licking her parched lips, she quickly pulled the blanket up farther, feeling suddenly . . . exposed. But that was silly—he was her betrothed. They had only done what countless engaged couples had done before them.

"Rodney?"

He turned in the doorway. "Tomorrow. Sleep now." And with that, he was gone.

She lay back against the down pillows, struggling to reclaim the sweet drowsiness that had almost claimed her. He was merely tired, as she was. And it wouldn't do to have her maid discover them together in the morning, betrothed or not. But the fingers of guilt played with her heart. Papa would certainly be disappointed if he knew what she'd done.

She hadn't expected this; she had expected gratification, fulfillment, completion.

Instead she felt robbed.

PAPA WASN'T FEELING WELL the next morning and sent a servant to ask Kathryn to come to him after mass. Though the guilt continued to nag as she walked to the chapel for mass, she pushed it aside. They were in love, Papa had obviously given Rodney his blessing, and God would surely forgive her. When such thoughts did little to pacify her conscience, she vowed to resist Rodney's temptation again until they were properly wed.

To her surprise, Rodney attended the service and sat next to her. She smiled in satisfaction. Already their impending marriage was working good in his heart. He whisked her out of the chapel as soon as the last prayer was finished. "Rodney!" she said with a giggle, "what is this rush?"

With a nervous smile he said, "Come. I've talked Cook into packing us a picnic." He took hold of her elbow and propelled her toward the stable.

She wrested her arm from him and stopped walking. "I must speak with my father, Rodney."

He scowled but quickly recovered with a charming smile. "Your father will understand if he is no longer first in your affections, love. And I am most anxious to get you alone again."

Rodney swung her into his arms and around a secluded corner, kissing her so passionately that she forgot about Papa, forgot about her decision to hold Rodney off until they were married. This pursuit, the thrill of desire—it was a difficult thing to say no to. No wonder the betrothed often gave up on their intentions to wait! She smiled in flirtatious, silent agreement and Rodney beamed his pleasure.

Hand in hand they ran to the stable and were about to saddle a horse when Cook's son, Fergus, came into the barn.

"Yer father wants to see ye, Lady Kathryn."

Rodney stepped between them. "The lady and I are going on a picnic. Tell her father she will see him when we return."

Fergus looked at Kathryn with uncertainty and said, "My lady?"

Before she could respond, Rodney grasped her elbow with more force than was necessary and she nearly yelped at the pain of his grip. She attempted to pull free but he didn't let go. "Rodney, you're hurting me."

Fergus stepped closer. "My lady, are ye all right?"

She nodded to Fergus but one look at Rodney's furious expression and she wondered for the first time if she was, indeed, all right.

Rodney said, "Be gone, boy. The lady will attend her father when we return."

Fergus stepped closer yet and stared meaningfully at Rodney's hand where it still clamped fast to her elbow. Boldly he glared at Rodney. "I'll not leave until ye release Kathryn's arm and allow her to talk with her father. I don't take my orders from ye. I take them from the earl."

Kathryn and Fergus had been friends all through their growing up and sometimes she and Fergus forgot that he was a servant. But Rodney wasn't likely to forget the distinction and Kathryn knew she must defray the tension between the two men.

"I'm all right, Fergus." She turned to Rodney and said, "I will only be a few minutes with Papa. Then we can go on our picnic." She smiled brightly, but Rodney continued to glower. His grip loosened but his resolve did not. "You'll obey *me* now, Kathryn."

Shocked at his tone of voice, she stared at him. Fergus unwisely pushed at Rodney's arm. "The devil she will. Who are ye to order Lady Kathryn about?"

Shrugging off Fergus's hand, Rodney declared, "I am the man who will be her husband."

"Ye forget I was tending to the earl when ye spoke to him last evening. He didn't seem too keen on a wedding."

Kathryn gasped. She fought for air, for understanding. "Is that true, Rodney? Papa did not give us his blessing?"

Rodney dismissed her concern with a wave of his hand. "Your father only wants you to tell him it's what you want before he'll sign the betrothal agreement."

"Then there's no harm in my going to him before we depart."

Looking rather pleased with himself, Rodney said, "I'm sure your father will see things differently this morning."

"What have ye done, Kat?" Fergus stared at her and she could feel her face turn crimson.

"The lady does not answer to you," Rodney said.

"I have done nothing wrong," she lied.

Fergus stared hard at her. "I hope not, for all our sakes. Don't go with him, today, Kat. He's using ye to get Homelea."

"That's enough!" Rodney shouted. He shoved Fergus out of the way and grabbed Kathryn's arm so tightly she cried out from the pain. Fergus dived at Rodney's legs and they went down in a tumble, Kathryn spared from a fall at the last second when Rodney let go of her arm. She stumbled backward and watched in horror as Rodney grabbed a riding crop and slapped Fergus across the face with it. The lash caught Fergus across his left eye, baring the brow bone and marking the lid.

Fergus fell away, stunned. Kathryn placed herself in front of Fergus to spare him another blow. When Rodney paused, wiping his upper lip of sweat, she turned to Fergus and nearly fainted at the sight of his blood pouring from the split skin. The eye was already swelling and she feared he would lose his sight.

Rodney stood and stared at Fergus with contempt. "Maybe now you will mind your betters."

"And is this how you intend to enforce *my* obedience, my laird?" she demanded, gesturing toward the crop still in his hand.

"Don't be ridiculous, Kathryn. There are better ways to inspire a wife to be compliant." The lecherous look he gave her had little to do with the gentleman he'd pretended to be these past weeks of his courtship.

Had she been played for a fool? It wasn't possible . . . was it? She loved him, though! And he loved her! But if that was so, what had made him lash out at Fergus, to speak to her with such contempt? Where was the kind suitor who'd sworn his undying love just hours ago in her chamber?

She looked at him now, at his smug air of superiority, so sure that she would bow to his will as everyone always seemed to do. Handsome Rodney, so sure the world would give him what he wanted simply because of his comeliness and charm. Disgust roiled through her at Rodney's behavior and was soon joined by guilt at her own complicity in what now became clear. Rodney's seduction had been aimed, not at her heart, but at her inheritance. Confused and unwilling to confront Rodney and the truth, she turned her attention to her friend; she ripped a strip of material from her chemise and held it to Fergus's wound, then helped him to sit up and lean against the stall.

Fergus put his hand on the makeshift bandage and said, "Send him away, Kathryn. He means ye no good."

"I should take you to Anna—"

"I'm all right for the moment."

She'd been so sure of herself last night that she'd given her heart and her body to Rodney. In light of what had taken place here in the stable her certainty crumbled. Rodney's temper had been both unprovoked and uncalled for under the circumstances.

She took a deep breath and straightened to face Rodney. "Did you speak to my father?"

"Of course I did."

"And did he or did he not give us his blessing?"

"We *will* marry, Kathryn," Rodney said.

"You haven't answered my question."

"He will say yes when you tell him you agree."

Rodney had lied. *Dear God, forgive me. What have I done?* He'd come to her as a husband and let her think that her father had said yes to his suit for marriage.

She'd committed an offense against her father and against God.

She looked at Rodney now and he seemed unaffected by her distress. She had given herself to a man who had no honor. He was smiling and she realized that his seduction had been planned all along. To ensure that she would have to marry him. Did he even love her? She doubted it. The thought of it, the breath-stealing ache of knowledge, threatened to take her to her knees. Her virtue, gone. Forever. And to a man who didn't truly love her!

But Kathryn knew that she must accept some responsibility for what she done. Rodney was not solely to blame. And she wanted no more bloodshed or violence.

"It isn't me you want, is it?" she asked, sure that her heart couldn't hurt worse. She fought to keep her chin up, her eyes steady. She had to face this.

"Marrying you will be no hardship, Kathryn. And it will bring me a title and wealth. The fees from the river crossing alone will make us very wealthy."

The river crossing. Papa and Rodney discussed the issue more than once and Papa was quite opposed to the idea. No wonder he hadn't given Rodney an answer until he was certain how Kathryn felt. Papa would not stand in the way of her happiness, she knew. But she seriously doubted that Rodney would make her happy. Not if he could harm someone the way he'd just lashed out at Fergus. Not if he could lie to her with his words and with his body in order to claim what he wanted. And she'd fallen for his lies, fallen as far as a women could fall.

But did she have the courage to turn Rodney away after last night? No other man would claim her, a used woman! But what was the alternative? Life with a man she could not trust?

Calling on God for the strength to see this through, she said with a shaking voice, "Leave Homelea, Rodney. I will not agree to marry a man who has so little honor."

"Don't be foolish. You cannot undo what's been done. I will speak to your father." He spun on his heel and stalked toward the keep.

She ran after him tugging his arm until he shook her hand off and stopped. "My father will not make me marry against my will, Rodney."

"But—"

"If you tell him what we did, I will paint you as the worst sort of seducer of an innocent maid. I will not agree to marry you and you will have gained the animosity of the Earl of Homelea. Papa is old and in poor health, but his name still counts for something at Edward's court."

Her last words got Rodney's attention—he valued his relationship with England's king above all else. "Are we to forget all that transpired between us, Kathryn? I care for you, though you seem to find that hard to believe."

How she wanted to believe him.

"If you find yourself with child, send for me."

She recoiled. "With child?"

"Yes, it isn't beyond possibility. I am not completely without honor, Kathryn. If there is a child I would want to do the right thing, despite our differences."

He sounded so sincere, so . . . hopeful. But of course, he sounded hopeful—a babe would give him exactly what he wanted—a way to force her to his will. A way to claim her and Homelea.

His charming idea for a picnic suddenly looked far less innocent. "Our picnic today—'twas just a way to get me alone and charm me into ensuring there would be child, wasn't it?"

He did not deny it.

Devastated that she'd ever thought herself in love with a man who would use his own child to further his ambitions, she said, "Leave before I tell my father what a charming deceiver you are."

"Very well, Kathryn. I will go quietly, this time. But rest assured I will return one day to claim Homelea." He strode to the keep to retrieve his baggage.

To claim Homelea. Not to claim Kathryn, but the title and the land.

With a heavy heart Kathryn returned to the stable to help her loyal friend, Fergus. A man who'd had nothing to gain by coming to her aid and might well have lost his eye for his trouble.

Year of Our Lord 1314

THE BELLS OF ST. MARY'S ABBEY rang *nones*, reminding Kathryn de Lindsay of the need to return home. How had the brisk spring day sped by so fast? She looked out the window of the visitors' chamber of the abbey and indeed, the light gave proof of the hour. Soon she must take Isobel back to the nursery the nuns had created in the safety of their quarters. Quarters where no man was allowed to enter.

Dreading yet another parting from her young daughter, Kathryn held the child in her arms and crooned a lullaby:

"Hushabye, hushabye, God will protect ye.
Hushabye, hushabye, the Black Knight shall not get ye."

From across the room Mother Superior looked up from her needlework. "'Tis a soothing melody, but I can't say the same for the words, lass."

Kathryn smiled ruefully. "The sentiment is what matters. I would protect my babe from all manner of evil, even the notorious Black Bryan, should he come raiding." She stroked the sleeping child's tiny hand. "I must go, Mother Philberta. I wish it were not so."

"It is still not safe to take her with you to Homelea?"

Kathryn shook her head. "Eventually I hope to raise her there. But not yet."

"You are determined not to tell the child's father of her existence?"

"Aye. I'll not add to my transgression by placing Isobel in danger."

"Surely Lord Carleton would not harm his own child."

"Rodney would use whatever he can, including an innocent babe, to gain control of Homelea. Of me. He cannot be trusted, certainly not with something as precious as this child."

Isobel awoke and began to fuss and Kathryn cooed to her. "She's hungry," Kathryn said.

"Come, you can carry her to the wet nurse before you leave."

Grateful that the older woman understood Kathryn's need to delay parting with Isobel as long as possible, she stood and followed Mother Philberta. They walked down the corridor to the room where Isobel lived with Nelda, the woman Kathryn had hired. Kathryn's eyes misted. "I don't know when I will visit again. Father's health is failing and I am needed at home."

The elderly nun said, "I'm sorry to hear of the earl's illness. He has been most generous to us at the abbey."

"As you have been generous to us." The nuns had welcomed her in her time of need, accepting her repentance and providing a safe haven for her child. "It grieves Papa that he isn't able to come visit his granddaughter. And that soon he will be unable to protect either of us from Sir Rodney. Already I have received word that Rodney is coming to Homelea at King Edward's request. As if either father or I cares to receive him."

"What brings him back?"

"I will become King Edward's ward when Papa dies and there will no longer be any obstacles in Rodney's path. Edward will force the marriage if I resist."

"So, he will renew his suit with you. What will you do?"

Kathryn shook her head. "I can't risk displeasing Rodney or the king, so I will bite my tongue and pray for God's intercession."

"I will add my prayers to yours. You know you are welcome to take refuge here, but perhaps our prayers will be answered and it won't come to that."

They reached the chamber, and Kathryn kissed Isobel's cheek before handing her to the nurse. The woman took the child to a three-legged stool and sat down to suckle the child.

As she looked on the scene, Kathryn thought of the brief weeks when she'd nourished the child herself. Weeks of healing and heartache knowing she must leave Isobel at the abbey to keep them both safe from Rodney. What would it be like to love a man as God ordained, to bring forth life and nourish it in partnership with a man who loved her?

Because she'd failed to resist temptation, she might never know.

"I would like nothing better than to hide here, Mother. To stay here with Isobel. But he would only come looking for me, and I want him nowhere near St. Mary's or Isobel."

"I will pray for you and your father, child."

They walked back through the stone-lined corridor, past the visitor's chamber where she'd rocked little Isobel and to the front gate. Kathryn turned to the older woman, suddenly desperate for reassurance. She grabbed the nun's arm. "Promise me you will keep Isobel here if I am forced to marry Lord Rodney."

"I am not young, Kathryn. I can only promise to see to her while I'm able. Perhaps you should have the papers prepared and give her to the Church."

Kathryn bowed her head momentarily, recognizing the truth of what Mother Superior said. "Aye. I may have no choice." Should she send Isobel away to become a nun in order to keep her safe? But how would Kathryn survive if she could not visit her each week? Not see her take her first steps or celebrate her birthdays?

Only God could hear her prayers and deliver Kathryn and Isobel.

Two

THE LAST FORLORN NOTES OF THE BAGPIPE echoed off the nearby Lammermuir hills. A numbing mist shrouded the late May sun as Kathryn de Lindsay crumbled a handful of thin Scottish soil over the fresh grave of her father. Homelea's small cemetery now held all of her family except Kathryn herself and Isobel. Precious Isobel, nearly a year old now and the light of Kathryn's life.

Crossing herself, Kathryn stared at the weathered headstones on either side. Mother. Sister. Knowing they were free from earth's toils did little to comfort Kathryn at the moment. It had been bad enough to lose them, but the loss of her father changed everything. Through the years he had protected her and in the hours since his death she'd come to realize just how much.

Father had indulged her independent spirit, had treated her more like the son he'd never had. But she was not a son; she was an unwed woman with an illegitimate child and no husband. Her father's indulgence now threatened to be her undoing.

How am I to go on?

Raising her gaze from the ground, she saw Lord Rodney Carleton standing on the other side of the gravesite, and despair swept through her, cold as the day's wind. Her unwanted suitor had arrived just yesterday, only a few hours after her father breathed his last.

For that Kathryn was grateful; Papa had always despised Rodney for the way he had treated Kathryn and Fergus. Not once had her wonderful father suggested she marry Rodney, not even when his child grew within her. And Papa had supported her decision not to tell Rodney about Isobel.

Rodney now stared at her as if to remind her that without her father to stand between them, she was powerless against him. How much longer could Kathryn avoid marrying him?

Numbed by that thought as well as the unseasonable weather, Kathryn stood motionless, at a loss to know what she could do to protect herself. To protect Isobel from the man who had fathered her.

Fergus gently took Kathryn's arm. "Come, my lady, 'tis time to leave. 'Twill do ye no good to catch a chill."

As the cold seeped under her woolen cloak, Kathryn hurried to do as Fergus asked. She did not want to risk another encounter between him and Rodney. "What am I going to do, Fergus?"

"Trust the Lord, lass. He will provide."

If only it could be that simple. Though she knew with all her heart that God would not desert her in this terrible time of grief and uncertainty, she felt just as strongly that she couldn't trust Rodney. If God intended to provide a protector, it would have to be someone else.

Avoiding Rodney's watchful gaze, she returned with Fergus to the main hall where many of the mourners sought shelter from the heavy mist before departing for their homes. A fire roared in the great fireplace, yet Kathryn could not shake off the depression that had settled over her. She was now the Countess of Homelea, heiress to a modest fortune, and utterly alone in this room full of people.

But her title would not protect her from Rodney and King Edward. Not a one of her guests would defend her—they each owed their own titles and lands to the whim of the king. He could take them away as easily as he bestowed them. He could give Homelea to Rodney and turn her out of her home if she refused to marry him. She knew it was coming. Why else would Rodney be here now?

Many of her guests belonged to that element of the Scottish nobility whose loyalty blew with the wind—or the fortunes of war—like her father. And like her father, they held lands and titles in both Scotland and England and owed allegiance to both kings. But the time was fast approaching, Kathryn knew, when they— and she—would have to choose sides once and for all.

Rodney Carleton, on the other hand, had firmly allied himself with England from the start. His family, though noble, lived on the edge of genteel poverty as a result of mismanagement by Rodney's late father. Rodney had only recently inherited to find that he had to marry a rich woman if he hoped to restore his estates. To that end he had ingratiated himself with Edward II.

She'd heard that Edward and Rodney were the two most profi- cient swordsmen in England. She wondered if the two also shared Rodney's rapier-quick temper.

Was it coincidence that Rodney arrived so soon after Papa's death? Had he somehow learned about Isobel? Kathryn's weariness gave way to fear, fear she fought to master as she saw him making his way to her side. If only she could have her men at arms remove him from her home. But that would bring down the wrath of Edward of England on Homelea and its inhabitants.

Rodney stood before her, and where once she had accepted his attentions eagerly, now she reluctantly offered her hand in greeting. It had been nearly two years since he had last left Homelea. She had hoped it would be forever.

"Kathryn." He held her hand to his lips, lingering overlong. "You are beautiful, as always."

Careful not to show her aversion to him, she said, "My laird, you are kind, as always." It made her stomach twist to be gracious to Rodney, but she dared not confront him. She had dared it once and Fergus had taken the brunt of Rodney's anger. God could not possibly intend for Rodney to be the answer to her fervent prayers for a protector. Not for her, and certainly not for Isobel.

"I'm sure his majesty, King Edward, would want me to extend his condolences along with my own, Lady Kathryn." He stroked her cheek with his finger in a chilling gesture of intimacy.

Withdrawing from his presumptuous touch, she said, "Thank you. I understand King Edward has given you another title. Congratulations."

"Yes, I am most fortunate. However, I still find myself in need of a wealthy wife. And you are still in need of a husband." A beguiling smile graced his face. "We felt something for each other once, Kathryn. Do not deny it. Perhaps Edward can provide for both of us with one betrothal."

Fresh shivers of dread chilled her deeper than the earlier frost in the graveyard. His charm had not diminished and she feared he would weave his spell around her again. Would she, in a moment of weakness, respond to him again? Kathryn withdrew from his touch, distancing herself from temptation. "You are presumptuous. Nothing has changed—I do not wish to be your wife. And I assure you I will not change my mind."

He took her hand and kissed it, then looked at her with such longing that Kathryn found herself bending toward him in sympathy. "That is unfortunate, Kathryn. I had hoped you would be more willing, in light of our past friendship. It pains me to tell you that Edward has already decided—our betrothal will be announced within the month. And this time you will not be able to deny me."

She paused a moment, struggling to maintain her composure. "You are the serpent himself, aren't you?"

"Ah, still so spirited. I shall enjoy taming you, my dear."

Reminding herself not say or do anything that would give Rodney an excuse to lose his temper, she forced her hands to let go of her skirt and clasped them together at her waist.

He stepped closer, attempting to regain her hand. "Come now, remember a time when we shared gentle kisses instead of barbed words?" he said in the tender voice she remembered so well. The one he'd used for seduction.

Any wickedness was carefully cloistered behind a mask of charm and perfect propriety. But an innocent child depended on her now—she must not fail again in her choices. He leaned forward, "I still think we are quite well suited."

Kathryn jerked her hand away from him. "We never suited, Rodney. I was simply too dazzled to see it."

"I apologize for my behavior, Kathryn. I wronged you and I'm here to make it right now that I've returned to my senses."

He seemed so sincere. Had he changed? Impossible!

"You not only wronged me, you wronged Fergus."

For a moment, he seemed at a loss for words. And then his expression became most contrite. "Yes, that was inexcusable." He took her hand and laid it in the crook of his arm and they began to walk around the room. He said, "I have not been able to forget our . . . interlude, Kathryn. As I said, I regret my behavior and I hope you will forgive me. I shall apologize to—what was his name?"

"Fergus."

He waved his hand in dismissal. "Yes, Fergus. I'll apologize to him as well if it will win me a place in your good graces once more."

Again, they moved forward together, and Rodney obviously assumed her silence was the beginning of compliance. Kathryn's mind raced. Was he sincere? She had heard of awakenings in men's hearts, especially after the deaths of their fathers. How could one tell when the devil spoke the truth? *The devil never speaks the truth.* She must not trust Rodney, and she mustn't allow him to provoke her into inadvertently revealing Isobel. Kathryn's head began to pound as she sought an excuse to get away from him.

"You may apologize all you want but it will not bring back Fergus's sight nor my virtue." She heard the stridency in her voice and paused to collect her emotions. More in control, she said quietly, "I find actions speak louder than words, Rodney, and yours made a lasting impression."

His smile was smug. "I am ready to redeem your virtue by marrying you. And do not forget you need my sword arm to protect you. Won't you allow me to do so?"

He was right. She most definitely needed a male protector. Perhaps she should just tell him about Isobel and accept his offer gracefully. In any case, she had to play this out, give herself some time to think. "I will give your suit consideration."

"There is nothing to consider, Kathryn."

She sighed. "Time to mourn, then. You will allow me that small favor, won't you?"

He kissed her hand again. "Of course."

Relieved, she said, "Now, if you will excuse me, I must attend to my other guests."

Kathryn forced herself to walk slowly across the room to speak with an acquaintance then fled to the kitchen before anyone could observe her shaking hands and obvious turmoil.

Not only did she have to deal with her father's death, but she also had to find a way to discourage Rodney from an inescapable marriage. He would do what suited him, with or without her consent. She had to have time to think, to devise a plan. Perhaps she could persuade the king against the union. But what argument could she use? Edward would not approve of her keeping Isobel from Rodney.

Homelea's kitchen, a wooden structure, was attached to the stone house by means of a covered wooden corridor. Kathryn entered the warmth of the kitchen, the room that, despite its separated location, seemed to Kathryn to be the heart of her home. Perhaps because of the woman who ruled there.

"Is there something amiss, lass? Are we running short of drink?" Anna, Homelea's cook and Fergus's mother, prodded.

Leaning against the wall for support, Kathryn took several deep breaths before answering her long-time servant and friend. "No, there is plenty."

"What brings ye to the kitchen, then?"

Away from Rodney, her headache began to recede. Kathryn rolled her eyes and, hoping to hide her turmoil and desperation, she made a face. Moving toward the older woman, she answered, "Too much overeager company."

Cook had served at Homelea since before the death of Kathryn's mother, and not much escaped her notice. "Lord Carleton, I would guess?" She snorted as if to punctuate her disapproval.

"Yes." Kathryn fought to control her agitation. "King Edward has betrothed us, and Rodney is counting the days until he gains control of Homelea. But I don't want to marry him. I can't."

"Aye, lass. He's a mean one. I fear for my son if you marry that man."

"I'm afraid Fergus would kill Lord Rodney first."

"I fear it, too."

Kathryn rubbed the tenseness in the back of her neck. She was not in the habit of questioning authority, or questioning God. But marriage to Rodney was more than she could bear. The need to escape overwhelmed her. "I cannot face him again, Anna. Not until I've had time to think."

"Running away never solved anything, lass. Ye're a countess now. Time to act like one."

"Maybe tomorrow, Anna." The kitchen no longer felt like a sanctuary, and Kathryn grabbed her work cloak from the pegs on the wall and hurried from the castle. Outside the mist had lightened somewhat although there was still no sign of the sun. Head bowed, she headed to the stable, shoulders slumped under a burden of responsibilities and emotions that threatened to overwhelm her.

In the stable with her beloved horses she sought solace. She opened a stall and stepped inside, idly stroking the sleek chestnut hide of her favorite mare, hoping to lose her confusion and her grief in the comfort of the familiar action. Despite the sure knowledge that she would one day be reunited with Papa, she missed him here. Needed him here, now.

"Please, God. Deliver me from Rodney. Please help me protect Isobel." She hugged the patient horse's neck and cried the first tears she had shed this endless, difficult week.

How long she stood thus, she didn't know. Eventually the horse in the next stall nickered. Kathryn raised her head to see Anna's son, Fergus, entering the stable. As her childhood friend came to stand by her, Kathryn dashed her sleeve across her eyes in a futile effort to erase the telltale signs of grief.

Fergus took her in his arms. "'Tis all right to cry, lassie. God knows ye've kept it inside these many days. And it will no' be getting any better, I'll wager."

He pulled a *shivereen* of cloth from the folds of his plaid and offered it to her. She thanked him and blew her nose as he led her to a bench outside the saddle room. The pleasant fragrance of hay and the earthy odor of the horses filled the barn. He sat beside her. "The mourners have left, except for that scum, Lord Rodney."

She didn't correct him for his slur upon the nobleman. Only a year in age separated them, and they'd long ago discarded the formalities between lady and servant. Their friendship ran deep— Fergus was as dear to her as any brother could be. And she knew he felt the same. "I didn't think Rodney would leave."

"Aye, that was too much to hope for. He ordered me to lower the portcullis. Rumor has it that some of Bruce's men are about." His hand tightened on her arm. "Did Rodney Carleton speak of marriage, Kat?"

Kathryn's stomach tensed. "Aye, he made it clear that he has Edward's support in the matter. How can he think I would have him after all that he's done?"

"I'll not allow him to touch ye again."

"Don't cross him, Fergus."

She looked to his scarred face and ruined eye. Rodney's handi-work. Fergus could see light and dark and movement, but only the blurry outline of objects. A boy no longer, Fergus gazed at her with a man's respectful appreciation and none of the resentment he might have felt.

Kathryn fought her guilt—now was not the time to wallow in useless recrimination. She stared at her hands in silence. "I want to live at St. Mary's and leave you here as castellan."

"The bairn is well?"

She smiled, thinking of Isobel. Fergus and his mother were the only ones at Homelea who knew of the child. "Aye, she's a bonny lass."

"Ye can't hide with her there forever."

"Aye, I know."

Fergus's face relayed his dismay. "I'd sooner ye became a nun than let him touch ye. But ye can't run from yer duty, from the people here who need ye."

She placed her hand on his arm. "'Twas only wishful thinking, Fergus. I won't desert Homelea or its people. But I swear I'd rather lose it all than become that man's wife. Or let him near Isobel."

Fergus shook his head. "More likely the wretch will force his way where he's not wanted."

"We must pray for a champion, someone who can protect us all from Rodney."

Wistfully, he said, "I wish it could be me."

"So do I." But it was impossible. Fergus had neither the social position to become her guardian nor the training in arms to take on a swordsman the caliber of Rodney.

A few years ago, when she and Fergus had grown old enough to understand the difference between lady and servant, woman and man, they'd discussed the implications of their friendship, accepted its limitations, and sworn their devotion to each other. Sworn to remain sister and brother of the heart, no matter what.

They sat in silence for a few minutes before Fergus suggested, "Perhaps ye could petition Scotland's king to come to yer aid. I'm sure he'd be glad to control Homelea's wealth."

"Perhaps."

Kathryn had no way of knowing what promises had been made between her father and England's king. She'd met King Edward II on a trip to London several years ago. People older and wiser than her were of the opinion that the son wasn't half the man his father, The Hammer of the Scots, had been. Still she found him to be an intimidating man, and she doubted she could persuade him to change his mind about giving Rodney control of Homelea.

She and Fergus sat in restrained silence, punctuated only by the sounds of the horses. Kathryn swiped at the tears that rolled down her cheeks as the realization of all she could lose came crashing down on her. If only Edward would have chosen someone other than Rodney.

Stifling her tears and hating the weakness they implied, she asked, "Do you really think Bruce would come to my aid?"

"Ye remember his decree? Scotland's landowners have less than a year to declare for him or be considered a sworn enemy. Aye, he might aid ye and provide a guardian, someone to protect and defend yer person."

"Probably marry me off to one of his nobles," she said gloomily.

"Most likely. One thing for certain, he wouldn't make ye marry Rodney Carleton."

That thought sparked hope. "Can we get a message to him?"

"Aye. But it would take time, and Rodney might insist on marrying before Bruce can answer."

Loud shouting and the clatter of approaching horses interrupted them. "What now?" She glanced at Fergus who rose to his feet and offered his hand, but she waved him off as she stood and headed toward the commotion.

A stable boy dashed through the doorway and ran headlong into her, nearly knocking her down.

"Pardon me, my lady, but ye must come quick. A knight and his warriors are demanding entrance. And he carries the king's own banner."

"Which king?" Fergus demanded.

"'Tis a red lion on a field of gold."

"Bruce," Kathryn whispered and moved closer to Fergus.

He faced her. "Aye, lass. I doubt he knows of yer father's death, but his timing is a godsend."

Kathryn grinned. "Aye, my prayers have been answered. It is beyond belief! I will yield to Bruce and be done with Rodney and England."

"Are ye certain, Kat? Perhaps it would be wise if ye'd be more cautious."

"'Tis the answer to my prayers, Fergus."

Fergus nodded. "All right. Let's hear what this knight has to say."

Duty required that she be sure those she loved would be safe. At least now she had an option other than Rodney. *Show me your will, God. Give me wisdom.* Gathering her resolve about her along with her cloak, Kathryn walked briskly toward the gatehouse guarding the entrance to Homelea.

Heart pounding in renewed optimism, she climbed the stairs leading to the guardroom, Fergus close behind. She crossed the small room and peered through the slotted window, saying another prayer for strength and wisdom. Fergus stood close by her, silently offering support.

There indeed flew Bruce's banner. She counted a small force of perhaps two score men, just beyond range of her archers, should she decide to deploy them.

Homelea was not a great castle but a large manor home surrounded by a curtain wall. The fortifications would not hold up to a determined siege, but provided security from marauding bands intent on stealing more than the occasional cow or sheep. The walls were surrounded on three sides by the Tweed River and by a bog on the fourth. A knight on a magnificent black stallion rode to the end of the causeway that had been built across the bog. She didn't recognize his pennon, only that it marked him as a bachelor.

The knight called out, "I am Sir Bryan Mackintosh and I come in the name of Scotland's King. I demand to speak to the Earl of Homelea."

Kathryn tripped over her skirt and nearly ran over Fergus in her haste to withdraw from the opening. *St. Columba save us. Bryan*

Dubh. Black Bryan Mackintosh, the Black Knight himself. He was certainly not the answer to anyone's prayer for protection.

She shuddered as she remembered the tales of the villages he'd burned and the castles he'd destroyed on both sides of the border. This warrior had earned the title Black Bryan from his many hapless victims. She'd also heard he was a natural son of Robert the Bruce, born while the then future king was still in his teens and well before Bruce had married his first wife, Isabella of Mar. The Black Knight's prowess with the mighty double-edged claymore sword was second only to his mentor, Bruce himself.

Bryan Dubh killed without mercy. What mercy could she hope for from a man such as him? She struggled to breathe, disappointment fogging her brain. This was not the champion she had prayed for! She had to think of some way to defend her home or they would all be dead before nightfall.

Fergus turned to Kathryn, "Ye should yield to him. I've heard it goes well for those who don't resist him. But he's the devil himself when opposed."

Kathryn braved another look. Even at a distance, she could see the size of the man. Those of his men who were mounted rode small, Scottish garrons. The menacing knight was mounted on a large, well-bred steed of considerable proportions.

The voice boomed once more. "Gatekeeper, fetch the earl at once!"

Frightened but determined, she took a deep breath and said, "He's but a man, Fergus. A very fearsome man, no doubt, but a man nonetheless." She smiled, and said a short, fervent prayer that her show of bravado made her appear more confident than she felt.

"Lord Carleton will be here any minute, Kathryn. Yield to the knight." His deepening scowl gave proof of his opinion of Rodney.

Gentling her voice, she said, "I understand your feelings for Sir Rodney, Fergus. I don't much care for him either. But allowing this warrior inside our gates might bring us all to death. We've both heard the horrible tales of his brutality."

The thought of Rodney caused her headache to return. The very real possibility of marriage awaited unless she yielded to the knight on the causeway. The knight whose legend had grown until he'd become the subject of the very lullaby she'd sung to Isobel not two weeks ago.

Isobel. Could she trust Rodney's avowal that he'd changed?

She would delay until her course became clear. "Tell Sir Bryan who holds Homelea."

Fergus reluctantly complied. "Sir Bryan, the earl was buried this morning. This stronghold is held by his daughter for her king, Edward of England."

The knight stood in his stirrups. "My condolences on the lady's loss. However, you should remind her that her home lies in Scotland, and Robert the Bruce is king of Scots and all who do dwell here."

Where was Rodney? Surely he'd heard the commotion by now. She said to Fergus, "Go see what is keeping Lord Carleton."

"I say we are in more danger from Lord Carleton than we'd be from the Black Knight."

"Enough. You overstep your place. Now do as I ask."

She'd never spoken with such authority before and Fergus looked suitably stunned. Kathryn watched him pivot on his heel and stalk away. Perhaps she would grow into the role of countess yet. She just hoped it wouldn't cost her Fergus's friendship. Though she was sorry to have been so curt, she had to believe that Rodney was a better choice than Bryan Dubh. Had he not killed every man, woman, and child at Roxborough when they resisted him? Heaven help her if she was wrong.

Black Bryan spoke again. "I grow weary of shouting." He paused to steady his restless horse. "Tell your lady she must yield to me. No one will be harmed, I give my word."

Kathryn's mind raced. According to the stories, Black Bryan had successfully captured several heavily fortified castles. How could they hope to hold him off with Homelea's modest defenses?

Finding no answer to her question she decided to speak with the man. She took a deep breath and willed her body to stop shaking, but still her voice quavered. "Sir Bryan, I am Countess Kathryn de Lindsay, and I hold my home for my liege laird, Edward. I am quite prepared to withstand a lengthy siege if you care to waste your time on such an endeavor."

The manor had been built during the peace and prosperity of Alexander III's reign. Just now Kathryn wished her father had built it for defense instead of comfort. She imagined Black Bryan laughing at her audacity—he must know how pitifully inadequate Homelea's walls would be against a protracted siege.

Still, she couldn't just give in. She might well be forced to yield, but not without a show of resistance. She couldn't allow his reputation alone to win the battle.

She had prayed for rescue—a champion to protect her home and person. As much as she didn't want her guardian to be Rodney, she was certain it couldn't be Black Bryan.

Could it?

THREE

KATHRYN REDIRECTED HER ATTENTION to the knight. Sir Bryan rode to the end of the causeway to converse with his men then returned to face the curtain wall.

"Lady Kathryn, you leave me no choice. Yield willingly and all will be spared. Otherwise I will order my men to attack."

Kathryn watched the equestrian warrior as she waited for Fergus to return with Rodney. Mackintosh's horse pawed the earth, mirroring Kathryn's restlessness. No more demands were shouted at her and a growing anxiety enveloped her as she paced the small space.

Fergus returned, grim faced. "My lady, Sir Rodney is on his way. He was . . . talking to one of the kitchen maids."

She stared back at him a moment, surely as grim-faced as her friend. Here was proof that Rodney hadn't changed as much as he wanted her to believe. How could she even consider him as a husband? Once she'd thought her love would change him, but she held little hope of that now.

Fergus said, "Kathryn, there is more you should know. The knight has nearly one hundred men surrounding the walls." With each castle that fell to the Black Knight, Bruce's army grew stronger. Bruce now controlled all but a few scattered pockets of resistance and the great castle at Stirling.

There were fewer than thirty men within Homelea. She had no doubt that the knight and his men could overpower her forces. To command them to defend Homelea would condemn many of them to death. They would die for naught, because in the end Black Bryan, with his superior numbers, would win.

At the sound of footsteps, Kathryn turned from the window and saw Rodney enter the small room. Fergus left, relieving Kathryn of the fear the two would come to blows. Rodney, his clothing disheveled as if he'd dressed hurriedly, went to the narrow window. He shouted to the mounted warrior, "This is Lord Rodney Carleton. Be gone, Mackintosh!" He turned to face her. "Go to your quarters, Kathryn. I'll deal with this nuisance."

Kathryn held her ground. "I remind you I am the Countess of Homelea and you are my guest. Do not order me about."

"You are my betrothed. Do as I say!"

"I haven't agreed to a betrothal—"

"You have no say in the matter. You and Homelea are mine, as of this day." With a withering glance, he dismissed her and turned back to shout at the warrior, "Leave now or face the might of the king of England."

Frustration welled up in Kathryn. How dare he treat her so, as if she had nothing worth saying about the future of her home and her people! Was this what marriage to him would mean—total submission to a tyrant? She knew the answer well enough— Rodney had shown his true character only too clearly two years ago. And contrary to his charming words this morning, he hadn't changed at all.

Tears threatened, for if she were ever to marry she wanted it to be to a man who cherished her. If she must face the prospect of dying in childbirth as her mother had, she wanted to at least be valued for the sacrifice.

Furthermore, her husband must live by God's Word. She knew enough of Rodney to know that God was of little or no importance to him. Yet she must yield to someone. Take Rodney as husband, or give herself and her home to Scotland's king and hope for better? Rodney or Black Bryan? England or Scotland?

A clamor outside caught her attention and she looked toward the window. She heard the knight say, "Carleton, I warn you, do not order those archers to fire on me. Now let me speak to the countess." Impatience sounded in the knight's bellow.

Rodney must have sent her archers to man the walls.

"The countess has no authority to bargain. Deal with me or be gone."

In that moment, Kathryn knew she could not allow Rodney to decide her fate or that of her daughter. If Rodney ever learned of Isobel's existence he would use the girl to exert his will over Kathryn. God must have sent the Black Knight for a reason, a reason she couldn't know. She must yield to him and trust in God. Although she would be at the mercy of Scotland's king, at least, as Fergus had said, he could not force her to marry Rodney. Bruce might be an unknown, but she certainly knew Rodney only too well.

That thought incited Kathryn to action. She shoved past Rodney, ducking under his outstretched arm and cried out, "I yield to Robert the Bruce!"

"How dare you defy me!" Rodney grabbed her by the hair and she screamed in terror. He clapped his hand hard across her mouth and her tongue tasted the coppery tang of blood. As he shoved her aside, Kathryn's head banged against the stone wall and she lay dazed upon the cold floor. She was dimly aware of someone's boots rushing past her.

When she regained her senses, she heard a grunt of pain. Pushing herself to a sitting position, she saw Fergus draw back his fist. Blood dripped from Rodney's nose—Fergus had already landed at least one punch.

Fearing more for Fergus than Rodney, she shouted, "Fergus, no! Stop." The thud of flesh on flesh answered her as the men tumbled to the floor, flailing at each other.

Kathryn struggled to her knees while the room filled with clamoring voices and jostling bodies. Evidently someone had sent for her steward, Peter, because he and several men at arms crowded the small room, pulling the adversaries apart.

Peter rushed to her side and asked, "My lady, what happened?" He looked at Fergus. "What have you done?"

Fergus ignored his question and stared with unmasked hatred at Rodney Carleton.

Kathryn rose shakily to her feet with Peter's help. "Do not rebuke Fergus, Peter. He came to my aid." Again. Thankfully he was uninjured this time, save for a bruise on the cheekbone below his bad eye and a bloody lip to match her own.

Rodney stepped forward, wiping his bloodied nose with a cloth. "I'll have the knave whipped. He interrupted a private matter between Lady Kathryn and myself. A matter we still must resolve. Take the boy to the bailey and hold him," he ordered.

No one moved except Fergus who crossed his arms across his chest.

Rodney glared at Peter. "Steward, take him and leave the lady and me in private. All of you."

"I will not; she is bleeding." Peter dabbed the blood from her face.

She pushed at his hand. "'Tis little, Peter. Stop fussing at me." To Fergus and the men at arms she said, "Escort Lord Carleton to the bailey. And see that he comes to no further harm," she warned Fergus. She glared at Rodney. "I will deal with you after I settle with Sir Bryan."

"Kathryn, I warn you!" Rodney growled. "Edward will not allow this treachery to go unpunished."

Kathryn watched impassively as the men at arms restrained Rodney. Strengthened by the growing hope that perhaps Sir Bryan was indeed the rescuer she'd prayed for, Kathryn said, "You will leave Homelea within the hour, Rodney. If Sir Bryan permits it." She paid no heed to Rodney's continued protests as he was forced down the stairs.

Fergus, arms still crossed, said, "I'm staying with ye."

Peter gently touched her arm. "I regret I am not a younger man. I'd have joined Fergus in thrashing that brute. Let Fergus stay with ye."

She nodded and Peter left her with Fergus.

"What are ye going to do?" he asked.

She shuddered. "I cannot marry Rodney. He is cruel and unrepentant. I . . . I have yielded Homelea to the Black Knight. That is why Rodney struck me."

Fergus remained silent for a moment. "So, ye believe it will go better for ye with Scotland's king?"

She raised her face to heaven. "I don't know," she whispered. "I only know marriage to Rodney is out of the question. I will not allow him to bully me, and I certainly won't give him Homelea. I must cast my lot with Bruce and pray he will treat us fairly."

"Can't be any worse than Lord Carleton."

They peered out the window slit at Bruce's warrior.

He bellowed once more. "Do you yield or not? If so, raise the portcullis. Now."

She shrank back and fear clutched Kathryn at the thought of what she was about to do. Had she simply traded one bully for another? Kathryn searched Fergus's face. "Am I doing the right thing?"

He nodded his agreement.

She made an attempt to put her hair to rights, then walked to the window and called out, "You will not harm my people?"

"I give you my word, lady. No one is to be harmed unless they take up weapons against me or my men."

"And my home? You won't destroy it?"

"The castle belongs to my liege laird. To do with as he sees fit."

She hesitated, frightened for Homelea's future. Bruce razed castles to the ground so they couldn't be held against him again. But this wasn't just a castle, it was a home. Surely he would spare her home. The people who depended on her would be safe as long as they didn't defend Homelea, and she would be safe from Rodney Carleton, God willing.

She nodded to Fergus, and he signaled the man at the gate. The portcullis chains groaned and clanked as the timbered gate slowly raised, placing Kathryn's future in the hands of Robert the Bruce.

And at the mercy of Bryan Dubh.

THE SOUND OF A WOMAN'S SCREAM had unnerved Bryan. "By the heavens, what treachery passes in there?" Bryan Mackintosh muttered as he stared at his latest conquest. Wary of a trap, Bryan remained mounted, instructing the men who would enter the bailey with him to be vigilant. Only those with chain mail would accompany him until he was sure the woman meant to yield.

His master at arms reined his mount to a stop beside Bryan. "They've withdrawn their archers from the walls. Looks as if they truly mean to yield."

"Aye, so it does."

"If the place is so poorly defended, why do you fear resistance?" his squire, Thomas, asked.

Bryan gazed at the fortress. The sixth sense that had saved him more than once in battle bade him to be cautious. "Something is amiss. The woman yielded, but I have no idea who actually wields the power, her or Carleton." Bryan calmed his horse as they awaited the slow progress of the lowering drawbridge. The countess should not have yielded without a fight and until he knew why she had, he would assume the worst.

The gate finally stopped its ascent. With a last caution to Adam and Thomas, Bryan led the way. The horses' hooves clomped upon the wooden bridge that spanned the ditch and they entered a courtyard. Bryan halted his horse while half a dozen men formed a defensive position around him. Each man faced his mount outward like the spokes of a wheel, three on each side. In short order and without resistance, the rest of Bryan's well-disciplined troops disarmed Homelea's defenders and secured the castle.

Thus assured, Bryan dismissed his guards and gave his attention to the question of who was in command. Bryan couldn't help the satisfied grin that creased his face at the sight of Rodney, held in the tight grip of two burly men at arms on the other side of the small bailey. An older man, the household steward by the quality of his clothing, stood next to them.

Bryan urged his horse forward and halted in front of Rodney. "Lord Carleton, why has the countess restrained you like a common thief?"

Carleton glared at him, dried blood marring his aristocratic nose. Someone had taken offense at Rodney. Bryan would like to hear more about the fight but it would have to wait until later. For now, he must deal with Carleton.

"Come, Sir Rodney, you've never been at a loss for words."

The nobleman drew himself up, not easy to do with a large man hanging on each arm, Bryan noted. Still, Rodney was always one to put up a good pretense.

"You will regret your actions today, *Sir* Bryan," Rodney sneered. "This castle is mine, and the countess is my betrothed."

"Ah. And if this is so why did the lady yield to me? To Bruce?" Why had the woman abandoned her betrothed and her king? Was she fickle and untrustworthy? Bryan grew anxious to meet her and take her measure. "Did you have a lover's quarrel?"

Carleton lunged, but the guards held him fast. "She is confused, a weak vessel. She and Homelea are mine, and I will have them while you share Wallace's fate."

Bryan dismissed Sir Rodney's threat with a wave of his hand even as he fought the images of William Wallace's execution. He would never forget, nor forgive, Carleton's part in the dishonorable affair.

"Let's see what the lady has to say." Bryan dismounted, handing the horse's reins to his squire.

The countess emerged from the guardhouse, a young man at her side. Bryan drew in a quick breath. He'd heard it said she was comely, but even at this distance it was clear the woman was beyond comely. Tall and graceful, her curving figure was clearly visible in a modest but flattering gown. Golden hair in a thick braid drooped from the top of her head, barely held in place with a gold band.

She stumbled and the man steadied her. Was she frail? Ill? Bryan dragged his gaze from her pleasing shape to her face. As he strode toward them he realized the man had a scar across the lid and brow of one eye and a bruised face. Bryan's attention returned to the woman, and his gaze took in her pallor and swollen lip. Blood glistened from a scrape on her forehead.

By the saints, someone had struck her. Bryan spun around to

glare at Carleton. The man's defiant stance and knowing look told him just who had done so. Bryan controlled his anger, willing himself not to walk over to Carleton and bloody the man's face further.

Instead, he stood before the lady. Scowling, Bryan removed his helm from his head and shoved it into the hands of the startled, one-eyed man beside her. The man defiantly shoved it back at him, and the expression on his face warned Bryan that he would defend the lady to the death.

An unarmed man defied the Black Knight. Interesting. The lady apparently provoked staunch loyalty from her retainers. Bryan raised his arm to signal his squire to take the helm, and the lady threw herself in front of the man at her side. "Nay, my laird. Do not strike him, please. I beg you, punish me. I am to blame."

Bryan stared at them. The man seemed displeased at her defense of him, the woman desperate. Bryan's squire now stood next to him and he handed the younger man the helm. Bryan pushed back his mail hood and said, "Lady, though I question his wisdom in challenging an armed knight, I took no offense. Indeed, I applaud your man's loyalty."

She looked astonished and disbelieving. Bryan knew he must establish some semblance of trust if they were going to accept him as a leader.

"What is your name?" he asked the man.

The young man straightened. "Fergus, my laird."

The man looked Bryan in the eye, giving Bryan the notion that he wore his wound with a certain amount of pride. And that his lady's defense had annoyed him, made him feel less of a man. As casually as he would have addressed any soldier Bryan asked, "How did you lose the eye?"

"Lord Carleton struck me."

"What did you do to anger him?"

"He was threatening Lady Kathryn, my laird, and I came to her defense. Which I have done today and would do again, should the need arise," he pronounced boldly.

The two men studied each other, taking measure. Perhaps Bryan had found an ally, someone who would protect the lady with his life. Satisfied that the man's belligerence was properly motivated, Bryan nodded and said, "As I would expect you to do, Fergus."

Bryan saw the man's shoulders relax and the woman's dawning realization that he was praising Fergus, encouraging him. "However, it would be unwise to challenge me again."

"Aye, my laird," Fergus said as he sketched a bow, still wary but with a show of grudging respect.

Bryan looked to the lady whose emotions played clearly on her beautiful face. She obviously had great affection for this Fergus, and her relief that the two of them settled their differences peaceably showed plainly. She dipped her head in unspoken acknowledgment, and without giving it a second thought, Bryan silently pledged himself to her protection.

BLACK BRYAN'S COAL BLACK HAIR shone in the sun, and Kathryn swallowed the lump of fear in her throat. Although his treatment of Fergus gave her hope that he would prove to be a man of honor, she didn't trust him. Sir Bryan's reputation as a fierce fighter and his unwavering loyalty to his king were renowned, and Kathryn feared he would not keep his word to her, might still consider her his enemy. She stared at the man's impassive face and prayed. *Lord, what have I done?*

Fergus said nothing, leaving Kathryn to further doubt the wisdom of her decision. Afraid to move or breathe, she was determined to maintain a tight rein on her clattering emotions. The warrior's angry dark eyes, rimmed with thick black lashes, transfixed her.

Somehow she managed to step forward and say, "I am Kathryn de Lindsay, Countess of Homelea." Sir Bryan brushed her hand lightly with his lips, and she withdrew from his touch as quickly as courtesy would permit. The man was huge and well armed with weapons.

"My lady, you are injured."

With surprise, she noted the concern in his voice. "It is nothing, my laird. I will attend it shortly."

His dispassionate features hid his emotions. "As you will. You were wise to allow me entrance, Lady Kathryn. You and yours are now under my protection. Robert the Bruce sends you his warmest regards."

"King Robert is most kind to send such an esteemed knight to convey his regards and offer protection." Kathryn nodded in Rodney's direction. "However, Lord Carleton has made the same offer on behalf of King Edward."

The knight glanced to where Rodney stood captive, then offered her his arm as they walked toward the nobleman. "Did you take insult at the offer?"

She was considered tall for a woman yet she felt small walking beside the knight. "King Edward would betroth me to him."

The man stopped walking, turned to face her, and frowned. "He speaks the truth, then. Your men are holding your betrothed at bay? What mischief is this?"

The coldness in his voice made her want to retreat from him, but she would not allow him to intimidate her. Because, despite her fear, Kathryn knew she must place her trust in this knight. He stood between her and Rodney here in the bailey. And she needed him to remain as a protective shield against Rodney's greed and whatever else drove him to covet Homelea. "I do not wish to marry him. I accept your offer of protection most gratefully."

She cringed when he lightly cupped her cheek with his gloved hand to inspect the damage Rodney had inflicted, but his touch was more gentle than she expected. "I can understand your dislike of Carleton." With quiet intensity, the knight dropped his hand to his sword hilt, bent his head to gaze directly into her eyes, and quietly vowed, "He will not harm you again. You need not fear."

Staring into his cold, dark eyes, she trembled with apprehension. "And should I not fear you, Black Bryan?"

His expression became more formal as he straightened to his full height. "I hope I will not give you or your people reason for such concern, Lady Kathryn."

Aye, one can hope. But he fairly radiated male confidence and restrained power, and Kathryn thought it wise to avoid provoking him in any way. She would admonish Fergus to do the same.

Sir Bryan's expression remained unreadable. Didn't he ever smile? It would make him seem more human. Less frightening.

He said, "I have been ordered to hold this castle for Robert the Bruce, and I am inclined to deal unkindly with those who stand in the way." He pointed toward Carleton. "He cannot stay."

Placing herself firmly under the authority of Black Bryan, she moved to stand at his side and said, "Nor do I wish him to." Emboldened by the presence of the formidable man standing next to her, she called to Rodney. "Lord Carleton, it seems I no longer require your company. You may go."

At a nod from her, the guards released him, and Rodney stalked toward her. Instinctively, she stepped closer to the protection of the knight while a large blond man at arms materialized at Sir Bryan's other side.

Rodney's crimson face and clenched fists betrayed him. Wisely he halted out of range of the Scots' weapons. "Kathryn, this is outrageous. Edward will not allow a prize like Homelea to be handed to his enemy. Nor will I." He stepped forward, but at the sound of a dozen swords leaving their scabbards he hastily retreated. Kathryn gathered her skirts, the better to run from the skirmish if necessary.

Black Bryan stepped between her and Rodney and drew his own sword. "Lucky for you I promised Lady Kathryn no blood-shed. She has made it clear you are no longer welcome. If you aren't convinced of her sincerity, let me remind you she has yielded to Bruce. To me."

Kathryn relaxed the grip on her clothing as he closed in on Rodney, placing the point of his sword on the man's neck. "But if you ever touch her again, I'll kill you."

The knight's resolute declaration let Kathryn know that God had chosen her champion well. Perhaps her fear of him wasn't justified.

The two men faced each other, a dark, powerful warrior and a tall, slender nobleman. Rodney repeated his earlier threat, though it was obvious who held the upper hand. "This isn't finished, Mackintosh. Beware."

Kathryn shuddered at the hatred seething between these two. She watched as Rodney, his expression malevolent, mounted his gelding and jerked the reins so hard Kathryn winced in sympathy for the horse. Her relief at seeing Rodney cross the bridge was soon replaced with the reminder that the scowling knight remained. What now? Had she relieved herself of one cruel master only to embrace another?

She brought her gaze from the knight to the red-headed squire at his side and was startled when he winked at her and grinned.

Caught off-balance by his obvious appreciation for the irony of her situation, she couldn't repress an answering smile.

Kathryn's mood lightened somewhat and she motioned to Peter and Fergus. "Please see to the needs of Sir Bryan's men and their horses."

As Peter and the blond-haired man turned to leave, Fergus protested. "I will stay with you, my lady."

"Yes, of course." He would provide a welcome buffer between her and the knight who now followed her into the hall. Servants were cleaning and putting up the trestles from the funeral feast. Gesturing for the knight to have a seat, she instructed a servant to bring food and drink then sat warily across from her unwanted, but necessary guest. Fergus and the knight's squire sat nearby.

"You should have your injuries tended, my lady," Black Bryan said.

Again, hearing his concern disconcerted her, because it seemed counter to his stoic features and what she knew about him. Bowing to the wisdom of his advice, she allowed one of the kitchen girls to wash the cuts as she studied the dark knight. At close range, Kathryn realized he might be considered handsome if he would allow his features to soften. The lilt of the highlands colored his voice when he wasn't angry.

His long wavy hair was parted in the middle, drawn back and secured with a leather lace. Not so much as a single hair dared to defy him by falling forward over his wide forehead. The only imperfection she could see was a hawklike nose that had obviously been broken at least once.

God had indeed chosen well—formidable, unapproachable— this warrior was an ideal champion. She would be safe in his care. But would he leave Homelea intact?

The servant finished tending Kathryn's injury and departed.

Kathryn realized the man was talking and dragged her attention back to what he was saying.

". . . you have suffered a terrible loss in the death of your father. Let me assure you, my king will see to your well being."

After a maid placed refreshments in front of them, Sir Bryan continued. "As you may know, several lowland chieftains and members of the nobility, including your father, have refused to align themselves with the crown of Scotland."

"My father had personal and business connections with England," she replied stiffly.

The knight tore off a piece of bread and chewed it. "Your father declared for England to save his English lands."

"Apparently, Papa expected England to succeed in the current conflict."

"Aye, and with such loyal retainers as the Earl of Homelea, Scotland's cause is jeopardized."

She could see his disdain for her father written in the hardness of his gaze. His accusation stung, though she knew it to be true. "My father is dead, sir. Am I to be held accountable for his actions?"

"In truth, lady, your allegiance will be decided by your husband."

"I do not wish to marry, my laird."

"Indeed."

He stared at her, and his ability to hide his emotions vexed her. How was she to deal with someone whose expression remained so stoic? Was he incapable of feeling or had he built a wall around his emotions to protect himself? And if so, why? An altogether intriguing man.

Her father's favorite hunting hound rose from under the table and laid its head on the warrior's thigh. Kathryn gently scolded, "Off with you, Maggie."

But the dog ignored her, and the man idly petted the beast's head, gently fondling the ears. "How do you plan to hold Homelea without a husband?" he asked as he slipped a morsel of cheese to the now devoted hound.

"Perhaps the king would appoint Fergus as castellan to see to the estate's affairs."

"And allow you to remain unmarried? Not likely."

The dog licked his hand clean; was that a smile she spied on Black Bryan's face? He was smiling at the dog? Kathryn stared at the way the smile transformed his face and instinctively raised a hand to cover her heart.

He patted Maggie's head, and by the time his gaze reached Kathryn's, the smile had disappeared and the stoic warrior had returned. Kathryn's hand dropped to her lap. "I would be happy to spend my days at the abbey at St. Mary's."

"You would take the veil?"

"No, simply live there in peace." Until Isobel was safely grown and married. Or Rodney was dead.

Sir Bryan took a drink and wiped a hand across his mouth. "'Tis more likely the king will reward some deserving fellow with your wealth and person." His gaze roved over her, and she felt herself blush.

Kathryn sat in stony silence. The man's frank appraisal reminded her she was powerless to affect her own future. In such discussions, her wishes would not be considered.

Black Bryan's lips softened into what Kathryn was beginning to recognize as the man's attempt to smile. It wasn't much of a smile, not nearly so bright as the one he'd bestowed on the dog. His eyes warmed briefly, from inky black to rich brown.

"Rest easy, Lady Kathryn. Bruce is a reasonable man. He will find you a good husband. Until we hear from him, you will remain inside the walls of Homelea."

"Oh, but I must visit St. Mary's." Her last visit had been two weeks ago and the child's first birthday was next week.

"Why?"

Stunned by his question, she struggled for an answer. "I visit every week."

"And again I ask, why must you risk your safety by going there?"

"My safety?"

"The English need access to the river crossing on your lands as much as Bruce does. Do you think they won't try to regain control of Homelea? Of you?"

"I care nothing for your plans for war. I simply wish to visit the abbey as I'm accustomed to. There is an elderly nun of whom I am very fond, and I take her food and other items to give her comfort." It wasn't exactly a lie, just not the whole truth, Kathryn assured herself.

"Very well. I will provide you with an armed escort and you may go."

"When?"

"In a few days."

Kathryn didn't want to wait, but from his forbidding expression, she knew better than to argue with a man who liked dogs better than people.

Four

Rodney carleton, newly named Earl of Fairfax, looked about the room at those Edward had hastily summoned to attend a war council. The Earls of Pembroke, Ulster, and Dunbar were in attendance. Edward seemed barely able to conceal his glee at whatever news he planned to share. The king quickly called his noblemen to order.

"Gentlemen, Bruce has finally given us the means to subdue the rebel Scots once and for all."

"What is the news, Your Majesty?" asked Ulster.

Ulster remained a valued member of the inner circle despite his daughter's imprisonment at the manor of Burstwick-in-Holderness. Edward's own father had arranged the marriage of Ulster's daughter, Elizabeth de Burgh, to Robert the Bruce in an effort to wed the Scotsman's loyalty to the English king. Only her father's continued loyalty to England had saved Elizabeth from being tried as a traitor.

Rodney returned his thoughts to the present as Edward continued. "We are still in command of Stirling. Our commander there, Sir Philip Mowbray, arrived here in London last week under a grant of safe conduct. It seems Bruce's impatient brother has committed Bruce to the capture of Stirling Castle."

A murmur arose among the gathering and the king raised his voice to be heard. "A bargain has been struck whereby, if I do not rescue Stirling from Bruce's siege by Midsummer's Day, then Mowbray will yield the castle to Bruce."

"And is Bruce bound by this agreement?" Dunbar inquired, his voice incredulous.

"Yes, he is. Mowbray and Edward Bruce pledged their sacred honor. Robert must see this through and meet us, at last, in a pitched battle he cannot win. No more must we abide his irregular warfare. He will meet the might of England and be vanquished."

Edward pounded the table in front of him. "We shall assemble a mighty army and defeat these vexing Scots once and for all. The relief of Stirling shall be our battle call and will cause all of England to rally to our cause."

"Here, here," shouted a chorus of voices.

At this, Carleton spoke up. "We shall prevail, Your Majesty. The Scots have seen much of war these past years, and it has taken a toll. How soon do we begin preparations?"

Edward smiled in malice. "Immediately. I have sent writs to eight earls, including the four of you here today, and eighty-seven barons, summoning you to appear with your forces at Berwick by June tenth."

Heads nodded as Edward continued. "I have also issued an open summons to any knight from any country who may wish to join our cause and so reap the fame and spoils of fortune."

"Here, here," the others shouted in excitement.

"I shall await you at Berwick, my lords. See to your duty." Edward dismissed them, all but Carleton.

As the others filed from the room, Lord Rodney Carleton straightened his sleeve and perused his finely tailored clothing, admiring this latest fashion from Paris. The new style suited his elegant body to perfection. In this, Rodney thought, he and the king of England had much in common. They both paid particular care to their appearance.

Indeed their mutual delight in the pursuit of life's pleasures was the glue that held their friendship together. His association with Edward provided prestige, privilege, and the opportunity to acquire the wealth needed to obtain life's finer possessions.

The young king, blond and fair of face, resembled his Plantagenet ancestors. Indeed, he favored his father physically, as Edward I had also been a towering man of great strength.

The similarities ended there; where the father had ruled with an iron fist, even Rodney would admit that the son was weak and surrounded himself with advisors of questionable character. Himself excluded, of course. The single idea the two Edwards held in common was a hatred of the rebellious Scots. In particular, Robert the Bruce and the baseborn knight, Bryan Mackintosh.

When they were alone, Rodney bowed and said, "Your Majesty, how good of you to see me privately."

"Nonsense, Rodney. Your message intrigued us, as you knew it would. We found the news quite interesting. It seems the Scottish rebel has stolen another jewel from our crown. And from you." He snickered. "Come, pour yourself some wine and let us sit."

Alerted to Edward's bad mood by the use of the royal pronoun, Rodney nervously filled a goblet from the side table, then sat in the chair next to his king.

Rodney waited for Edward to begin the conversation, reminding himself he didn't care one way or the other if the Scots were subdued or not. Politics only interested him in so far as it affected his ability to accumulate wealth and power. However, he did want revenge against Bryan Mackintosh for taking what was his.

Edward eyed him over the top of his goblet. "I expected you to convince Lady Kathryn, by force, if necessary, to yield her Scottish lands and wealth to England."

"Yes, my lord." He'd had plenty of time to dread Edward's

reaction in the six days it had taken him to return to London. So far Edward's behavior was more reasonable than he'd hoped.

Edward slapped the arm of his chair. "Confound it. How did Mackintosh take the castle?"

Rodney swallowed. "Lady Kathryn yielded to Mackintosh, not to me. Her people are loyal to her and they refused to obey me."

"Perhaps the young countess has not yet had time to take note of your numerous attributes."

"Perhaps not." Rodney refused to rise to the bait and give the king more reason to be angry with him. Kathryn's refusal of his marriage proposal had caused quite a stir among his social set. He'd been biding his time, waiting for the aging earl to oblige him by dying. But Mackintosh had spoiled his plans.

Given another chance, Rodney would make Kathryn pay for her most recent behavior. Her treachery might cost him the king's favor unless he thought of some way to make amends.

"Well, Rodney, what are we to do? Her Scottish estates are worth far more than those she holds here. The wealth will only be used against England's cause if it remains in the hands of that Scottish rebel." Edward brushed at his sleeve. "She must be punished to prove to my detractors that I can be ruthless when necessary."

Rodney stiffened. "Punished how?"

"Use your imagination, can't you, Rodney?"

"Of course." Best to change the subject quickly before Edward used his. "And what of my desires, sire?"

"You will be rewarded according to your success in getting me what I want." He leaned forward. "I want Homelea and its river crossing."

"And the woman?"

"Why must you have the one woman in my kingdom who doesn't want you?" He leaned back again. "There are others just as wealthy as Lady Kathryn who would willingly grace your arm, you know."

"No doubt. But 'tis her I want." *She will bow to my will.*

Edward speared him with a look. "In all likelihood, Bruce will give the woman to one of his nobles. We probably cannot stop such a marriage, but time is running short for Bruce and his rabble army." He made a quick decision. "You will accompany me north to Stirling."

Rodney felt ill at the suggestion. "I'm a swordsman, not a warrior."

"You can sit a horse while you wield your sword, can't you? If you want the countess, you will seek out Mackintosh and kill him."

"But what if she's already married?"

"We will seek an annulment. Nothing is impossible when one has money and the ear of the pope."

"Yes, Your Majesty."

"As to Mackintosh, it shouldn't be hard to find him on the field of battle after we tear Bruce's army into shreds. Indeed, Black Bryan is always in the ranks that protect his nefarious sire, and I want *him* dead, too."

Edward stood and Rodney followed suit, replacing his goblet on the table. "My liege, perhaps we can use Kathryn to lure Mackintosh, and even Bruce himself, into a trap and thus avoid a battle at Stirling altogether."

Edward clapped his hands together. "Yes, just the thing, Rodney. Your devious mind is always working. See how it can be done. One way or another, I will rid my kingdom of that trumped up king."

KATHRYN SAW LITTLE OF HER GUARDIAN the next week. From Fergus she learned that the knight's squire was named

Thomas and his man at arms was named Adam. All three were recruiting men for the Scottish army. When she saw them enter the hall on Saturday evening, she quickly sent a servant to invite them to join her at the high table.

She awaited them by the fireplace, Fergus at her side. She wasn't surprised to see Maggie the hound at Sir Bryan's heels.

"So that's where the dog has been all day," Fergus said.

"Aye, she's taken to Sir Bryan, it seems."

She feared her distrust of the knight must have shown in her tone of voice and Fergus defended him. "A man who inspires such canine loyalty can't be all bad, can he?"

Kathryn frowned. "Don't trust a dog to judge a man's character, Fergus. Will you join us for the meal?"

"I will stay in the hall, aye. But not at table with you."

Sir Bryan and the blond man walked to where Kathryn and Fergus stood. The men nodded curtly to one another before Fergus took his leave while the squire went to sit with Sir Bryan's soldiers. She saw Fergus give orders to several of the castle guards before finding an empty spot at a table near the kitchen doorway.

Her attention was soon captured by Sir Bryan's man at arms. His smiling face certainly contrasted with the dour knight's. Bending over her proffered hand, he said, "We have not been properly introduced, my lady. Adam Mackintosh, at your service. I have the misfortune to be this brute's foster brother as well as his master at arms."

He straightened and clapped Sir Bryan on the back. The smile that accompanied such impertinence assured Kathryn the men were the best of friends, despite the difference in age. Adam looked to be at least five years older and was as fair as the other man was dark, their coloring presumably mirroring their dispositions.

"Good evening, Lady Kathryn," Sir Bryan said as he offered her his arm and led her to the dais. They took their seats, one man on either side of her and she said, "Are you cousins, then, Sir Bryan?"

"No. My mother married a Mackintosh. I lived at Moy until her death." Bryan cut the meat on the trencher they shared and gave her the first bite on the end of his knife.

At least he has good table manners. She finished chewing and asked, "And how did you come to train as a knight?"

"I was sent to Lochmaben to train as a page with the Earl of Carrick." The Earl of Carrick, who now reigned as Robert the Bruce of Scotland.

Without thinking, she asked, "Your father sent for you?" For a brief second some emotion raced across his face and she quickly said, "I'm sorry, my laird. I should not have spoken so."

He calmly resumed cutting the meat and offered her another piece. "The only father I have known was William Mackintosh. And he is dead."

Adam cleared his throat and said, "'Tis hard to lose a parent under the best of circumstances."

"You have shared my experience," she replied, glad to move the conversation to a safer topic.

Bryan filled their glasses. "He has."

"Aye," Adam said. "My father died six years ago. But as I've often said, the love of a good woman can soothe all manner of heartache."

Kathryn smiled at Adam's declaration. "And you speak from experience again?"

Bryan said, "Adam is disgustingly happily married. And how many bairns have you and Gwenyth now? I can't keep track."

"There's only the three, Bryan."

Kathryn relaxed in their company, enjoying the banter she had always imagined flowed between siblings. The awkwardness caused by her reference to Bryan's parentage seemed forgotten, thankfully.

As the table was being cleared for the serving of sweets, Adam's tone became more somber. "Ceallach should arrive any day and we'll be called to Stirling. In the meantime, let's enjoy good food and warm beds while we can."

"Aye, we'll be eating army food and sleeping on the ground once we leave here."

Somehow Sir Bryan didn't sound as unhappy at the prospect of leaving as Adam did.

"And there won't be such a lovely lady to grace our meals, either." Adam grinned and Kathryn felt her face blush at his compliment. Adam continued to jest with her and rib his foster brother until a traveling troubadour carrying a harp walked over to their table.

"Gawen," Adam said, "it's good to see you again. Lady Kathryn, have you ever heard young Gawen sing?"

"No, I haven't."

"He has the voice of an angel."

The man bowed over her hand. "Your servant, my lady." He indicated his harp. "I know of your father's recent death. Would you prefer not to have song this evening?"

"How thoughtful of you to ask, Gawen. My father loved a well-sung tale, and I'm sure your song would be an appropriate remembrance of him."

"With your permission, then?"

Kathryn inclined her head and smiled at his courtly manners. "Of course, Gawen. Tell us a fine tale this evening."

Conversations gradually halted throughout the hall as Gawen took a seat before the great fireplace and strummed the harp. His clear tenor voice enchanted them. Kathryn leaned over and asked Bryan if he would interpret.

"Do you mean to tell me you don't speak the Gaelic?" he asked.

"I do, but not well enough to follow in song."

"Very well, then." He moved closer to her on the bench. She glanced to where Fergus sat, and saw him scowling. Now what? The man seemed constantly cross with her lately.

Sir Bryan bent down closer to her ear. Kathryn felt his breath stir her hair. She detected the fragrance of mint and a musky, masculine scent that, coupled with his chest touching her shoulder, she found disconcerting. She forced her thoughts back to the singer and his tale.

"Scotland's current troubles began over the love of a woman," Sir Bryan spoke softly. "For hundreds of years, royal descendants of *Ceann-Mor* ruled our fair land. Gawen is now listing each of those kings. Shall I repeat them for you?"

She shook her head, content to listen to Gawen's strong, clear voice as he counted the great, and not so great, past kings of Scotland.

"Come, Bryan," Adam said. "'Tis my turn to regale the lady." Adam picked up the story. "All through these times, England and Scotland were good neighbors and friends. Tonight we hear the tale of Alexander III, well beloved king, whose wife bore him two sons and a daughter. None, alas, who outlived their sire. Upon his first wife's death, Alexander took a second, much younger wife. He was quite delighted with her, and took every opportunity to attempt to create an heir."

Kathryn heard the mirth in Adam's voice and looked at him to confirm it. He made a comical face and she felt herself blush. Black Bryan did not join in the frivolity, and Kathryn wondered that such a stern man could be a friend with a man such as Adam.

She brought her thoughts back to Alexander, the king who had found delight in being a husband. Would Kathryn ever elicit such devotion from a man?

Bryan shifted in his seat, and now his thigh touched hers.

Deliberate or not, it made her uncomfortable, and she pulled away.

Seeming not to notice her retreat, Sir Bryan interrupted Adam and continued with the story. "One winter night, the king met with his advisors some distance from his home. The meeting ended well after dark, on a cold, blustery evening. His squire and others tried to persuade Alexander to wait until morning, but visions of his lovely young wife rose in his head, and he started for home.

"When the king's riderless horse arrived at the castle later that night, a search party set forth. But it wasn't until morn that they found his body lying at the foot of a cliff. He had apparently urged his horse forward, but the beast, sensing danger, had stopped suddenly and Alexander tumbled over the animal's head to his death."

"And how did this lead to our present difficulties with England?" Kathryn asked, as Gawen sang the final verse.

"Alexander's heir, an infant granddaughter, died before taking the throne. With the monarchy in chaos, the nobles fought amongst themselves and are still trying to regain control a quarter century later."

"And I take it you blame all this on the love of a woman?"

Black Bryan's scowl returned. "Aye." The tone of his voice cooled dramatically. "If Alexander hadn't been so besotted over his wife and her charms, perhaps he would have listened to reason and lived long enough to father a suitable heir."

"So, duty comes before love? Or do you not approve of a man loving his wife?"

Bryan answered, "A house divided cannot stand, nor can a man see to his duty if his loyalties are divided."

Adam said, "Come, brother. Kings have a duty to produce heirs." At this a look passed between the two men that Kathryn couldn't unravel.

"So they do," Sir Bryan agreed.

Kathryn knew that Bruce's only legitimate heir was a young

daughter about Kathryn's age. Was Bryan her older half brother? Did he entertain hopes of inheriting Bruce's crown? If he did it would create as much instability as had the death of King Alexander's granddaughter.

He had moved to the other side of the bench and turned his back to her, deep in conversation with Adam. She glanced at him and wondered if he ever laughed in the company of people or if he was only so forbidding around her.

Returning her thoughts to the night's entertainment, she saw many of those present had now joined Gawen in another song.

Kathryn stifled a yawn just as Sir Bryan turned to face her, emotions masked, as usual, beneath a scowl. "You are tired, my lady. Do you wish to retire?"

"Aye, my laird, if it please you."

His face remained expressionless. "I have enjoyed your company this evening."

His confession surprised her. "And I yours, my laird." Though the polite response came automatically, she realized the words were true. Were his words more than required etiquette as well? His stoic countenance made clear that he desired no further conversation. She rose, bid him goodnight, and retired to her chamber to a restless night's sleep.

KATHRYN SPENT THE NEXT MORNING with her steward and her chief shepherd, tallying the lambs born this spring. Homelea's wealth derived mainly from the fine wool produced by its flock of sheep, and Kathryn had much to learn about their care. If she had hoped her protector would also oversee the estate, she was doomed to disappointment.

Over the past week Sir Bryan and Adam had been far too busy

to attend to the day-to-day decisions of managing a castle and its occupants. Messengers arrived at all hours and often Sir Bryan had ridden out with them.

As the time for the noonday meal approached, the sound of horses on the drawbridge startled her. By the time she crossed the hall, she saw Fergus usher a man into the solar, which Sir Bryan now occupied as a temporary headquarters.

Fergus closed the door and Kathryn inquired, "Do you know who sent him?"

"King Robert, my lady. Most likely the man has news of the war."

"He doesn't look like a messenger." The man had been as large as the Black Knight and carried an unusual number of weapons.

Kathryn went to see to refreshments for the man, whoever or whatever he might be.

Curiosity aroused, Kathryn returned to the hall and lingered about the doorway of the solar for several minutes. Something was brewing, something more than the confrontation at Stirling. And their plotting seemed to put Homelea and its inhabitants directly in the middle, making her fear for their safety.

Twice she walked toward the door intending to knock, but voices raised in anger could clearly be heard from behind the heavy oak door. Actually, only one voice sounded angry—Sir Bryan's. The other voice was pleading.

The sound of crashing furniture sent Kathryn scurrying to the other side of the hall. Whatever the messenger had told Sir Bryan had obviously not pleased the knight. The door would no doubt open soon and disgorge the hapless messenger. Rather than risk being near the angry knight, she hastened out of the hall to the stable. She had just begun to groom her mare when a servant found her. "My lady, Sir Bryan would like a word with ye."

Reluctantly Kathryn set down the brush and walked back

toward the keep, entering through the kitchen. She crossed the hall and hesitated outside the solar. Finally, she pushed the door open, barely concealing a gasp when she spied the scowl on Black Bryan's face.

Adam stood next to him, and only the kindness in his smile kept Kathryn from retracing her steps to the stable. A fast ride on a willing horse appealed to her far more than facing the grim-faced man in front of her. The messenger had already left the room.

Recovering her composure, Kathryn asked, "You sent for me, sir?"

"Aye, come have a seat." He averted his gaze.

Why wouldn't he look at her?

He brought his gaze back to her and something in his eyes made her shiver involuntarily.

She sat in the chair Adam offered as Sir Bryan picked up a parchment from the table. Her heart hammered in her chest. She could see the muscle work in his jaw as he clenched and un-clenched it.

"The king has chosen a husband for you." The knight's voice sounded strained.

"But I don't wish to marry, my laird. You said you would make that clear to His Majesty."

The fierce warrior stared at the document in his hands. After clearing his throat, Sir Bryan spoke. "I am instructed to assure you His Majesty King Robert is not insensitive to your person or your position. But he feels it is in your best interest to have the protection of a husband. Therefore he has chosen . . . It seems he wishes to strengthen his claim to Homelea by wedding you to one of his knights."

He raised an eyebrow and regarded her intently. For once his face divulged his emotions only too clearly and he didn't look any

ier about the situation than she felt. Who had the king chosen
l how would it affect her and Isobel? Fighting panic, Kathryn
rayed that this was somehow part of God's plan.

What does that parchment say?

Sir Bryan averted his gaze. Obviously at a loss to continue, the
dark-haired knight faced her again, then turned to his man at arms
with an imploring look. Such hesitation was so out of character for
the man that she caught herself biting her thumbnail in agitation.

Adam stepped forward. "The rest of our king's message concerns
my foster brother, which is why he's stumbling about. King Robert is
aware of your youth and praises your beauty. An opinion, by the way,
which I share with our sovereign."

Adam's grin was infectious and Kathryn found herself amused
by his efforts to put her at ease. The warmth of his expression and
the kindness in his voice gave her hope that he, at least, approved
of the king's choice. But the scowl on Black Bryan's face told her he
didn't share his brother's opinion.

She could only hope that whomever the king had chosen, he
would protect her and Isobel from Rodney Carleton. Her breathing
became shallow. Her heart raced. *Please God. Send someone kind who
will love Isobel and cherish me. A man who knows you and your son.*
Despite the coolness of the room, moisture beaded on her forehead.

"Perhaps you should hear what the king has to say." Adam took
the parchment and opened it, and Kathryn's future unfolded as
Adam smoothed the pages.

The knight appeared as uneasy as she felt. Then Adam said,
"My lady, you will retain one third of this estate as your dowry, all
rents and payments to remain under your control. There is a
complete listing of those payments—"

Black Bryan erupted. "Adam, for the love of heaven, get on
with it."

"Yes. My apologies to both of you." With a nod to Sir Bryan, lips twitching, Adam continued. "In the name of King Robert the Bruce of Scotland, Sir Bryan Robert Mackintosh is hereby named as the new Earl of Homelea."

Kathryn gasped in indignation. Robert the Bruce was taking her birthright. Who would marry her without her title and lands? Her eyes widened in shock as the obvious answer to that question was confirmed.

"To seal Sir Bryan's claim to the title, His Majesty announces the betrothal of his ward, Kathryn Rose de Lindsay to the new Earl of Homelea. The marriage is to take place within the week—"

"Absolutely not." Kathryn jumped up from her chair and shook her head in disbelief. The sudden rise to her feet caused a wave of dizziness and she all but fainted. "Out of the question. I do not accept this betrothal."

He wasn't the one, the answer to her prayers. The king had made a mistake. Sir Bryan was her champion, not her husband. He was not God's choice . . . he couldn't be. Kathryn struggled to maintain her wits while she considered how to halt this nightmare. In the heat of her emotions, she didn't think before she said, "I'll not be forced to marry anyone, let alone some baseborn knight."

Immediately she wished to retract the harsh words that condemned her own precious daughter. But 'twas too late.

At the murderous look on Black Bryan's face, she nearly panicked. That remark had certainly gone beyond the bounds of courtesy. How to diffuse the tangible tension in the room and give herself time to think? To pray. If ever she'd needed time alone to seek God's will, it was now.

A fainting spell. Yes, that would put an end to this ridiculous conversation. Not the most original idea, she knew, but it was the best solution she could manage at the moment. Without further thought, Kathryn let her body go limp in what she hoped was a graceful fall that wouldn't end with her head crashing into the furniture. Just before she closed her eyes she saw Sir Bryan reach for her, his scowl replaced by apparent concern for her welfare.

Mercifully, he caught her before she hit anything, although the pins holding her braided hair came loose. Relief that her hair was the only casualty of her folly was short-lived. Kathryn now found herself held securely in the brute's arms. She fought down her panic, but not before she stiffened for a telltale instant. He must be peering into her face because she could feel his warm breath on her cheek, smell the mint he chewed after meals. Barely refraining from an errant shudder, she focused on staying limp.

"Well, brother, it seems you have the lady swooning at your feet," Adam chided.

Kathryn wished she could peek at the expression on Sir Bryan's face. "Fetch the matron to tend her," he said.

Just put me down and go away. Please.

But all he did was sit down on a bench and set her weight on his thigh. She heard Anna bustle in and her indignant, "What have ye done to my lady?"

"She appears to have fainted, though Lady Kathryn doesn't strike me as the fainting sort," he said. "What ails her?"

"I don't know—did ye have words with her?" Anna asked.

As he explained the king's message, Kathryn wondered how much longer she could feign her fainting spell.

She heard Anna's intake of breath at the announcement of the betrothal. "One too many shocks, I dare say. Come, let's take her to her chamber."

Kathryn's head lolled against his chest as he climbed the stairs. He laid her gently on the bed in her chamber. Anna placed a cool cloth on her forehead.

"I assure you I am no more pleased than Lady Kathryn at marrying against my will. However, this fainting spell will not deter me from my duty."

Knowing that if she didn't "revive" soon they would know she'd faked the spell, she moved her head and pushed at the cloth with her hand.

A silent moment passed and she peered through nearly closed eyelids. "Is he gone?"

"No, my lady, I'm still here."

She could swear she heard something like amusement in his voice. Kathryn groaned. "Leave me, please."

Silence. "We will speak when you have recovered."

FIVE

THE NEXT DAY KATHRYN WAS NO CLOSER to a solution to her dilemma. She decided to check on a mare due to foal soon, thinking the company of the horses would soothe her as it so often did. The stable door was slightly ajar and as she pushed it open she heard a voice crooning in a Gaelic lilt. She stepped quietly inside, unprepared for the sight of Bryan Mackintosh leading his stallion from its stall. Kathryn watched him tie the horse and then run his hands down a foreleg.

He was so intent on what he was doing he didn't notice her in the shadows. Feeling slightly guilty for spying, nevertheless she watched in fascination as he continued to run his hands over each of the horse's legs in turn, all the while speaking softly to the animal. Now and then his face came into her view and she marveled at the difference. Gone was the seemingly perpetual scowl, replaced by concern and then relief when his hands detected no heat or swelling. And more than that, his expression was that of a man who loved and admired horses as much as she did herself.

Encouraged by this glimpse of the man, she shuffled her feet to make it appear as if she'd just entered the door. He stopped mid-stride as their gazes met and almost immediately his face became a mask. How did he do that? And why? Intrigued, she stared at him before recovering her manners.

He recovered first. Laying a hand on the animal's croup, he said, "Good morrow, lady. You are feeling better today, I see."

"Good morrow to you, my laird. I am quite recovered, thank you," she said.

He walked to the animal's head and with practiced ease, untied him and circled him until horse and man faced her. Standing to the horse's left, he watched as she approached.

She walked to the horse's head, but mindful of the antics of feisty stallions, stayed out of reach of its teeth.

Sir Bryan stood at the quiet stallion's shoulder, the rope acting as a barrier between Kathryn and him. As if in answer to her unspoken question, he explained his presence in the stable. "My horse was lame. I thought I'd take a look to see if he's recovered."

The stallion docilely accepted the man's hand as he ran it down its neck. The horse's rich, black coat glistened, nearly identical in color to its master's hair. She carefully extended her hand to stroke the white, star-shaped hair between the wide-set eyes. The horse accepted her touch just as quietly. "Such a beautiful animal. And with a nice disposition for a stallion."

Sir Bryan straightened to his full height and looked at her, eyes cold and distant. "Aye, his manners are good."

For a moment, Kathryn forgot if they were discussing the horse or the man. Her confusion must have been apparent on her face. Disconcerted she blurted, "Perhaps better than his master's."

Hand over his heart he said, straight-faced, "You wound me, lady."

She couldn't help but smile, even though his foolery made her feel off-balance. So, he *could* let down his guard around people after all. Pointing to the horse's leg, she asked, "Doesn't your squire take care of such things?"

"He does, but I prefer to care for Cerin myself."

Her gaze shifted back to the man. He wore a saffron sark, loosely laced at the neck. The small plaid draped across his broad chest was belted at his waist and pinned in place at his left shoulder. His muscular legs were well defined by the woven trews . . . She hastened her gaze to his face to find him assessing her with similar interest, and she felt her cheeks flush under his appraising stare.

How ill-mannered of him. She turned and walked toward the stall of the expectant mare.

She thought she heard a smile in his voice as he said, "And you, my lady, do you prefer to care for your own horse as well?"

She swiveled back to face him. "I find comfort in the company of these beasts." As soon as she said the words, she was sorry she'd shared even that small bit of herself with this bewildering stranger.

"Aye, that I understand." The horse tossed its head, jiggling the ropes, and Sir Bryan quieted it with a touch to its neck. "You miss your father, then?"

There was genuine sympathy in his tone, and she did not want sympathy or kindness or anything else from him. So she must fight the impulse to accept those very things from him. God had not sent him—he was not the answer to her prayers. She used the only weapons she had at hand—words of anger. "Aye, well. Papa's death makes one less enemy for your king."

His expression darkened, and for a moment she regretted the words. But he recovered quickly, though his voice was strained. "One less man whose loyalty could be bought."

Why had she given in to anger? Lashing him verbally wouldn't resolve her issues with King Robert's plan for them to marry. Nor had Sir Bryan done or said anything to deserve it. Indeed the man had actually been kind, and tears threatened as she repented of her uncharitable behavior.

Her anguish must have shown, because his voice gentled once again. "We've gotten off to a rather poor start, haven't we?"

She nodded, all she felt capable of at the moment. His tenderness was totally out of character for the Bryan Dubh of legend. How dare he speak so kindly, this destroyer of villages and dreams? How dare he make her wish for what couldn't be?

He frowned.

Much better. *Don't confuse me with kindness.*

"My lady, there are things that must be said between us, and we cannot wait on a more convenient time. The king's plans obviously don't suit either of us, so I will ride to Bruce's camp and ask him to rescind the betrothal."

Hope arose. "Do you have some influence with him? I mean, because you are . . . he is. . . ." Flustered, she gave up.

He shrugged. Apparently satisfied his horse was sound, he returned the animal to its stall, then faced her. "I cannot make any promises, Lady Kathryn. My relationship with King Robert is that of a knight to his liege laird. Nothing more. I'm not privy to his reasons for suggesting the marriage in the first place."

She drew in a deep breath. "But he is your father, isn't he?"

He looped the leading rope in his hand, studying it. In the quiet she could hear horses munching hay and the occasional stomp of an equine foot. "Would it change your mind about marrying me if I told you the king was indeed my sire?"

"Not at all."

"Then there is no need to discuss this further. I will do my best to convey your wishes to His Majesty. But I warn you, we may have no choice. I obey my liege, in this and all other matters." He hung the leading rope on a peg. "Tell me, what is your objection to marriage?"

Anna had asked the same thing and the answer remained the same. "Marriage to a man who doesn't love me, who doesn't love

God above all else, would be no marriage at all but prison." She would need to marry for love, because only a man who truly loved her and God might be able to forgive her lack of virginity.

And above all other considerations, she couldn't marry anyone who wouldn't protect Isobel. She'd had no time to learn anything about this man other than his love for animals and his belief that duty came before love. She must protect the child, even if it meant lying to the knight.

"I would prefer to have Fergus manage my affairs rather than acquire a husband." And now for the blow she hated to give, but must if she had any hope of persuading him against the union. "And if I must marry, I would prefer it be with someone more in keeping with my station." *God forgive me for saying such a thing.*

LADY KATHRYN HAD A rather exalted opinion of herself. There were many women who would gladly marry a royal by-blow such as him. Bryan struggled to control his emotions. He wasn't sure of anything at the moment, especially how he felt about the aggravating woman standing before him. One minute he wanted only to shelter her in his arms and stave off all who would bring her harm, and the next she made him so angry he wanted to throttle her.

Fighting the impulse to do just that, he let his gaze rove over her. "Be careful, my lady. A man such as I, of such distasteful birth, could be very tempted by the title of earl. I could decide this marriage suits me after all."

He grasped her arm and pulled her close. Her frightened eyes told him she feared him, and he regretted it. But if she would not respect him, then she could very well fear him instead. "You see, I have earned this reward from my king, with my loyalty and my blood. And you may yet provoke me to take what my king offers."

She shook loose of his grip but did not back away. "'Tis all that's important to one such as you, isn't it? A legitimate title and fortune?"

Losing all patience with her, he replied, "You may believe what you wish, Lady Kathryn. It changes naught. I will do my best to persuade King Robert to free you from sullying your precious bloodline with the likes of me. But make no mistake: If he insists, then we will marry."

"Whether I wish to or not."

"Aye. And whether I wish to or not."

She stared in disbelief. "You would force me?"

He didn't answer.

"You are a cruel, unfeeling brute."

"And you, Countess, would do well to remember your manners."

They stood toe to toe, glaring at each other, neither giving an inch. Because of her unusual height, her head reached his chin; she barely had to look up to meet his gaze. Her eyes blazed with indignation.

Her willingness to confront him—Black Bryan, warrior knight—kindled his admiration. Admiration soon turned to longing, for what he did not know. He fought the urge to seize her shoulders and kiss her, to mark her as his. To prove she desired him as much as he desired her. *Insanity.* Then he strode past her and out of the stable, shaken, confused, and badly in need of his father's advice.

BRYAN RETREATED TO THE SOLAR where he paced the room from end to end, seeking to escape his tangled emotions. Her rejection had stung, especially since she'd found his most vulnerable point and, like a skilled warrior, had stabbed hard at the weak link in his armor.

His relationship to Bruce had never been publicly acknowl-edged. Bryan had gained a reputation as a fierce warrior and a man of honor. Few people, whether they knew his parentage or not, dared to insult him for any reason.

Yet this woman had the audacity to do just that. And he'd completely lost his senses and made marriage sound like a merce-nary payment, a duty to be performed. No woman wanted to hear such a thing. They wanted declarations of undying love, or at the least, gentle words of kindness. Hadn't she said as much?

But he feared soft words and kindness—they would weaken him—weaken his resolve to keep his emotions disengaged.

The room seemed to shrink; he craved open space and fresh air. Bryan found Adam and Thomas and in as few words as possible told them he was going to Bruce's camp and would return tomorrow night.

Thomas objected. "I'll go with you."

"I'm in no mood for company, Thomas."

"Fine. I won't talk to you. But you'll not ride out alone."

Adam said, "He's right—"

"All right. All right. Saddle up, Thomas, and be quick about it."

Then Bryan fled the castle, looking neither right nor left, and returned to the stable. He needed to put time and space between himself and that woman, time to clear his head and rein in his temper.

And any other misbegotten emotions that threatened to surface.

His stallion whinnied a welcome at Bryan's return. "Steady, lad. Since you seem to be sound again, let's take a good run today," he said. He placed the bit in the stallion's mouth and pulled the bridle stall over the animal's ears. With practiced movements he finished saddling, led the horse out of the barn and then mounted and urged the horse into a trot. When they'd cleared the drawbridge he set his heels to the animal's side and Cerin responded with a spirited canter, Thomas following behind.

Despite the distraction of the powerful horse beneath him and the scenery passing by, Bryan's thoughts returned to his confrontation with Kathryn. He leaned low over the great beast's neck and said, "By the saints, Cerin, why didn't I tell her about my vow?"

Bryan had never told anyone of his resolve not to marry until the war was over. Until Kathryn, he'd never been tempted, so there'd been no need. Now, saints help him, Robert the Bruce had placed temptation squarely in Bryan's path.

Angrily, he cursed his king and the sky above for handing him such provocation—honeyed tresses, gold-flecked brown eyes, and a feminine form that made him long for the intimacies of marriage.

Obviously Kathryn didn't want him. Fine. He didn't need a woman to complicate his life. And Kathryn would surely disturb his ordered existence—she'd already disturbed him more than he'd thought possible.

Robert would understand—Bryan would explain everything. He wasn't sure it would do any good, but he had to try. Aye, he'd explain how he couldn't marry such a beautiful, wealthy, exciting woman, if he could just find a way to put it into words.

He spurred Cerin on and arrived at the hideout just before evening. Thomas took the horse and, knowing the animal would be well cared for, Bryan strode toward the tent where the king's standard blew lazily in the breeze.

Not surprisingly, the king met him at the tent's entrance and invited him in. Bruce clapped Bryan on the shoulder. "Come in, join us. Ceallach is here."

Bryan entered, knowing his discussion would have to wait until the other man left. He nodded to Ceallach and took a seat at the table. The open cask of wine and half-empty chalices indicated a celebration in progress.

"What news, my laird?" Bryan had left the main force to take Homelea and despite his need to resolve his problem with Kathryn, now hungered for a report on how Bruce's army had fared during his absence. He poured himself some water as Ceallach said, "Perth has fallen."

Bryan's instincts as a soldier overcame his personal needs. "You had the town surrounded when I left—no access in or out!" he said incredulously. Bruce had no artillery or siege weapons to batter down the walls. And many of his troops were highlanders such as himself who didn't take well to static warfare. "How did you get inside?"

Bruce grinned. Even the taciturn Ceallach smiled, and Bryan knew he was going to regret not being part of this particular adventure.

Ceallach continued. "Actually, Bruce ordered us to retreat and we packed up and marched away. You'll recall the heavy woods two miles off?"

Bryan nodded, eager to hear the rest.

"We hid there and constructed rope ladders to scale the ramparts. We spent eight days there in the woods to allow the garrison at Perth to let down their guard. Then on a pitch-dark night we sneaked back to the edge of the moat. The king himself crept through the icy water, testing the depth with his spear until he crossed to the other side. The rest of us followed, climbed the ropes, and took the town by surprise!"

"Well done!" Bryan exclaimed.

"That's not all," Bruce added. "In addition to Homelea, the castles of Buittle and Caerlavrock are now ours as well. All that remains is Stirling."

At mention of this great fortress the mood of all three men

dampened somewhat. No one wanted to mention the impossible agreement Bruce's brother had made with the commander there. The Scots had learned their lesson early on at Methven that England's superior numbers and armament would triumph on a traditional battlefield. When Bruce observed that spider in the cave at Carrick, he'd devised the strategy he'd used for the next seven years. Bruce had waged war against the English, on his terms—fighting in small skirmishes, with strategic targets, and using the lay of the land to their advantage.

Then last April Robert had sent his brother Edward—always an impatient and hotheaded warrior—to lay siege to the impregnable fortress at Stirling. After three months Edward, bored with the static nature of a siege, had made a foolish bargain with Sir Philip Mowbray, the castle's commander. If Edward of England did not come to Stirling's rescue by midsummer a year hence, then Mowbray would yield the castle freely. When Mowbray agreed, Edward took his troops off to find more exciting work. Without consulting either of their monarchs, the two men pledged their honor to fulfill this treaty.

Robert had been outraged at his brother's actions, but there was nothing to be done without sacrificing his brother's honor. Bruce was now compelled to meet Edward II in pitched battle, and the odds were very much against the Scots.

Bryan broke the silence with a change of subject. "What of our negotiations with Ceallach's . . . friends?"

Bruce answered, "The arms will arrive at Homelea within the week. I need you and Adam to secure the weapons and make sure the wagons reach Stirling. Keith will take command of the cavalry in your absence. Ceallach and I will leave for Stirling in two days to begin training the men and to plan our strategy."

"Am I to ride with you?"

"You should be busy with wedding preparations," Bruce said.

"We need to talk about that, Your Majesty." Bruce nodded in acknowledgment. The men emptied their goblets and then they stood as Ceallach bid them goodbye and departed the tent, leaving an uncomfortable silence behind him.

Robert paused, studying Bryan's face. "You are angry."

Angry and, if Bryan cared to admit it, confused. Even the long ride here and the discussion of the battle facing them hadn't eased his conflict. "Why didn't you offer Homelea to Douglas? Or Randolph?" he asked bluntly.

"I have already made Randolph the Earl of Moray and have given him lordship of the Isle of Man. Douglas has his own lands and title."

"Why me, then?"

"As I told you, I wish to reward a loyal and worthy retainer. You deserve the earldom, Bryan, and none would begrudge you." Robert frowned. "You may have to rebuild before you can retire there in peace, but it is yours nonetheless."

Robert indicated the chairs next to a somewhat wobbly table. "Come, sit down and tell me what troubles you about becoming an earl."

Bryan returned to his seat, trying to formulate his objections to wedding Kathryn. The king poured himself a goblet of wine before suggesting, "Perhaps it's the title of husband that doesn't suit. Is she not comely?" Robert asked.

Bryan groaned. If only she weren't. "She is beautiful," he admitted quietly.

"Then she's a shrew?" Robert jested.

"She is more than a little stubborn, quite intelligent, and desperately in need of protection." The truth was, he wanted her —wanted her in a way he'd never desired a woman before. His vow at Carrick might easily disappear on the wind unless he held tight to it.

And then there was the vow he'd made in Homelea's courtyard when he'd first set eyes on Kathryn. Kathryn, with Carleton's mark still fresh upon her beautiful face. Did the second vow cancel the first? Of course not. He could certainly protect her from harm without relinquishing his heart.

Couldn't he? That was a very good question—one he wasn't sure he could answer at the moment. Not with the vision of her standing toe to toe with him in defiance clouding his brain.

"So, you care for her. It could be worse."

"She doesn't want anything to do with someone so far beneath her station. Nor do I need to be bothered with the baggage of a wife," Bryan declared.

"Ah, her opinion must have stung. So you do care for her."

Bryan stood and paced. "If you're asking do I want to . . . am I attracted to her, then yes, I care for her."

"Physical craving and caring are different."

"So you've told me." Bryan studied his king. His father. The memory of that day in the hills of Carrick came back to him. The news of death and capture and his vow not to marry were all vivid in his mind. "What do you hear from the queen?"

Bruce hesitated. "She fares as well as one might expect after eight years of captivity. She has little in the way of furniture or clothing." Bruce hid his pain well but Bryan ached for him.

"And the others?"

Bruce said, "Mercifully they've been treated kindly enough since those bitter months spent in cages. Marjory," he hesitated, drew a breath. "My daughter is at the nunnery at Walton. Her health is precarious."

Bryan stared at his hands a moment. "If you had it to do over again, knowing she would be taken from you, would you still have married Elizabeth?"

Bryan saw the shadow pass over Robert's face, and regretted the pain his question had caused. But Robert must be made to realize what he asked of Bryan in arranging this marriage. He did care for Lady Kathryn, far more than he wanted to admit. However, he wasn't sure marriage to him was in her best interest, under the circumstances.

The two men stared at each other, then Bruce answered Bryan's question. "I'm glad I didn't know then how it would all come to pass, because in truth, I might not have married Elizabeth and thus would have denied myself her love. But sometimes, the hope of seeing her again is all that keeps me going."

Bryan sat back down. He didn't know how to respond to such a candid answer.

Robert broke the uncomfortable silence. "Now, explain to me why you can't marry a beautiful, intelligent, and wealthy woman. Surely your pride was not so wounded that you cannot get past it. Surely you can find a way to persuade the lady?"

Bryan shook his head. "I'm a warrior. What have I to offer her?" He huffed. "I've sworn to safeguard her. Isn't that enough?"

Robert's gaze was direct. "Perhaps. But the war can't last forever, Bryan. When it is done, you will need a woman to come home to, somewhere to reside in peace to nurse your wounds and heal your soul."

Bryan sipped his water. "I could just as easily make a widow of her. Already Rodney Carleton has sworn to seek revenge for taking what he considers his." He had never spoken of his vow. Now he must. "That day in the hills of Carrick, when Lady Christian came to us?"

"I remember."

"You . . . I . . . 'twas the darkest moment of my life, my laird."

"And mine." Bruce's voice was somber.

Bryan gripped the table until his knuckles turned white. "I vowed that day I would not marry until Scotland is free. I don't know if I can face what you have endured and still go on."

Robert studied him before replying, "So that is why you've guarded your heart so closely." He bowed his head and toyed with his wedding ring. "The woman finds your lack of noble lineage distasteful?"

"So she says."

Robert rubbed his forehead above his brows, head bowed. When he looked up, he said, "I told you I have no regrets about marrying Elizabeth. But I am not proud of all my actions, Bryan. I have not always acted according to God's will when it came to my . . . carnal appetites."

Bruce jerked to his feet and now he paced the confines of the tent. "Do you remember your mother, Bryan?"

Shocked speechless, Bryan stammered, "Yes, of course."

"What do you know of her?"

Bryan swallowed. "That she was gently born but impoverished and served in your father's house." There would have been no question of Robert marrying her—she was little more than a servant and could not bring wealth or a political alliance to Bruce's powerful family. "Such relationships are not uncommon among the nobility."

"That doesn't make them right."

"No. But you didn't abandon her." *Or me.* Many noblemen ignored their by-blows, but despite his youth, Bruce had accepted responsibility for Bryan's welfare. Even when Bryan's mother married William Mackintosh and moved to Moy, Bruce sent money.

And when Bryan's mother died, Bruce had sent for him, made him part of the Bruce household as Robert's page. Robert himself had taught him to wield the claymore and battle-axe along with the other skills necessary to become a successful warrior.

Bruce ran his fingers through his hair. "No, I didn't abandon her. I cared for her just as I care, have always cared, for her son."

Bryan didn't know what to say or where the conversation was leading.

"I have regrets, Bryan. But loving Elizabeth isn't one of them." The king ceased pacing and sat back down in the chair facing Bryan, head bowed. "I regret that three of my four brothers have died in this struggle against England. I regret that I am nearly forty years old with my wife imprisoned." Robert raised his head and looked at Bryan. "I regret Elizabeth and I have no son that I may acknowledge before the world as my rightful heir. Aye, that I regret deeply."

Bryan took his father's hand and kissed the back of it. "You have been more than generous to me, my laird."

The king grasped Bryan's fingers fleetingly and released them. "You don't aspire to take my place on the throne?"

"In truth, I've considered what it might be like."

"But?"

"If you were to name me as your heir, or even simply acknowledge me, it would just create more instability and strife. Our current woes came about as a result of controversy over who should rule. Your brother Edward would rightly contest me. And you may yet have a son with your wife, my laird. I must consider what is best for Scotland."

Bruce nodded in approval. "Well said. Then you are content that our relationship remain unspoken?"

"It is enough to have had this conversation with you. To be silently acknowledged by your family, as I always have been."

The king smiled. "I am very pleased with the man you've

become, Bryan. And while I may take some credit for it, 'tis your heart that has always been true. Please accept the earldom as a small measure of my esteem for you."

"As you wish." They sat in companionable silence. "But what of the woman?"

After a pause, the king said, "I'm sorry to ask you to go against a solemn pledge, but it is my wish that you wed the countess." Robert fiddled with his wineglass, staring at the table. "When the shipment has passed safely across the river Tweed, you will desert Homelea and go to Stirling to prepare for battle."

"You will leave Homelea defenseless."

"I cannot spare the men or arms, Bryan. If you wish to keep Lady Kathryn safe, you will have to take her with you. Either that, or leave her there for Edward."

"Edward and Rodney. What a tangle this turned out to be."

"Bryan, I'm sorry. Lady Kathryn must either be protected or abandoned. Shall I look elsewhere for a husband for her?"

No other man shall have her. She is mine. Surprised by the intensity of his reaction, and troubled by the impossible situation he was being forced into, Bryan willed his face to mask his feelings.

"No, Your Majesty. I will do as you ask."

"Bryan, I can coerce you into marriage, but no one can force you to engage your emotions. Do you understand what I'm saying?"

"Aye." A marriage of convenience—a chaste union until such time as he could give his heart freely. What Robert suggested allowed Bryan to keep both vows—he could protect Kathryn while remaining emotionally detached.

"I have sworn to protect her. If my name is needed as well as my sword, so be it."

But how will I protect my heart?

SIX

THE CONFRONTATION IN THE STABLE had frightened
Kathryn. Sir Bryan's size and strength spoke more eloquently than
even his words. He could take what he wanted—indeed he *would*
take what he wanted. She had been warned.

In despair, she sought out Fergus. Kathryn found him with
Lachlan the Smith, who was trimming the hooves on one of the
donkeys used to pull the wool carts to market. Lachlan's sullen
expression and the donkey's loud braying did little to improve
Kathryn's spirits. But Fergus's face lit up when he spied Kathryn,
making her feel welcome and special as he always did. With a nod
toward the noisy donkey he said, "Come, let us find a quieter spot."

They walked toward the keep's entrance, and Fergus guided
them toward Homelea's chapel, a small room on the second floor
of the keep. The altar stood on the eastern wall, and soft morning
light filtered through the stained glass window behind it, creating
a rainbow on the polished stone floor.

The room was plain and simple, the only adornment being the
embroidered cloth and a pair of pewter candlesticks on the altar.
Homelea had no priest in residence since Father Munro's death six
months ago. Services were held sporadically, whenever a traveling
priest showed up. But castle residents came to the chapel each
morning for prayers before breaking their fast.

Although they had no priest, Homelea's chapel did boast two rows of wooden benches, and Kathryn sat down on one of them. Fergus joined her and Kathryn asked, "What ails Lachlan? Seems he's in a sour mood every time I see him lately."

"Lachlan isn't happy with the amount of time his wife spends as a nursemaid at the abbey."

Alarmed by this revelation, she said, "Nelda has never mentioned anything to me. She seems content to earn extra coin this way, although she did ask why I'd taken such an interest in a foundling child."

"Was she satisfied with yer explanation?"

"Aye, I think so." No one had questioned her desire to retreat to St. Mary's after that disastrous confrontation with Rodney. Indeed, she'd gone there before she'd had any idea she carried his child and had simply remained in seclusion. Her heart and soul had truly been shaken and she'd used the time to right herself with God while she awaited Isobel's birth.

Fergus nodded. "How soon can Isobel be weaned?"

Although it was hard to believe so much time had passed, Isobel's first birthday was next week. Kathryn returned her thoughts to Fergus's question. "Isobel could drink from a cup if she had to."

"It might be wise to release Nelda from her duties as soon as ye can, then."

"Sir Bryan said I could go to the abbey in a few days." Remembering their confrontation, she said, "Unless he changes his mind."

"Is that all that's troubling ye this morning? Isobel?"

"No. I have been unwise." She stood and paced the short distance across the room and back and as she did, she confessed to Fergus her conversation with the knight about their potential wedding, her dismissal, and his anger.

"Ye insulted him, Kathryn. Of course he'd be angry. Lucky for ye he is a man who can control his emotions."

"Oh, he's very good at that. Anger is the only emotion I've seen him feel since he came here."

Fergus looked at her acutely. "Then ye don't watch him closely enough."

"Why would I watch him at all? Nothing he does interests me."

Fergus smiled and quickly hid it. "But ye've seen him with the dogs and now with his horse, haven't ye?"

She didn't care to answer; to do so she might have to admit that, yes, she had observed the knight and her observations unsettled her.

"There is more to the Black Knight than meets the eye, Kathryn."

"You are quick to defend him."

"Aye, he has treated me as a man, not an injured pet."

"How can you say such a thing?"

He stood up and faced her. "It's true, though I'm sorry to phrase it so bluntly."

She stared at him, controlling her irritation at his accusation. Finally, realizing he was right, she said, "I'm sorry if I embarrassed you, Fergus. 'Twas not my intent." She sighed. "We aren't children anymore, are we?"

"No, those days are behind us, Kat. And we must also accept the fact that our country is at war. Homelea has been spared until now, but we're going to have to do our part if Scotland is to defeat her enemy."

"You won't fight, will you? Please, tell me that you won't!" Her strident voice echoed in the small room.

He took her hands in his. "I may have no choice, Kathryn."

"But I couldn't bear it if you were hurt again."

"Perhaps it will ease ye to know that ll be better prepared next time. Adam is teaching me sword play." He moved away from her, left arm held up behind his head, right arm swishing an imaginary sword in the air between them. "Did ye know he was wounded at Dalry Pass?" He parried and stepped neatly aside, apparently dodging his opponent's thrust.

Kathryn hid a smile behind her hand.

"Nearly died. And he thought he'd never fight again but he learned new strategies. He's teaching me how to make up for my lack of vision—I may never be a great swordsman but," he stabbed at her playfully, "he thinks I can become adept despite my injury. He's even teaching me how to use that to my advantage!" He crossed his chest with his imaginary weapon and bowed to her.

Kathryn clapped her hands and chuckled. "Well done!" She looked at him with new understanding. "You are happy, Fergus. For the first time since Rodney's blow to your eye, you are happy." She stood and hugged him. "I didn't realize how difficult it must have been to be unsure if you could defend yourself."

He sat down again and pulled her down beside him, taking her hand in his. "And ye, sister of my heart. To be helpless when ye need protection, it tears at me. But no more. Thanks to Adam and the Black Knight."

"Ah, we are back to him." She pulled her hands away from Fergus.

"I saw him leave Homelea in haste."

"I told you he was very angry with me. Which is just as well. He should have no trouble persuading the king to free us from this marriage neither of us wants."

Fergus looked thoughtful.

She didn't like what Fergus wasn't saying. "What? You think it is only I? I can assure you Sir Bryan is just as unhappy with the situation."

"Perhaps so." They sat in silence, the distant noises of the castle folk bustling about their work muffled by the stone walls. "Have ye prayed on this?"

Kathryn twisted her hands in her lap. "I fear the Lord isn't listening."

"God always listens, Kat. Perhaps ye just can't hear the answer."

"More likely I don't like the answer I hear."

"Even if Bruce doesn't insist on the marriage, I sincerely doubt he'll take the earldom from Sir Bryan. Have ye thought of that?"

Kathryn rose to her feet and paced in agitation. "You are saying I have no real choice if I want to keep Homelea."

"Aye."

She stopped pacing as an idea came to her. "There is one possibility. I could send a messenger to Cousin Richard. Perhaps he could intercede on my behalf."

"If I'd thought he could help I'd have suggested him when the knight was pounding at the gate. But Richard is not in favor with Bruce," Fergus reminded her.

"Perhaps they've come to an agreement. Then Bruce might allow Richard to be my protector," she said in desperation.

"Not very likely."

She frowned.

"Aye, it's worth a try if ye are truly so set against marrying Sir Bryan."

"I am. Oh, Fergus. Why are women treated like chattel, as if we have no feelings or . . . or the intelligence to handle our own affairs? Doesn't the Bible say we are all equal in Christ?"

"Equal before the Lord, Kat. Yes, we are all equal before him. But we each have earthly duties to perform the best we can. Even Sir Bryan has duties he must perform in obedience to his liege laird, whether he likes them or not."

She grimaced. "I'm not sure that makes me feel any better, Fergus. Either he is marrying me for my inheritance or because it is his duty."

"Ah, lass, ye were hoping to find love, weren't ye?"

"Aye. Love. Or at least mutual affection."

"Come, Kathryn. Ye would have found little of either with Sir Rodney. Edward of England will come north and Carleton will come with him. Ye made your choice when ye yielded to Sir Bryan and Scotland's king. Be fully truthful with Sir Bryan. And see if love will bloom."

"It will take a very special man to overlook what I've done, won't it?"

"Aye, it will."

"And you think Black Bryan is such a man?"

"Only time will tell."

"Perhaps. But I would still like you to send for Cousin Richard."

"All right. But it will take some time. If the king insists on a wedding, ye're going to have to delay it as long as ye can." They walked out of the chapel and down the steps. "Surely Sir Bryan has some redeeming qualities that ye could admire if ye tried."

"You may judge for yourself. Thus far *I* have found none."

KING ROBERT insisted on sending his priest with Bryan so the ceremony could be held without delay. Bryan returned to Homelea the next day resigned to the marriage. And mindful that Ceallach would arrive in a matter of days with the arms shipment. Bryan had sent word to Kathryn that the wedding would take place the next day. They must marry and prepare to leave within the week so that the inhabitants of Homelea could accompany Ceallach and the wagons north to Stirling.

Bryan asked for his evening meal to be served in the solar, which opened off the great hall at the end farthest from the kitchen. Apparently the old earl had used it as his office, for it boasted a large table and sturdy benches.

He pushed the food around his trencher with a knife as he considered his conversation with the king. A conversation with his father. How strange it seemed to freely think of Robert the Bruce as his father. He'd always known of the relationship, and nothing had really changed. Still, he was gratified at the man's admission and by his praise.

But the conversation had ended with Bryan's agreement to wed Lady Kathryn.

A shadow graced the doorway. "Would you care for some company, brother?"

"No."

Adam walked in and sat down.

Evidently Adam's question was not a sincere request for information. Bryan smiled. He found it difficult to be angry in the man's presence.

Without preliminary, Adam asked, "When do you plan to tell her that we must leave?"

"First we must marry."

Although they spoke French in the company of others, Adam now conversed in their native Gaelic. "Am I to be your witness, then?" He took a drink.

"Aye, if there's a wedding."

Adam coughed and sputtered.

Bryan pounded his back. "Are you all right?"

"Aye, no thanks to you." Adam took another sip of water. "What do you mean, if there's a wedding?" Adam managed to croak.

Bryan examined his food, then spoke quietly. "She made it clear that I am not suitable for her station. I'm not noble or even a landed knight."

"Well, someone needs to talk some sense to her. Once we desert Homelea, she will have a difficult time reclaiming it as a single woman."

"The fact is, she'd be better off as my widow."

"Aye, but do try not to be killed, Bryan."

"At least as a widow no one could force her to marry, not even Rodney."

"Aye."

They ate in silence for a few minutes before Bryan spoke. "We are to accompany the arms to Stirling and leave nothing here for Edward when he marches through."

"That isn't going to endear you to your betrothed, Bryan. She expects you to protect her home. Though she may not be happy with you, she does seem relieved to be rid of Carleton. Why didn't you kill the man when you had the chance?"

"If he'd challenged me, I would have tried. But I'd given the lady my word not to harm anyone within the castle."

"Then you should have followed him outside the walls," Adam stated with fervor.

"Perhaps you're right, but it's too late now."

"I'm sure you'll meet up with him again. In the meantime, you will have the joys of marriage to occupy your mind."

Bryan wasn't about to admit to Adam or anyone his decision to have a chaste marriage. "I'm not so sure this marriage is in the lady's best interest. My enemies become hers . . . and Edward of England is a formidable enemy."

"Don't let Robert's troubles unsettle you."

"Curse it, man. Even he couldn't protect his wife. Our queen remains in Edward's prison, and Robert is helpless to release her. I've seen how it tears at him."

Adam put a hand on his foster brother's shoulder. Somberly, he replied, "We will win this fight and free our queen, God willing."

"Yes, and in the meantime I'm supposed to marry and protect this woman. And I don't know if I can." The admission clawed at Bryan's innards. "Adam, promise me you will look after Kathryn if I cannot."

Adam's expression grew more solemn. "I will guard her with my life, Bryan. Not only because she is deserving, but because you ask it."

A load lifted from Bryan's heart. With both of them seeing to her welfare, Kathryn would be safer than if Bryan alone was pledged to her. "You should return home before the battle. See to your wife and bairns."

"I will if there's time."

"Good. And you'll stand with me at the ceremony tomorrow evening?"

"Of course. The event promises to be interesting."

Bryan grinned. "Aye, she's a spirited lass."

They stood, and Adam clapped him on the back. "Mayhap she'll save us the trouble and refuse to marry you."

IN THE HOUR BEFORE VESPERS, Bryan waited with Bruce's priest at the altar of Homelea's tiny chapel, Adam and Thomas at his side. His thoughts weren't on the forthcoming ceremony as much as they dwelt on his encounter with Kathryn. He rolled his shoulders as if to shift a weight. Perhaps with time she would come to accept the circumstances of his birth as he had done long ago. Somehow, they would make the marriage work despite their differences.

After months of wearing trews and his small plaid to accommodate a life spent on horseback, the great plaid kilted about his hips felt strange. But he'd dressed for the occasion, hoping to appease Kathryn with his effort, because he regretted his behavior in the stable. Kathryn's defiance had fueled his temper, and like a fool he'd tried to conquer by force. He certainly knew better—even on the battlefield it was sometimes necessary to retreat to gain an advantage.

Adam leaned toward him. "You're sure you want to go through with this?"

"Yes." His terse response in no way told his true feelings. He was not sure at all. The late afternoon's dark clouds reminded him of the cave in Carrick and his vow not to marry. Yet here he stood about to pledge himself to a woman. A woman who was at least half an hour late for her wedding.

Tugging at his plaid, he growled, "What keeps her?"

"She made it plain the thought of wedding you makes her swoon. Perhaps she's had another fit." Adam wisely said this without a trace of a grin, because Bryan was in no mood for levity.

"Aggravating woman. Go see what keeps her." As he waited for Adam to return with his reluctant bride, Bryan glanced about at the few people in attendance. Dressing in his finest clothes was the least he could offer to the woman in return for this pitiful ceremony.

As an earl's daughter, she had probably expected to have a fine wedding. She would have ridden on a white horse to the steps of the village kirk while the many distinguished guests lining the way wished her well. Somehow, he would make it up to her, for although she did indeed aggravate him, he'd certainly given her cause to return the sentiment.

When Adam returned shortly, Bryan feared his foster brother would choke on the grin he was obviously trying to suppress. "Well?"

Adam stopped several arm-lengths away and drew a deep breath.

"The lady refuses to leave her chamber. She has barred the door." Adam struggled to keep a straight face. Thomas was less successful at withholding a loud guffaw and Bryan turned and cuffed his arm. "See to your duties," he growled.

"What—"

"Go clean out Cerin's stall!"

Thomas smirked but hurried off.

Bryan's jaw tensed as his temper rose, good intentions sinking rapidly to the bottom of his priorities.

Adam hurriedly continued. "She bade me tell you that she will bring the castle down with screams of protest if you force her to wed."

Clenching his teeth in what he hoped passed for a smile, Bryan muttered, "Bring the castle down? She has gone too far." He strode to the stairway, taking the steps two at a time until he stood outside the obstinate woman's chamber.

Pounding on the door, he demanded entrance. Silence. Not a sound from within.

"Is this the only exit?" he demanded of a cowering servant.

"Aye, my laird."

"And she remains inside?"

"Aye. This chamber, ah . . ." The young boy swallowed deeply.

"Out with it."

"The door has been heavily fortified, my laird. I fear it would take a battering ram to open it."

Despite that warning Bryan drove his shoulder against the door with all his considerable might. Neither door nor hinge nor lock gave way in the slightest.

Rubbing his bruised joint, his temper on a very short rein, Bryan bellowed for the edification of the silent room's occupant. "My lady will marry me if I must starve her into submission."

Adam cleared his throat. "Is this a good idea, Bryan? Surely there are better ways to subdue a headstrong woman."

"She has insulted me, defied me, fainted to get her way—now she shall taste *my* dislike of this marriage. She will not eat until she opens this door and takes the vows."

He stormed away, leaving orders that his wishes best be obeyed unless Adam wanted to share her fate.

Bryan ranted against his king, England's king, and his unwilling bride as he marched to the solar, slamming the door behind him. He went directly to a table that held *uisgebeatha*, wishing with all his strength that he was a drinking man. Still he poured himself some whiskey but only stared at the glass in his hand.

Why had he made such a foolish threat? How could he in all good conscience starve a woman to gain acquiescence? Again he wished he could just get drunk and forget war and death, kings and royal decrees, and a pair of bewitching, defiant brown eyes.

Aye, drink himself into oblivion. He hadn't done so in years, having promised Adam not to give in to the temptation. But tonight he didn't know where else to turn.

Just as he was about to raise the glass to his lips a knock came at the door. Carrying the glass over to it, he opened the door to admit his foster brother. "Ah, Adam. Come to tell me of the folly of my ways, have you?"

"As if you'd listen."

"Just say what you came to say. You'll not leave me be until you've said your piece."

"Are you going to drink that?" Adam asked, pointing to the glass.

Bryan shrugged. "It will do about as much good as praying, which is what you're about to suggest, isn't it?"

"Have you even tried it? Honestly tried prayer?"

Bryan had attended church and prayed as a child. But he'd become a man that day in the hills of Carrick and he'd put away childish things. He stared at Adam. "Nothing has changed. I simply can't give myself up to a God that deserts the innocent when they most need him."

"God didn't desert Bruce's women or his brothers. He has taken the dead to be with him in heaven and stands beside the living through their trials."

"Aye, so you've said."

Adam just looked at him for a minute. "What would it take for you to believe, to trust God?"

"Something miraculous, Adam."

"You see miracles everyday but you don't recognize them."

"Like what?"

"Laughter; the beauty of a sunrise or a woman's face; the joy of riding a magnificent animal like Cerin. Life is full of small miracles if you aren't too blind to see them."

Bryan set the whiskey down, untouched. "I've given up whiskey. Don't expect more of me."

Adam stood before Bryan. "Good. You're going to need a clear head to deal with her."

"I'm still tempted to strangle her as well as starve her."

Adam shook his head. "You can't mean to follow through with either of those threats."

"I'll be forced to, unless you have a better idea."

Adam smiled wickedly. "Aye, I do at that."

"Well, out with it."

"Nay, you need to come with me. There's someone you should meet."

Shrugging, Bryan gestured toward the door. "All right, then. Lead on."

Bryan followed Adam through the main hall to the entrance to the dungeons. The sounds of a bagpipe playing a lively tune could be heard as they descended the narrow steps. "What is that—"

"You'll see, or rather hear, in a minute."

The piper's tune ended, then the drones filled again and the tune was repeated. At least Bryan thought it was the same tune. He shook his head to clear his ears but it didn't help.

By now they had reached the lower level, deep beneath the castle, where the castle piper and his young pupil stood. And as the boy continued to struggle with his playing, Bryan understood why the lessons were held in such a remote spot.

The sounds coming from the pipe were . . . awful. Either this was a very new pupil or a horridly inept one.

Seeing Bryan, the boy quit playing, much to Bryan's relief. Adam introduced everyone and Bryan made polite inquiries before he and Adam returned to the solar.

Puzzled, Bryan asked, "What was that all about?"

"The lady *did* threaten to bring the castle down with her screams."

"Aye, well she better hurry before that boy beats her to it." He chuckled. "He's bad but he's loud."

With a knowing wink, Adam replied, "Yes, he is."

Bryan furrowed his brow but by the time Adam explained his plan, Bryan was laughing and pounding the man's back. "It could just work, Adam. It's certainly worth a try. Come, let's put your fiendish idea to the test."

BY THE NEXT MORNING Bryan was having second thoughts. Denying her food and water had seemed reasonable yesterday in his anger, but he probably would have capitulated by now.

However, Adam argued that he must make it seem as if he truly meant to stick with his threat if their plan was to work.

Now that she was good and hungry, Bryan could send a tray to her along with a note of apology.

And a surprise.

SEVEN

JUST PAST MIDDAY a knock at the chamber door startled
Kathryn. She and Anna had heard nothing since the barbarian's
attempt to force the door yesterday. Aye, force. The man knew no
other way to get what he wanted but to take, to coerce with sheer
physical power. But she would not be intimidated. She only wished
Anna wasn't also sentenced to starve.

The knock came again, and she bid Anna look through the
small hatch set within the larger, fortified door. "'Tis Gunna with
a tray of food and water." Anna reached for the bolt.

"Wait." Kathryn's stomach rumbled. "No one is with her?"

"Nay." She leaned her ear closer to the opening, then turned
back to Kathryn with a look of triumph. "She says she has a written
apology from Sir Bryan."

It was past time the man came to his senses. "Let me see it—
have her pass it through."

Anna looked hopeful. "And the food?"

"Don't open the door just yet. I don't trust Sir Bryan."

With a resigned sigh, Anna reached through the opening and
then handed her the parchment.

Kathryn smiled in satisfaction when she'd finished reading it.
"Sir Bryan is most sorry for his behavior. He does not want to force
me into anything and has asked King Robert to reconsider the

marriage." She smiled at the small victory the knight's apology revealed. She'd locked herself away in hopes that her cousin Richard would arrive in time to rescue her. But if Sir Bryan persuaded the king to change his mind about the marriage, all the better.

The smell of warm bread wafted through the small opening, and Kathryn's mouth watered. A final peek through the trap door satisfied Kathryn that the servant was alone. She and Anna lifted the heavy timber that barred the door.

The door leaped open as if an army pushed against it. Kathryn and Anna strained to shove it closed but the door and the women were propelled backward as the Black Knight burst into the room. Just when she had gathered her wits enough to realize Sir Bryan wasn't alone, a bagpiper began to play.

Loudly. And very, very badly.

And standing next to this incredible source of noise was an elderly cleric she'd never seen before.

"What is the meaning of this?" Kathryn shouted.

There was no answer. Thomas gently but firmly escorted Anna from the room before the door slammed shut and Adam bolted it, then stood with arms crossed to further bar the way.

At a signal from the knight, the piper quit playing and in blessed silence, Sir Bryan stepped toward her. Without thinking, she backed away from him until she could go no farther. Trapped against the far wall, she mustered her voice to sound as cold and disdaining as she could. "What is the meaning of this?" she repeated.

"We will wed this day, my lady."

She shook her head, sure that she had heard wrong. "But your note—you said you'd sent a messenger to the king to reconsider."

"No. I wrote that I'd asked the king to reconsider the marriage. Which I did in person. Two days ago."

Furious at this deception, she restrained herself from flinging the nearby water pitcher at his head. How dare he twist his words so? But the note held a more incriminating promise. Triumphant, she accused him. "You said you wouldn't force me. Here." She fumbled for the note, opened it and pointed. "Here, in your own handwriting it says so."

"Nay, lady."

The regret in his voice confused her.

"The note very clearly states that I don't want to force you. But I will if I must. 'Tis up to you."

She stared at him dumbfounded. "I won't marry you."

"Will you dare to throw my birth in my face again?"

"It isn't that."

"What then?"

The man was menacing, even without his weapons. "My cousin Richard. I . . . sent word to him, asking him to be my benefactor."

"Who is this cousin?" His voice sounded disbelieving, as if she'd conjured a cousin out of the air somehow, just to thwart him.

"Richard of Badenoch. A distant cousin but acceptable to be my guardian, if he agrees."

"Acceptable to whom? Why would you think Bruce would allow such a thing—the Comyns of Badenoch are traitors."

"Not Richard! He has sworn allegiance to Bruce."

"Aye, he had no choice—it was that or the gallows. There is no love lost between Bruce and any of the Comyn clan."

"Still, what harm can there be to wait until this possible solution—"

"I don't have time to wait for your cousin's reply, especially knowing that Bruce almost certainly will not agree. I must leave for Stirling and you will go with me." He took hold of her arm.

She pulled free of his grip. "But—"

"You cannot stay here. I can't spare enough men to defend the castle and keep you safe. Now, let us proceed with the ceremony. Shall we adjourn to the chapel and have a civilized wedding or—"

"I will not marry—"

Bryan signaled the piper and he began to play again. Apparently Sir Bryan had no intention of listening to her reasons for opposing the marriage. Someone in the hallway pounded on the door, but their words were drowned by the sounds coming from the bagpipe.

The priest opened his prayer book and began to speak—she shrieked louder. The piper played louder—she hadn't known the pipes could be played at such a volume. Or so poorly.

Her back pressed against the solid stone wall as she faced the smiling priest and a grim Sir Bryan. She could barely hear the priest's words.

Sir Bryan said something and nodded, then the priest looked to her.

"I do not," she screamed. The priest cupped his ear with his hand, shrugged, and then made the sign of the cross.

Abruptly the noise ceased as the priest said, "I now pronounce you man and wife. Go with God."

Kathryn bowed her head and hid her face in her hands. She wanted to weep. The grim-faced warrior was her husband, despite her protests. Protests that could not have been heard outside of this room. Probably hadn't been heard even within the room over the noise of those awful pipes. The witnesses could honestly say they'd heard no objection on her part.

She lifted her head and looked at the traitorous priest, the young piper, and the well-guarded door. No escape—not from this room, and not from the man who stood before her.

Sir Bryan took her hand and moved to the table by the window, towing Kathryn with him. He signed the marriage agreement and handed the quill to Kathryn. She refused to take it.

Glowering, he whispered, "Sign the contract. 'Tis a marriage in name only, I promise."

Anger gave way to surprise as she struggled to grasp his meaning. So, the marriage was to be a sham in every way? She shook her head and hissed, "Why should I trust you after this farce of a ceremony?"

Moving closer, he spoke in an undertone. "Shall I tear up the parchment and send you to Carleton?"

She recoiled physically from his suggestion, shaking her head. "You gave your word to protect me from him."

"Aye. And making you my wife seals that promise, Kathryn. This farce of a ceremony will enable you to claim you were forced and thus you can be released from the vows."

He would release her? "Released? When?"

"When Scotland is free."

The sincerity of his voice and expression could not be denied. What choice did she have? It was still Black Bryan or Rodney. And a chaste marriage freed her from the necessity of admitting her lack of maidenhood.

"You may kiss the bride," the priest said helpfully.

Before she could react, the rogue took her hands and bent his head. He brushed her lips with a gentle kiss. Kathryn jerked away. Kissing Rodney had led to her downfall. She would not make the same mistake again.

"Leave us," Sir Bryan ordered, and the others made a hasty exit, closing the door behind them.

Now what? What further mischief did he intend?

HER ASHEN FACE AND CLENCHED FISTS betrayed her fear and confusion, and he hastened to reassure her. "This is a marriage in name only, I promise. I only meant to show you respect by heeding the priest's request to kiss the bride. Nothing more, I swear."

Her chin came up. "Then there will be no more kisses."

Good. He preferred defiance to fear. "No. No more kissing, with or without witnesses." Her look of relief both wounded and amused him. His constant state of confusion toward the woman was wearing thin, and they'd only been married a few short minutes. "Will you sign the contract?"

She made no move toward the pen and parchment. "You will agree to a loveless, chaste marriage. Why?"

"I have pledged to keep you safe and to keep you and your wealth for my king. But neither of us wants this union. Am I correct in that?"

She nodded.

Relieved at her answer, he replied, "So, as I said, a marriage in name only will give us both our freedom, eventually. In the event I don't survive the upcoming battle, you will have far more control over your life as my widow than you would as an unmarried maid."

She hadn't considered that he might die. The thought of his death saddened her, because despite her anger with him, she couldn't wish any harm to come to him. "How can you face death so calmly?"

"'Tis the price men of honor pay for freedom. I don't welcome it, but I am willing to die for what I believe in."

In that moment, she glimpsed the man beneath the cool exterior, because she understood the willingness to sacrifice for others. She was willing to make any sacrifice that would keep Isobel and Homelea safe. Even a sham marriage to this man.

"I will pray for your safe keeping, my laird."

She walked to the narrow window slit, staring out of it, lost for a brief time in her own thoughts. He barely heard her next question. "And what do you derive from such a marriage?"

His answer was quick. "My king's gratitude. And if you are agreeable to this arrangement, I will fulfill my duty to my king without having to break an earlier vow."

She spun to face him. "What vow was that?"

He shifted his weight. "I have no desire to encumber myself with an emotional attachment so long as Scotland is at war."

She said nothing for several seconds. "I see."

"I ask only that you put aside your animosity toward me so that we may give the impression of resignation to a marriage neither of us wants. As my wife, you receive not only my protection, but also the enmity of the English."

She straightened her shoulders and held her head in an imperious pose he was beginning to recognize. "I alone am to put aside my feelings?"

Her bravado delighted him and he stifled a grin. "We will both play our part."

She took a backward step, and held up her hand as if to ward off an evil spirit. "And you will forego your husband's rights?" Despite her rigid posture, her voice quivered.

Looking at her lovely face, it was the last thing he wanted to promise. Yet something about her demeanor told him his promise meant more to her than met the eye. "I will not touch you. Aside from the reasons I've already told you, I would not endanger you with conceiving a child when the future is so uncertain."

Her features relaxed in obvious relief, and Bryan wondered why.

"Thank you, my laird." She dipped the pen in the ink and signed her name next to his. "My laird, husband."

It was done. Bryan didn't know how to feel or what to think. Married and yet not. How would they get through the next weeks? Best just to get on with it, he supposed.

"I took the liberty of arranging a meal and entertainment I hope you will enjoy."

"And if I refuse to join you? What then? Will you starve me into submission?" A tentative smile accompanied her words.

Relieved that she was no longer angry but apparently resigned to make the best of the situation, he considered that perhaps now they could at least be cordial. "Nay, I think locking you in this room with that piper would be far more effective."

She laughed, and the enchanting sound overwhelmed the warning signals his brain tried to send his way. Bryan's resolve to remain detached slipped a notch. He offered his arm. "Will you join me?"

She stared at him boldly. "Aye, but I need a few moments to prepare. I wasn't planning on a wedding when I dressed this morning."

The reminder of their forced nuptials dulled the accord between them. He dipped his head in acknowledgment. "I'll send your maid to help you and will return for you within the hour." He closed the door gently behind him.

KATHRYN BREATHED A DEEP SIGH even as she fought against the softening of her opinion of the dark knight. Where had her anger fled? She sank to the stool by the fireplace, shaking her head in amazement. At first, his assurance that he would not seek the marriage bed relieved her.

Then perversely, she wondered if his heart were engaged elsewhere. But she didn't think his sentiments were involved with another woman. More likely, from what she'd learned about him, he held his duty like a shield before his heart. A warrior's spirit, no doubt torn between his needs as a man and the demands of his profession. Kathryn sensed that here was a man of deeply felt emotions and deeply held beliefs. One who would love as powerfully as he hated. She shuddered. What would it be like to be cherished by such a man?

Deep within her own heart, she yearned to know.

His thoughtfulness concerning the risks of childbirth had touched her deeply. As she changed into her best dress, she gave thanks to God for the admirable champion he'd sent her.

Bryan came for her just as her maid finished arranging her hair. Perhaps it was her earlier musing that made Kathryn more aware, but only now as he stepped into the room did she realize the effort he'd taken to look his best on his wedding day.

His broad shoulders and deep chest strained the seams of his saffron shirt. And the plaid kilted on his lean hips—the excess draped across his shoulder and pinned in place—gave an impression of wildness, lent boldness to his movements.

Aye, he was fearful, even frightening at times. But she was drawn to him, to the loneliness she sensed in him. Taking a deep breath, she vowed to pray daily for a swift end to the war with England before she did something foolish. She dare not fall in love with this man.

But when she tried to remember why not, her mind went blank. Isobel, that was it. Who knew what he would do when he discovered she had a child?

"My lady?" He offered his arm and for a moment, his face betrayed his approval of her appearance. But just as quickly his mask returned. Kathryn laid her hand on his arm and allowed him to escort her to the great hall.

"You arranged this?" she asked as she stared at the small gathering of people and the food that awaited them.

"Aye, I asked the cook to prepare a modest meal. A troop of traveling minstrels will provide music and entertainment."

Resentment of his highhanded actions conflicted with pleasure at his thoughtfulness. "You must have been certain we would marry today to have made such arrangements ahead of time."

"Not certain; determined to carry out my king's wishes."

AS HE LOOKED ABOUT at the handful of guests, Bryan thought of the chapel at Castle Moy, home of the Mackintosh clan. He remembered a similar ceremony last year when one of Adam's many cousins and her bridegroom had taken their vows. For a moment, Bryan wished his foster family could be here to celebrate this important occasion. Thomas and Adam's familiar faces reminded him he wasn't completely alone.

He led Kathryn to the table on the dais, where Adam awaited them. None of Kathryn's social circle had been invited to this hasty gathering. The company consisted of the two knights who served with Bryan as well as various castle residents. Thomas sat with Fergus, a common sight these days, as they were very close in age.

A woman of Kathryn's social standing certainly deserved more than this, but it was the best he could contrive on such short notice. They arrived at their places and greeted Adam. Bryan assisted Kathryn into her chair as the musicians sounded a fanfare. Bowls of water and towels were brought to each table. Bryan took up the towel and attempted to dry his wife's hands, but she pulled away from his touch.

Gently, he reclaimed her hand, determined to reconcile her to the role they each must play. "I will not bite."

"I'm not so sure," she retorted.

"Am I so frightening?"

"Aye, you are that."

He would have to let down his guard enough to allay her fear of him. He smiled; at least he hoped it was a smile. "We are being watched, lady wife."

She seemed taken aback. But he had to admire her quick wit and composure.

She allowed him to dry her hands. "Do our guests know about the piper—about how this marriage came to be?"

He said, "No one outside of Adam, Thomas, and the priest . . . And Anna, of course. Will she tell tales?"

"No, she can be trusted. I had a word with her as I dressed."

Bryan laid down the towel and washed his own hands in the bowl. "Then it is our secret until we choose to make it public."

Lips pursed, Kathryn dried his hands. With the ceremony completed, a great cheer went up from their audience. He gave her hand a squeeze.

"You are kind, my laird. Perhaps this play-acting will improve your temper."

"Am I such a bully you thought I'd beat you in front of the wedding guests?"

She rewarded him with a smile—a warm smile—and his heart twisted at the beauty of it. The accord they'd reached earlier returned, and they acted as any agreeable couple might, feeding each other from a shared trencher. Her fingertips brushed his lips when she fed him a morsel and his hand skimmed hers as they both reached for the goblet.

And Kathryn's blushing face told him she was aware of him, too. Here, then, was one of Adam's miracles—the way of a man and a maid. Aye, looking at her lovely face and hearing her laughter could go a long way toward making a man believe.

For the first time in many years, Bryan prayed to a God he wasn't sure existed. He prayed for an end to the war; but he feared his heart would surrender long before England did.

KATHRYN'S CHURNING EMOTIONS nearly overwhelmed her. She cast about for an excuse to leave Sir Bryan's presence, to escape from his touch and his flashing dark eyes. These fluttery feelings were exactly what she'd felt with Rodney and could not be trusted.

She was about to give her attention to Adam when a servant hurried to Sir Bryan and bent close to speak privately.

The knight sprang to his feet. "The devil you say." Pivoting to her he said, "Excuse me, Kathryn, but we have unexpected guests. I will return shortly." He strode to the hall's entrance, which was at the opposite end of the room. She asked Adam, "Who can it be to agitate him so?"

"I don't know."

Kathryn heard uneasiness in his voice and she feared trouble was afoot. Adam evidently shared her apprehension because he moved off to stand between her and the new arrivals.

A burst from the minstrel's trumpets announced the arrival of the visitors. She heard Adam chuckle but he stood too far away to ask what he found so amusing about the situation.

She stood in order to see better but the visitors had their backs to her. Still she didn't think she'd ever seen either of the two men before. She watched as Sir Bryan paid obeisance to one of the men. He was nearly the same height as Sir Bryan and had the same broad shoulders and powerful chest of a soldier. The three men clasped hands and greeted one another. Sir Bryan obviously knew them well.

Even from a distance Kathryn could discern the fine cloth of their traveling clothes. The knight nodded toward the dais and the man and his companion turned to face her. Only then did she notice the golden circlet on his hat and the red lion on his surcoat. Her face drained of blood. Somehow she managed to stay standing as Sir Bryan led the king of Scotland toward her.

When they stood before her, Bryan said, "Your Majesty, may I present my bride, Lady Kathryn Mackintosh, Countess of Homelea."

The king brought her hand to his lips and brushed the back of it lightly as Kathryn contrived a curtsy. "Your Majesty," she said coolly, unsure how she felt about the man who'd freed her from Rodney Carleton only to impose a marriage to Black Bryan upon her.

The king didn't release her hand, and she dared not withdraw it. He stared at her and she feared she had offended him with her tone of voice. "Forgive me, Countess," Robert said as he let go of her fingers. "Your beauty reminded me of my own wedding and how lovely my wife was on that day."

A look of sadness crossed his face, and Kathryn recalled that the king's wife was held captive. Clearly this pained him, and Kathryn's hostility toward him felt out of place in the face of his obvious devotion.

"I hope your wife will be returned to you soon, Sire," she said with reluctant warmth. She reminded herself that because of this man, she was now wed against her will. And she was not happy about it. Truly, she was not.

"You are kind, lass. Some day Elizabeth and I will be reunited. I only pray that the reunion takes place first here on earth." He clapped Sir Bryan on the back. "But enough of such musings. I've brought Douglas to enliven this happy occasion. Let's celebrate your marriage with all due indulgence."

So saying, Sir Bryan introduced Kathryn to James Douglas, another of Robert's fearsome lieutenants. Unlike Bryan, Douglas appeared harmless and spoke with a slight lisp. But she noted the man had permission to carry his sword in his king's presence. Apparently he was a trusted and competent bodyguard.

Then the king took Kathryn's arm and escorted her to her seat, he on one side, Bryan on the other. Never had Kathryn envisioned having a king attend her wedding feast. Bruce honored her, and even more, Bryan by coming here. Perhaps that was his purpose.

Evidently Douglas's purpose for being here was more one of protection than levity, for he declined to join them. He and Adam took themselves to the table near the door where Fergus sat.

With another flourish of trumpets the celebration resumed and food was served to the new arrivals. Sir Bryan leaned close to her and quietly said, "Thank you for your graciousness to Robert. I must admit, I rather feared your reaction to him."

"He is a likable man, not at all what I expected."

"Aye." Bryan agreed. "He does have that effect, especially on the ladies." His expression softened into a grin and his gaze traveled to her neck and below, lingering briefly before returning to rest on her face. "I haven't had a chance to tell you how beautiful you look. You honor me by wearing such finery."

She blushed at his frank appraisal. "Did you think I would wear my stable clothes?"

"I never know what to expect from you," he admitted.

He smiled, a smile with more warmth than she'd yet seen from him, and Kathryn's senses reeled. He was much less dangerous when he scowled, since the smile softened his features and made his face appealing. Very appealing. Much too appealing for a man who was to be a husband in name only.

Still, she grinned at his confession. She didn't know what to expect from him either. He was frightening and . . . intriguing.

Obviously King Robert held this knight, his son, in high esteem or he wouldn't have rewarded the man with an earldom. Or come to his wedding. Fergus's defense of the knight echoed in Kathryn's mind—perhaps she should look beneath the surface of this fascinating man she'd married. And his king.

Courteous and charming, Bruce entertained her with stories of Bryan's exploits much as any proud parent might.

At the end of this last tale, Sir Bryan rolled his eyes. "Please don't believe half these stories, lady wife. I fear my king exaggerates."

Robert sipped from his cup. "You call me false, then?" he said with obvious fondness.

"Nay, my laird. I only wonder who told you such outrageous tales."

"I suspect I don't know the half of it." Bruce's look became pensive. "I am a king blessed with able lieutenants, Lady Kathryn. I would be proud to call any one of them my son. But none more so than Bryan here."

She stared at Bruce and he gave her an almost imperceptible nod. When she recovered from the shock, she dipped her head in silent acknowledgment of his admission. Kathryn sipped her drink and Bryan remained silent, probably as surprised as Kathryn by the turn of the conversation.

Bruce said, "You have chosen your wife well, Bryan."

Kathryn nearly choked on her water. Bryan stared at the king and then laughed out loud. She hadn't heard him laugh before, and the sound was infectious. Soon the three of them were laughing at the absurdity of Bruce's statement.

Watching the two of them, Kathryn marveled at how much they resembled each other. She studied her husband's profile. *I have married a stranger. A handsome, charming, frightening stranger.* She must not allow him to disarm her as Rodney once had.

Despite these misgivings, the evening passed pleasantly and soon it grew late.

"Lady Kathryn, it has been a pleasure to share this occasion with you," Bruce said. He stood and lifted his tankard toward the guests and toasted them. "To long life and God's blessing on your marriage."

"Hear, hear!" came a hearty reply.

The king turned to Sir Bryan. "And now James and I bid you goodnight."

"Come, lady wife. 'Tis time to retire." Sir Bryan took her hand. Only then did Kathryn remember she hadn't made arrangements for a room for them.

"First I must rouse Anna and make rooms ready—"

"I saw to it earlier. Adam will give Bruce his room, and Douglas will stand watch at the door."

"They don't trust you?"

"The king has learned to be cautious—I take no offense. Now, come. I'm tired, as I know you must be. Let us retire."

When she realized the full implications of Sir Bryan's suggestion, she withdrew her hand from his.

Perhaps sensing her distress, his scowl softened and he leaned closer. "It is past time. Will you play along or would you rather risk the fainting ruse again?"

Despite his frown, his voice held a trace of the warmth he'd displayed earlier. His acknowledgment of her subterfuge lightened her fears and she covered a smile with her fingers. "How far do you expect me to play, my laird?"

He reclaimed her hand and held it to his lips. "I won't rescind our agreement, no matter how tempting the circumstances."

"Will you spend the night in the stable, then?"

He chuckled, and the rich warm sound tugged at her spirit in a way that Rodney at his most charming had not. "No, indeed. That would not be appropriate." Bryan stood and drew her to her feet. "Come, my lady. There's nothing to be done about it—we shall have to endure the bedding ceremony."

Kathryn's protests went unheard as they were quickly surrounded and pushed up the steps to the upper floor. A knowing look passed between Sir Bryan and Adam, but neither made any effort to halt the proceedings. Did Adam know of Bryan's agreement with her? Would Bryan truly honor it now the time had come?

Striving not to panic, Kathryn allowed the women to propel her into the master chamber. As they undressed her, Anna let down Kathryn's hair, unwinding the braids and brushing the strands until they shone in the firelight. With gentle hands and not a few giggles, the women helped Kathryn climb into bed, then covered her with a white coverlet Anna had quilted in an intricate circle design.

Not wanting to be left alone, anxious to forestall Sir Bryan's arrival, Kathryn grabbed Anna's hand. "Anna, please."

The older woman looked tenderly upon her. "There's naught to fear, Kathryn. I spied your husband gazing at ye tonight—he'll not hurt ye, lass. 'Tisn't in him to harm a woman. Just tell him the truth, lass, and all will go well."

Unwilling to confess that the marriage was in name only, Kathryn watched as Anna laid a bottle of wine and a loaf of bread on the bed beside her. "What are you doing?"

With a mischievous grin Anna replied, "The wine will help ye relax, and the bread will keep up yer husband's strength." Looking quite pleased with herself, Anna quickly left the room before Kathryn could make a suitably indignant reply.

The door had barely closed on Anna before the men entered the chamber, shoving Bryan before them. Kathryn's face warmed, as he stood before her clad only in his knee length saffron colored shirt. With many suggestions to enjoy themselves, the others soon left, and Kathryn stared at the man who had promised to leave her untouched.

Kathryn was sure her face couldn't get any warmer. Sir Bryan shook his head and walked toward her. Kathryn drew back into the pillows and pulled the cover higher.

EIGHT

Bryan stopped, dismayed at his wife's apprehensive expression. "You need not fear, Lady Kathryn. This is a marriage of convenience. For appearance."

Kathryn's chin came up in a show of bravado. "I only wanted to be sure you remembered."

"I remember." The sight of her with her dark blond hair hanging loose upon the bed coverings gave him a moment to regret the condition of their marriage. He'd never been in a woman's chamber before and like any man, he'd looked forward to his wedding night and the secrets it held.

But that was not to be. He scrubbed a hand through his hair and walked to the window opening, in hopes a cool breeze would bring some order to his confused senses. Saints above, why couldn't she be an ugly hag?

Feeling more in control, he faced her again but avoided looking directly at her. "Although our friends will no doubt grow tired of listening at the door—"

She gasped. "They are listening?"

"No doubt." He sat on the edge of the bed. He made no move to touch her, but she did not relax her rigid grip on the blanket. "They'll leave soon, but come the morning they will look for . . . evidence . . . that the marriage was consummated."

"Aye, they will." Such was the custom and the only other explanation they could give would impugn Kathryn's virtue. "I will take care of it."

"You know . . .?" his face grew warm.

She blushed as well. "I know enough."

He reached for her hand and she shrank from his touch. "Have you been wronged in some way, my lady?" He saw her go pale and could hide his curiosity no longer. "Who has frightened you so?"

She turned away from him.

Gently he tugged her back to face him. "The day you yielded to me, Carleton hit you."

She nodded.

Restraining his anger he asked as tenderly as he could, "What else did he do?" He wasn't sure he wanted to know the answer, but until he understood, he couldn't help her.

Her voice was calm. "While he was courting me, I gave him offense and angered him. He made to strike me and Fergus came to my rescue. Rodney hit him and injured his eye."

Now he understood her defense of Fergus that first day. Silently cursing Rodney Carleton, Bryan said, "And do you think you will anger me somehow and be rewarded with the back of my hand?"

She studied him, perhaps weighing what she knew of him. "Nay, I think not."

"I'm glad to hear you say that." He took one of her hands in his. "'Twill be all right. He won't hurt you or yours again. Nor will I." Bryan suspected there was more to her story, for why else would she be so unsettled? But now was not the time to find out. It could wait.

After a time, he sat back and watched her settle into the pillows once more. Having been so close to her, his warrior's body clamored for more of her womanly comfort. More softness. More affection. The respite and peace Robert had spoken of and that Bryan longed to experience.

Abruptly he stood to leave, but she grabbed his hand, nearly losing the blanket in the process. She let go of his hand and clutching the covers back in place she said, "I don't understand you at all, but I thank you. I didn't quite believe that you would honor our agreement."

Her lack of trust pierced him.

Taking a deep breath to steady his emotions, he answered, "Why would I be other than honest with my wife?"

"But I am not—"

"You are. You are my lawfully wedded wife, for the foreseeable future, and I will honor you as such." Could he expect the same from her? She'd yielded to him to save herself from Rodney. Would she return to Edward's loyalty if given the chance? Knowing that demanding her loyalty would in no way ensure it, he forced a detachment he didn't truly feel and changed the subject. "I will make my bed in front of the fireplace. Good night."

"Oh, no, my laird. You mustn't do that. This bed is huge—couldn't we share it?"

"I'm not experienced in these matters, my lady, but I suspect that would not be a good idea."

Her expression was one of surprise and perhaps, disbelief. Her face flushed bright red. "Not experienced? Then you have never . . .?"

He shook his head. "Tonight is the first I've ever been in a lady's chamber other than my mother's."

"Oh. I see. I suppose you're right," she said. "But I do hate to see you sleep on the floor."

"I'm a warrior—a hard bed won't be strange to me." He looked at her, at the softness of her features, and knew this marriage had been a mistake. His heart was not going to survive it.

"Good night, Lady Kathryn." He blew out the candles and settled into a pallet on the floor.

KATHRYN LAY IN THE DARKNESS listening to the Black Knight as he made himself comfortable. Guiltily she shifted onto her side on the soft mattress, knowing he'd been right. How foolish to suggest he sleep in the same bed. He had been entirely charming throughout the evening, charming and thoughtful. He hadn't even asked for another kiss. *What kind of man is he?*

Certainly he was nothing like Rodney. Although she felt quivery in Black Bryan's presence, just as she had with Rodney, she did not feel pressured to give in. Of course, now she knew the consequences. But more than that. The knight had kept his promise. He was an honorable man. Someone she could depend upon.

She said a prayer of thanksgiving for her husband's thoughtfulness, for it gave rise to hopes he would understand. Her thoughts drifted to the abbey, and the small, blond-haired child who lived there.

Perhaps Sir Bryan would accept the child, for despite his reputation as a warrior, it was plain from his comportment this day that he had admirable qualities, just as Anna and Fergus had said. Was he, perhaps, the answer to her prayers after all?

No, this marriage could never be more than it was tonight. An honorable and virtuous man such as Sir Bryan wouldn't want Kathryn when he learned she had a child.

BY THE TIME KATHRYN SAT DOWN to break her fast two days after the wedding, the day was well under way and she had worked up the courage to ask Sir Bryan to take her to the abbey to fetch

Isobel. She knew that the time they must leave for Stirling grew near. She would not go until she was sure the child would be safe at the abbey or if not, had been taken under the knight's protection.

She entered the great hall and walked to where Sir Bryan sat with Adam. Though the two men were deep in discussion, she sat across the table from them and wished them good morrow. Adam acknowledged her with a brief nod and the knight with his usual scowl.

This did not bode well for what she had to say to him. Perhaps she should choose another time. But as she ate the porridge a servant placed in front of her, Kathryn decided to wait until they'd finished their discussion and then she would ask him. If he agreed to take her, then she would find the courage to explain about Isobel. In any case, she was determined to visit the child to celebrate her birthday.

"Ceallach has not arrived with the . . . promised shipment," Adam said, glancing warily at her.

"Aye, and I have no way of knowing if he's been successful in obtaining . . . what he was sent for or what is delaying him."

"How much longer can we wait?"

"'Tis already the first week of June. I've begun preparations for our departure—we can leave within a day or two of Ceallach's arrival." Sir Bryan looked up at her and quickly away, obviously uncomfortable with her presence. What didn't he and Adam want her to know? Perhaps she wasn't the only one with secrets.

"Shall I send a messenger to look for him?"

Sir Bryan hesitated. "Nay, let's give him another day."

Adam nodded and, having finished his meal, left the table. Sir Bryan rose to follow but Kathryn said, "If you have a moment, I need to speak with you on a matter of importance."

His scowl deepened and seeing his reluctance made her cross. But she held back her animosity and said, "I need to go to the abbey."

"I don't have time to take you. It will have to wait."

She stared at him. "Then Fergus can accompany me," she said reasonably. If he wouldn't go with her, she and Fergus could fetch the child.

"Fergus isn't your husband, I am." In name only, which she suspected made all the difference this morning. Apparently Sir Bryan chafed to be gone, to be released from sleeping on the floor in Kathryn's chamber in order to keep their sham marriage a secret. She didn't blame him, but he needn't be so churlish about it. How could she tell him why she wanted to go to the abbey when he was so obviously out of sorts?

Her voice took on an edge. "Fergus is perfectly capable of accompanying me. He's done so in the past."

"Well, now I am responsible for you and I say you shall wait until I can take you."

"You promised."

"Let it rest."

"It is important that I go or I wouldn't ask—"

"I said no. Not until I can accompany you." He rose to leave and she stood as well.

"You are being unreasonable."

"Try to be an obedient wife, Lady Kathryn," he nearly shouted.

They were interrupted when Anna approached. She didn't let the knight's obvious temper deter her. She said, "As eldest woman, 'twas my duty to inspect the marriage bed." She spoke loud enough so others could hear.

Kathryn's face grew hot as Bryan asked impatiently, "And have you done so?"

"Aye, my laird. Each morning. Today it appears the marriage is legal." Anna gazed piercingly at Kathryn.

When Anna had retreated, Sir Bryan said quietly, for Kathryn's ears alone, "What is she talking about?"

"There is no need to fear. I stubbed my toe this morning and broke the skin, so I . . . I dabbed the injury with the sheet."

"I want no evidence to be used against us when the time comes to part, for that is still my intent." He paused, as if allowing his words to take their mark. "Burn those cursed sheets."

She stared at him, angry and hurt. "Fine." Barely keeping her anger in check she said, "Answer me one thing. Will the nuns be safe at the abbey when the English come through on their way to Stirling?"

"Certainly. They can bar the gate. Even Edward isn't so depraved he would allow his army to break in and molest servants of God."

But Rodney might, if he learned about Isobel. With that thought, her course was set. Isobel would be safer with Kathryn and the knight.

"When will you accompany me to the abbey?"

He huffed a breath in exasperation. "*If* there is time, I will take you to say your good-byes before we leave. I can promise no more than that." With a brusque "Good day" he stalked off toward the lists.

KATHRYN SPENT THE DAY IN THE GARDEN, weeding and cultivating the vegetables that provided welcome variety to their diet after the long winter. The sun was unusually warm and made for a fine day to spend in one of her favorite pastimes. And the repetitive work helped soothe her after her argument with Sir Bryan. Somehow she would find a way to see Isobel for her birthday, despite the knight's heavy hand.

By late afternoon, satisfied with her work, Kathryn dismissed her helpers and walked the short distance to the small rose garden, sheltered in the southwest corner of the garden. It was too early for them to bloom though some of the earliest had buds that already showed color. She smiled as she envisioned what it would look like here in another week.

Years ago her father had built a stone bench in the middle of the roses. In her childhood Kathryn had sat there with her mother, learning how to care for these beautiful plants. Kathryn rested on the bench now, remembering those early years. Her mother had been regarded as a true beauty, of both countenance and spirit. Sadly, Kathryn realized she couldn't remember her mother's face. But she did remember sitting on this very bench with Rodney Carleton and falling for his charms. If her mother had lived, would she have taught Kathryn to know her heart, to resist a deceiver such as Rodney?

What would her mother have thought of the man Kathryn had married? Kathryn was at a loss to know how she felt about him. After his tirade this morning, she looked forward to the end of their disagreeable union. He was difficult and demanding and . . . altogether charming when he chose to be. He'd been decidedly irritable and less than charming this morning!

With or without his permission, she would visit St. Mary's. She wanted to celebrate the first anniversary of Isobel's birth with the nuns and then bring her to Homelea. If he hadn't been so stubborn this morning, she'd have told him then. The snapping of a twig startled her. She jumped up and spun about to see who intruded.

Black Bryan halted. "I'm sorry if I frightened you."

Heart pounding with a combination of fright and guilt, she said, "No. Yes. I was . . . rather lost in thought."

He gestured with his hand. "This is a pretty spot. May I join you?"

She hesitated, troubled by the need to talk to him about the child but unwilling to confront him yet again today. Glancing at her work-stained clothes and his dusty clothing, she said, "We are both in need of some water and clean clothes, so we can hardly offend one another in that regard."

"No, and with some effort, perhaps we can converse without offending in some other manner." His face conveyed no clue as to his feelings, and she resented his ability to keep his emotions so well hidden. How was she to deal with him when he could shut her out so effectively?

Sir Bryan followed her as she walked about in the early evening light, asking her about the different varieties of roses. "Do you have a favorite?" he asked.

"Yes, the white ones. They were my mother's favorites, too."

In a voice filled with genuine concern, he asked, "Were you very young when she died?"

"Four."

"'Tis difficult, losing your mother so young." At the unexpected wistful quality in his voice, she raised an eyebrow in question.

"I was twelve. Not so young, but it was still hard." He looked away, hiding feelings she sensed he rarely allowed others to witness.

Touched by his sharing of something so private, Kathryn hesitated to question him more. But curiosity won out and she asked, "Do you remember her?"

"Aye. Some." Apparently ready to change the subject, he reached out and touched one of the buds. "Isn't the white rose the symbol of the Virgin Mary?"

She looked up at him, and her face must have betrayed her surprise.

His expression darkened. "Just because I was raised in the highlands doesn't mean I am a heathen."

She felt herself blush. "I never . . ." *I never said as much but I certainly thought it.* "I've never seen you in the chapel."

"Nor are you likely to."

"You don't believe?" she asked, saddened by his attitude.

"I'm waiting for a miracle," he said without a trace of amusement.

"You need a miracle to believe in God?"

"No. I think he exists. I just don't happen to believe that he cares all that much about his creation."

"Oh, but—"

He raised his hand. "Don't, my lady. I get enough from Adam."

The tentative warmth between them disappeared, to Kathryn's regret.

He stared at the keep. "Perhaps we should go inside."

"Yes," she agreed, wanting to do just the opposite, to stay here and assure him of God's love. But his stern face let her know he would not be receptive. Perhaps another time. If ever she were to give him her heart, he would have to believe. "Yes, I need to wash up before the evening meal." She squared her shoulders and turned to leave.

"Lady Kathryn."

The entreaty in his voice touched her. She stopped and swung around to face him. "Aye, my laird?"

He tugged at his plaid and squirmed for a moment like a small boy caught sneaking a sweet. "I am sorry."

"For what?"

"For being so short with you this morning. For not explaining my reasons . . . for ordering you about like a servant instead of treating you with the respect due as my wife. This marriage that isn't a marriage may prove more difficult than either of us expected." He treated her to a small smile and she could feel her heart thawing against her will.

Bryan knelt and plucked some stems of the yellow heartsease that grew at will throughout the garden. The little heart-shaped faces of the flowers had always delighted her. He offered them to her, seeming sincere and somewhat embarrassed by his spur-of-the-moment action. He didn't look at all fierce just now with the tiny yellow flowers lying in his tanned, outstretched hand.

She took the flowers from him. "A peace offering, my laird?"

"Aye, I suppose. I have good reason to ask you to remain within the walls, Lady Kathryn. You must trust me on this." He put his hands behind his back. "I hope you and Adam are right, you know."

"About what?"

"That God cares about what is happening in Scotland. Because in a few short weeks we will either be living in a free country or we may very well be dead. Or wish we were."

She laid her hand on his arm. "Surely it isn't as grim as all that?"

"No. It's worse."

She shook her head. "How can you face such a battle without hope in God's promises, my laird?"

He looked at her with a yearning that stunned her. "When I look at you, at Homelea, I am made all too aware of what may be lost."

"Then I will pray for us both, Sir Bryan. And for a future that brings peace to those we love." She looked down at the flowers in her hand, then back to the knight. "Thank you. This is a most thoughtful gesture."

There were depths to him that she longed to know. But would they be given the time or would these days at Homelea be all they would have? Again she wondered what it might be like to be such a man's cherished wife. She prayed that God would grant them time. She should tell him about Isobel now, even if it broke the accord they'd just reached.

But before she could do so he said, "I'm glad you liked them. But do not mistake the gesture for a lessening of my resolve to end our marriage. Or my decision to keep you safe within Homelea's walls."

A man who wanted no emotional ties would certainly not welcome the demands of a small child. If she told him now he might make it impossible for her to slip away without him.

Reluctantly, she kept quiet about Isobel. "As you wish, my laird." Fleeing his powerful presence she strode with purpose toward the keep. Her mind was made up. She would go to St. Mary's with or without his permission.

BRYAN WATCHED HER HURRY UP THE PATH, her head bent to the flowers he'd given her. How he hoped she and Adam were right. Perhaps a prayer now and then on his part wouldn't be remiss.

And while he prayed for victory at Stirling, he would also ask for time to know his wife. He'd never met any woman whose intelligence matched her beauty the way the two combined in Kathryn. How was he to protect his heart from such as she? Aye, even though they had agreed to a temporary union, he couldn't stop wondering what it might be like to be truly married to Kathryn. She was a prize, and he wanted to win her.

But it would have to wait. A messenger had come an hour ago to tell him that tomorrow night Ceallach would arrive from the coast with wagons loaded with supplies and armament. The sooner they moved it to Bruce's new headquarters, the less chance of Edward's learning about it.

Bryan should have told her the rest of it. Delaying the news would not make it any easier on her. The peace he and Kathryn had found between them here among the rosebushes would soon be ruined along with the garden.

The time for Homelea's destruction grew near.

THE NUMBER OF MEN GATHERED in Homelea's hall increased each day and they spoke of Stirling and the battle to come. Kathryn spent the early morning among them, overseeing preparations to depart. She must question the knight on his plans for Homelea's defense.

Somehow, despite all the activity and work to be done, she was determined to visit St. Mary's tomorrow. Knowing she would need help in slipping from the castle, Kathryn asked Fergus to go with her to the stable to check on her mare's newborn foal.

"How are your lessons with Adam going?" she asked as they walked toward the stable. She smiled, remembering Fergus's demonstration of his new skills.

"Better than expected."

"And have you seen Sir Bryan this morning?"

"Aye. He spends most mornings in the lists training the men. Did you need to speak with him?"

"No, what I need can wait."

They entered the stable and stood in front of the mare's stall. "Easy lass," Kathryn crooned as she entered the stall. Keeping one eye on the nervous mare, Kathryn stroked the perfect little body of the chestnut filly.

"She's a beauty," Fergus observed as he entered the stall as well. Kathryn moved away to let him closer. He'd only taken two steps when the mare snorted and laid back her ears in warning. Aiming a lethal kick, she whirled and struck at Fergus, who made a hasty retreat, dragging Kathryn with him. She crashed into his chest and for a brief moment, his arm encircled her as she caught her balance.

At the look on Fergus's face, she burst out laughing. "Don't tell me you've never been spurned by a lady before." Kathryn pulled away and held onto his hand.

"On the contrary, more often than I'd care to admit. But none have ever tried to disembowel me."

They stood facing one another, and Fergus dropped her hand as if it scalded and walked several paces away.

He did not look at her. "We should return to the hall."

Confused by his behavior, Kathryn thought to protest, then changed her mind. "I'm sure you will recover from my mare's disapproval."

He didn't appear to share her lighthearted mood. "Aye, my lady, but Sir Bryan would not be pleased with me just now."

His expression made his meaning suddenly clear to Kathryn.

She placed her hand on his arm. "Fergus, we did nothing wrong."

He pulled away from her touch. Kathryn gazed at the floor before raising her head to say, "I would be deeply saddened to cause a breach between us or to lose the pleasure of your company."

"Aye. We have long been friends and I'm glad to hear you say your marriage won't change that. But we must take care not to provoke your husband with our friendship."

"You think he'd be jealous?"

"Oh, yes. And unforgiving where you are concerned."

Kathryn found that hard to believe, but let it pass. "Then I'll give him no reason to play the part of jealous husband. Now, friend, perhaps you'd be willing to grant me a boon?"

THAT NIGHT THE VILLAGE OF HOMELEA lay quietly sleeping except for the revelers at the tavern. Most were far too intoxicated to note or take exception to the presence of a stranger. At any rate, he didn't tarry long. Leaving payment for his drink, he left and wandered to the stable, all the while looking about as if searching for something.

Lachlan the Smith watched the stranger leave the tavern and make his way down the street. He followed, staying in the shadows, until they reached the appointed meeting place.

Inside the stable, the stranger faced him, although in the darkness Lachlan couldn't make out his features.

"What news?" the man asked.

Lachlan glanced about nervously. "Yer time is come. I overheard Lady Kathryn talking in the stable today. She plans to visit St. Mary's tomorrow—'tis the child's birthday." Aye, the blasted foundling child who kept his wife busy at the abbey, too busy to see to his meals and his home. Well, he'd soon put an end to that. It was all the lady's fault. As soon as she was gone, Nelda would come to her senses and return home. "All ye need do is keep a watch on the trail and wait for her."

"His lordship will be very pleased with this news."

Lachlan stood taller. "To be sure, I can make myself very valuable in the future."

"Good. Here is your purse. You remember how to contact me?"

"Aye."

"Then do so if you learn more that would be of interest to his lordship."

Lachlan scratched his chin. "You won't harm the child?"

"No, we want the lady only."

Lachlan breathed easier. His wife wouldn't forgive him if something were to happen to the brat.

"Wait here for a few minutes before leaving," the man ordered. Then he slipped into the night and was gone.

Lachlan waited as instructed then made his way back to Homelea. He approached the river crossing, tossing the coin purse from hand to hand and whistling at his good fortune. Had he been a truly competent spy, he would not have had the misfortune to stumble upon something Rodney Carleton would have paid even more dearly to know about.

But Lachlan barely glimpsed the heavily loaded wagons splashing through the water before his world went black.

"THAT WAS NOT WELL DONE," Bryan said when he strode over to Ceallach and stared down at the body.

"No, it was not," Ceallach agreed. "I only meant to knock him to the ground, not kill him."

Bryan heard the remorse in the other man's voice and said, "Looks like he struck his head when he fell. Perhaps 'tis just as well—how would we have explained our activities to him?"

"I'd have thought of something. Do you recognize him?" Ceallach asked.

Bryan pointed at the body. "Aye, he's Kathryn's blacksmith. A disgruntled sort I didn't trust."

Ceallach stooped to pick up the leather purse and pulled the strings open. He shook the contents into his hand. "There's a year's wages here. Where do you suppose he came into such a sum?"

Bryan took the purse Ceallach pressed into his hands. "I don't like it—who paid him and for what? Did he know what's in the wagons? I would have liked to get the answers from him."

"So would I." Ceallach walked toward the wagons, all of which had forded the stream by now and awaited the signal to move on. When Bryan joined him, the other man said, "We can't take a chance on hiding them at Homelea now."

Bryan considered the situation. They had intended to take the wagons north along with the inhabitants of Homelea in a few days. That plan now must change. "You had best start for Stirling yet tonight. I will follow with Kathryn and the rest in a few days."

"Have you told her?"

"Aye, she knows we must go north."

"Nay, have you told her of Homelea's fate?"

"There hasn't been time." He was definitely not looking forward to telling Kathryn they could leave nothing behind that would aid Edward in his trek through Scotland—no food or shelter for his army.

Ceallach shook his head. "I don't envy you the task."

"I told her from the beginning that Homelea is Bruce's to do with as he wishes."

"I don't know much about women, Bryan, but 'tis likely she expects protection for her home as well as her person."

"You may be right. I'll keep that in mind."

Mounting their horses, they moved to the trail and headed north, Ceallach bringing up the rear. At the edge of Homelea's lands, they halted and Bryan drew his horse abreast of Ceallach's. The men clasped hands.

Bryan said, "Go in peace."

"And you also."

Ceallach turned his horse and ordered the wagons to move out.

Bryan felt uneasy watching him ride away. Much as he hated to do it, he must ask Adam not to leave to see his family. He needed him close to help keep Kathryn safe from Rodney. The mystery of Lachlan's purse and who had filled it added to Bryan's unease. But he assured himself that Kathryn would be safe inside the castle's walls for the short time until they would head north.

NINE

Homelea castle sat atop a riverside cliff, commanding the best spot to ford the river Tweed on the road between Edinburgh and Stirling. To the north lay open land where sheep grazed peacefully in the pastures adjacent to the village of the same name. The ancient abbey of St. Mary's rested in the forested hills just east of the village.

As they headed their horses to the river crossing, Kathryn smiled, anticipating the celebration of Isobel's birthday. She would take the child back to Homelea with her today.

Kathryn watched as the late-morning rays of sunlight shone through the leaves of passing trees, dappling the ground with uneven light. The air began to warm as the sun rose higher.

Fergus reined in his mount until Kathryn's horse drew abreast of him. With Bryan engaged in training his men, she and Fergus and three men loyal to her had been able to convince the guard on duty that she had Bryan's permission to leave. They'd slipped out the main gate and headed for St. Mary's.

But Fergus had been on edge from the moment they left the castle walls behind. He'd expressed grave misgivings about this boon Kathryn had wheedled from him, had at first refused when she suggested the trip to visit Isobel. Finally he'd agreed but insisted that they take additional men for protection.

Kathryn smiled at him. "Thank you for making this trip today."

"Aye, well, keep the visit short so that we are safely behind Homelea's walls before Sir Bryan realizes we've left."

Kathryn laid a hand on his sleeve. "We are on our own lands; we have additional men for protection. Surely you are overly cautious."

"Perhaps I am, but your safety is my concern. God help me if I fail and the earl finds out about this."

She pulled her hand back. This was the first time anyone had referred to the Black Knight as earl, and it stunned her. Her father had been the earl for all of her life and it felt somehow disloyal to call someone else by the name. "Really, Fergus, you act as if Sir Bryan truly cared about me."

"You are his wife. Of course he cares."

"Aye, he cares for what belongs to him, like his stallion and his chain mail. I don't flatter myself in thinking I rank higher than his horse."

Fergus's voice took on an edge she'd never heard before. "You do your husband injustice with your words, my lady. Come, let us move out faster." Had Fergus become an admirer of the knight? He signaled the others and all urged their horses into a brisk trot.

Kathryn prodded her horse to a faster pace, the other riders following close behind. Soon the road narrowed and paralleled the river as it led through the woods to the abbey, then edged it, perilously close. Her horse's ears lay flattened to its head and she felt its apprehension. She shouted to get Fergus's attention, but the rushing water made it difficult to be heard, and her shouts went unanswered.

Fergus's horse disappeared as the road curved sharply to the left behind a large boulder on the river's edge. Kathryn heard a strangled cry and drove her mare forward. As she approached the giant rock, a horse appeared from the trees on Kathryn's right and the rider grabbed at her bridle. She quickly turned her frightened animal's head and the stranger missed.

But on every side, men shouted and startled horses whinnied. Her guardians' defense was scattered at best. She searched frantically for Fergus, while struggling to regain control of her frightened horse.

"Fergus!" she shouted. "Fergus, where are you?"

Kathryn's mount threw back its head as someone snatched the reins. Kathryn held on, only to realize the bandit was leading her away.

Where is Fergus? She searched frantically as she disengaged her foot from the stirrup to dismount. The man yanked the reins from her hand and pulled them over the horse's head. Then, as her horse leaped to the side to follow where it was led, she saw Fergus's unconscious form lying in a heap by the boulder. She wanted desperately to get to Fergus and help him, but dared not jump from the horse for fear of being trampled.

"Let me go!" A low-hanging branch stung her face and tore her veil. A fingernail was ripped to the quick as she tried to wrest the reins back to no avail. Finally, the bandit stopped his horse long enough to pull her onto his own horse, rip her veil in half and use it to bind her hands and gag her. Kathryn struggled until a long, sharp knife nicked at her throat. Defeated for the moment, Kathryn remained still. Hands and mouth secure, her kidnappers returned her to her mount and headed out again.

The horses broke into a canter. She sat the horse the best she could, clinging with her hands bound in front of her. The English accents of her captors left no doubt where they were headed.

BRYAN HALTED THE TRAINING AT MIDDAY to find the castle in an uproar—Kathryn was nowhere to be found. He ordered the grounds to be thoroughly searched and wasn't surprised when someone discovered that horses were missing. He'd underestimated her determination to go to the abbey; no doubt that was where he'd find her. He'd fetch her back himself.

Bryan saddled Cerin and had just mounted the horse when a horse and rider raced into the bailey. The rider, one of Kathryn's men, threw himself off his barely checked animal and ran to where Bryan sat his horse.

"My laird, we were ambushed and the lady seized by English reivers."

Bryan pounded the saddle so hard Cerin tossed his head. How was he to protect the woman if she disobeyed him? "Ambushed? Where? Never mind, explain while we ride." Fearing the worst, Bryan ordered his troops to prepare for a three-day absence. While they packed food and shelter, he gave orders to Adam. "Secure the castle after I leave, and open it to no one but me. Understood?"

"Aye, my laird."

"Good. Who knows what other mischief is afoot."

"Take care, brother." He put his hand on Bryan's knee. "And bring the lady home."

Bryan turned Cerin and followed the messenger out of Homelea's gates, shouting questions and not liking the answers.

When they reached the ambush site, one man was attempting to round up the scattered horses. Another was bent over a figure propped against a giant boulder. Bryan spoke to his squire. "Thomas, see if you can find any tracks."

"Aye, my laird." Taking several men with him, Thomas began a search of the area for the tracks of the marauders.

Bryan dismounted and walked over to Fergus, who appeared to be disoriented from a bloody wound at his temple. Bryan wanted answers. No, he wanted to throttle Fergus, then Kathryn, for leaving the safety of Homelea.

Fergus glanced upward and cringed. "My laird, she is taken." His shoulders slumped, and Bryan feared the man would pass out. But Fergus rallied to face him once more.

"Tell me what happened," Bryan demanded.

"Lady Kathryn wished to visit St. Mary's. To visit an aging nun as she is accustomed to doing each week. I saw no harm."

Something in the way the man bowed his head made Bryan suspect there was more to the story, but he was more interested in what had happened to Kathryn.

"We were ambushed. They wore no insignia, Sir Bryan. All I can tell you is that the accents were English. I must have struck the rock and by the time I came to my senses, they were gone," he explained, holding his head as he raised his gaze.

"Who knew of your plans?"

"Only Kathryn and I."

"Why the devil did you give in to her? Had you completely lost your senses before you hit the rock? Was Kathryn hurt? So help me, if any harm comes to her, Fergus—"

"Kathryn." Fergus's voice caught and he bowed his head. "I believe she was trying to warn me when the ambush struck. I'm sorry, my laird. I'm terribly sorry."

Bryan clenched his fists to keep from striking out with them or his temper. "Lot of good that will do."

Those words hung between the two men for several minutes.

The return of Thomas and his trackers broke the silence. "It appears they rode their horses into the river. We found where they entered, but not where they left. The stream can be ridden for a good mile or more before they must leave it."

Bryan didn't answer, so his squire continued. "We found this on yon wee bush."

He handed Bryan a scrap of material from a lady's veil. Bryan took the fluttering material from the man, noting the large tear and speck of fresh blood at one end. Whose blood was this?

Kathryn. I have failed to protect you, just as I feared. Hadn't he known he couldn't keep her safe? He'd tried to tell his father that he didn't want such responsibility. And now here he stood exactly where Bruce had—someone had captured Bryan's wife. He found it difficult to control his voice. "Can you track them?"

Thomas nodded. "Aye. 'Twill be difficult and slow once they reach the road."

Bryan ranted in frustration until the worst of his temper passed. His tantrum didn't change the situation, but at least he could look at Fergus without strangling him.

"Take your men and go home, Fergus."

"Nay, my laird. I will help you find Lady Kathryn."

Bryan doubted that time spent on a horse would improve the man's headache, but he grudgingly admired him for his insistence on helping.

They spent the next two hours combing the banks of the stream for the trail of Kathryn's abductors. Once they discovered where they exited the water, Thomas easily tracked the group for several more miles before the tracks joined others on the rough road leading south to England. Now it became nearly impossible to determine which tracks were which.

Evening set in; weary and frustrated, Bryan refused to stop even to eat. As darkness enveloped them, Thomas rode up beside him. "We need to call a halt for the night."

Bryan kept his eyes on the ground, ignoring him.

Thomas muttered under his breath, and Bryan finally reined in Cerin. "You're right, Thomas. No sense risking the horses in the dark. I'm not so daft and stubborn that I can't heed good advice when it's given."

Looking somewhat abashed to know that Bryan had heard him, Thomas nodded.

"But no campfires. We don't want to give ourselves away."

"Aye. No need to chance it."

After a cold supper Bryan and his companions wrapped their plaids about them and settled in for a few hours of sleep.

But sleep wouldn't come for Bryan. Too many unanswered questions plagued him. They had not parted on good terms. He'd dismissed Kathryn's desire to go to the abbey as unimportant, even though she'd tried to tell him how serious she was about going. Did Kathryn know her abductors—had she contrived to visit the abbey in order to flee a marriage she didn't want? But if that were the case, why had she bothered to seek his permission?

KATHRYN CRIED OUT AGAINST THE GAG as her horse slipped down the stream bank, causing her leg to jam into the pommel once again. With a lunge that threw Kathryn backward, the beast surged through the water, climbed the opposite bank and found solid footing.

They made their way to a small clearing within a copse of pines and halted. No one dismounted.

After several minutes they were joined by another man, who reported, "They are following but slowly. Shall we stop here, Simon, or move on?"

The man called Simon answered, "We'll return to the road and put some distance behind us before resting the beasts."

They urged their horses through the dense undergrowth, eventually coming out on the road that led north to Homelea. They turned south and headed at a canter for the English border, fifteen miles away.

Mercifully, the horses could not keep up such a pace and soon slowed to a walk again. By now Kathryn's legs were chafed and each jolt of the horse sent twinges of pain from her full bladder. Unwillingly, she cried out when the horse stumbled on a rock and the man she now thought of as her jailer led the group into the trees at the side of the road and called a halt.

It was growing dark and there would be no moon tonight. Simon dismounted and told the others to do the same. He turned and lifted Kathryn off the horse and set her none too gently on the ground. To her relief, her legs didn't buckle.

Her jailer untied her hands. "Leave the gag in place, my lady. None of us are interested in your opinions, and I know well enough what your problem is. We could all use some relief."

The men fanned out into a circle a discreet distance away and turned their backs to her, as much for their own privacy as hers. Grateful for their consideration, she took care of her needs. Before she stood up, she quietly ripped a piece of material from the hem of her chemise and laid it within a nearby bush.

She stood and moved away from the spot, praying the men would not see the telltale scrap of fabric in the darkness, but that Bryan somehow would notice it.

But her act of defiance did not go unnoticed. One of the men brought Simon the strip of cloth. Shaking his head as if disgusted with her, Simon bound her hands again before lifting her into the saddle.

"Mount up," Simon ordered his men. "We've still an hour or more to the border."

They'd been riding for nearly three hours, and Kathryn's skin chafed where her skirt bunched under her knees. The time dragged by. Finally they came to Norham Castle. Someone must have been expecting them, for they gained entrance quickly. Once inside the other men scattered to obey Simon's crisply given orders.

He removed the gag.

"Whose prisoner am I?" she asked, her mouth dry.

"Mine for now."

Pins and needles shot through her feet and legs from the hours astride as Kathryn moved about, returning blood to her limbs. She stumbled but regained her balance as Simon pushed her before him, indicating she was to enter the keep.

A young woman, perhaps a few years older than Kathryn, awaited them at the door. She spoke with Simon and though Kathryn strained to hear, they kept their conversation private. Who had planned this kidnapping? She suspected her captors were someone else's henchmen. But it couldn't be . . . he certainly wouldn't . . .

The room she was led to was clean and modestly furnished, and the bed looked most inviting after the long, uncomfortable ride. The woman would not make eye contact. "My name is Peggy. If ye have need of anything, let me know." Peggy hurried out, closing the door behind her. Kathryn heard scratching and bumping outside the door and concluded Simon or one of his men would sleep there. Glancing about the room, she noticed the only window in her room—high, narrow, and shuttered tightly.

Somehow she must discover a means to escape. But sleep would have to come first. Wearily Kathryn crawled into the bed, and slept fitfully.

BRYAN'S MOOD HAD NOT IMPROVED by dawn. The lack of sleep and nagging questions compounded his frustration at Kathryn's disappearance. He nearly saddled up to ride on alone until reason prevailed.

As the dawn became daylight, they ate a cold breakfast. Bryan glared at Fergus, who kept his head down, not meeting Bryan's gaze. A huge bruise purpled the left side of Fergus's face, and a blood-tinged bandage covered what Bryan suspected was a painful gash just above his ear.

But as bad as the injury must feel this morning, Fergus would be far more pained by Kathryn's abduction. The man was loyal to her first and above all others. Bryan felt a moment's remorse for his harsh words the night before. Knowing he must make the first move to heal the rift, he asked gruffly, "From the looks of your face, I wonder how your head feels this morning."

"I'm fine."

"You don't look fine."

Fergus wouldn't look at him. "Do you think they're headed for Norham?"

"'Tis most likely. It's close."

"Then Edward must have taken her." Fergus looked up, finally.

"Or Carleton." Bryan could feel his own agitation rising.

Fergus winced, as if the thought pained him, too.

"If you had obeyed my orders . . ." Bryan slammed his fist into his palm. "You placed her in danger. How could you be so careless?"

"Are you worried about her, or is it that you don't want Rodney to have her?" Fergus shot back.

"How dare you say that? She is my wife—of course I care about her."

"As much as you care for your horse?"

Annoyed and puzzled, he roared, "What does my horse have to do with this?"

"Kathryn believes she is lower in your esteem than Cerin."

"You go too far, Fergus." He lowered his voice, and the menace was clear. "She is my wife. I vowed to protect her and I have failed. Because of *your* carelessness."

Thomas walked over and took a seat between them. Bryan suspected the younger man feared he and Fergus would come to blows. And well they might before this was over.

Bryan heaved a sigh. "No sense sitting here blaming ourselves. Let's mount up."

They broke camp and followed the tracks south until they reached a clearing within sight of Norham. Thomas scouted ahead while the rest of them dismounted and waited in the cover of the trees.

He returned shortly. "The tracks lead straight to Norham."

"If 'tis Carleton, I swear I'll kill him if he so much as touches her."

"Will we mount a rescue?" Fergus asked.

Bryan paced. Had Kathryn gone willingly? He didn't want to believe it but he couldn't be sure. Mayhap she'd played him for a fool, seeking permission to go to St. Mary's then acting resigned to his refusal in order to defray suspicion. He stood in front of Fergus and Thomas. "Are we in agreement that no matter who holds her, it is most likely at Carleton's order and that Kathryn is in danger?"

The others nodded.

"Do we also agree that Kathryn wants to be rescued?"

"What are you implying?" Fergus growled.

In a calmer voice Thomas asked, "What reason do ye have to question yer lady's loyalty?"

Bryan shot a glance at Kathryn's friend, but Fergus's expression was unreadable. If he knew anything about the intricacies of Bryan's relationship with Kathryn, he was not going to share it.

Returning his glance to Thomas, he answered the man's question. "Kathryn and I have been married but a short while, and I don't know her feelings about many things. I do know that she didn't want to marry and she has continued to . . . she does not seem reconciled to the marriage. When last we met, I was less than a patient, loving husband."

Thomas nodded.

Bryan continued. "I have no way of knowing Kathryn's true desire in this matter of marriage." Again Bryan glanced at Fergus. Fergus met his gaze and didn't back down, even as Bryan said, "She does not confide in me. Perhaps her affection lies elsewhere."

Fergus defended her, tight-lipped and obviously angry. "I can assure ye it doesn't lie with Carleton."

"How do you know this?"

"She despises the man. Surely ye must know at least that much about yer wife!"

"You seem to know as much or more about the lady than I do. How is that?"

Fergus jumped up, fists raised. "What are ye accusing me of?"

"Stop it, both of ye," Thomas thundered. "Ye're actin' like a couple of dogs with a bone." He glared at Bryan. "Are ye goin' to rescue the lass or not?"

Bryan shoved his hand through his hair, taking time to let his anger cool. "Aye, let's be about it. Have the men mount up. We need to move deeper into the woods and devise a plan."

Fergus put a hand on his arm. "That ye question my loyalty is bad enough, but why do ye question Kathryn's?"

"Are you so sure, Fergus? Are you sure we aren't riding into a cleverly laid English trap? Not only do they gain Homelea and its mistress, but Black Bryan as well."

"If it is a trap, it's not of Kathryn's doing!"

Fergus stalked away, and Bryan threw his saddle over Cerin's broad back.

How could he be sure? He couldn't be sure of anything! And he needed to be sure.

KATHRYN AWOKE, CONFUSED AT FIRST by the unfamiliar room. *Where am I? And whose prisoner?*

She climbed out of bed and gratefully washed in the basin of tepid water on the table. Having made herself presentable, she paced the room, hoping someone would soon bring food. She hadn't eaten since before leaving Homelea yesterday afternoon.

When Simon showed up at her door she said, "I demand to speak to your leader."

"His lordship won't be here for a few days. Just relax and enjoy yourself, lady."

"And who is his lordship?"

"Sir Rodney Carleton. We're to stay here and see if your Scottish rebel comes a calling."

He refused to answer any more of her questions, and Kathryn was once again alone with her anxiety. A small window high on the wall allowed the only light and made it difficult to judge the passage of time.

Kathryn wondered for the hundredth time if Sir Bryan would come for her. In truth, she feared he would be lured here to his death. The thought twisted her stomach into a knot. Though she hadn't wanted to marry him, still she would not wish for any harm to come to him. The knight was at least honorable, more than she could say for Rodney.

She thought of Rodney's handsome face with its straight nose and lively blue eyes. Black Bryan and his ruddy skin and intense dark eyes. Rodney—whipcord lean and fast. Bryan—strong and true. The two men couldn't be more different.

Isobel's safety depended on the knight—Rodney must not be given the chance to use the child for his own self-interest. He knew Kathryn well enough to know she would bend to his will if that's what it took to keep the child safe.

If she had to choose—if she were free to choose—it wouldn't be difficult.

Would that she'd be given a choice.

TEN

Bᴙʏᴀɴ ᴏʙsᴇʀᴠᴇᴅ ɴᴏʀʜᴀᴍ ᴄᴀsᴛʟᴇ from a tree line some distance away. No one had entered or left since early this morning and now, as he waited for the midday meal, he recalled the role the imposing keep had played in Scotland's history. Here the nobles of Scotland had foolishly acknowledged Edward I of England as the supreme and direct laird of Scotland in 1291, the year of Bryan's birth. Then the nobles had accepted Edward's choice for Scotland's king, John Balliol, thus setting in motion the events that had fueled the war Bryan had fought in since he was barely fifteen.

Within five years, Edward removed his puppet from Scotland's throne, and Robert the Bruce inherited his father's title as Earl of Carrick. He also inherited his family's claim to the crown, a crown Edward usurped as his own. Edward's first act as Scotland's king had been to sack the town of Berwick, a town just north of them now, ordering his men to spare no one. Thousands were hacked to death over a two-day period; even women and children had not been spared.

God have mercy, Kathryn was now imprisoned at Norham under English authority. And although this Edward was not the butcher his father had been, Bryan feared for her life. He had every reason to believe Rodney Carleton was at Norham, which meant her virtue was in danger as well. Bryan noted the reassuring weight of his claymore at his back and grasped the handle of the dirk on his belt, as if to withdraw it and storm the castle in his frustration.

"It's a trap," Fergus said, startling Bryan back to reality.

"So you've said, several times. I agree." He released the knife and dropped his fists to his sides. "Edward and Rodney hope to lure me, and perhaps even Robert, to Norham. And see, here I am, just as they hoped."

Fergus's grim expression matched his own dark humor. "Ye don't still believe Kathryn lured ye here, do ye?"

"Let's just say that I would rather believe better of her." Bryan continued, "You should return to Homelea."

"I'm not leaving until Kathryn is free. As ye've been so willing to point out, 'tis my fault Kathryn is held in yonder keep."

"Aye, so it is." At the moment, Bryan wasn't sure who he was more angry with—Fergus, for allowing Kathryn to be abducted— or Robert, for forcing him to marry her in the first place. All his fears had come to pass.

Fergus must have sensed how tightly strung Bryan's emotions were because he didn't press for details of Bryan's plan to breach the stern walls of the keep. Which showed excellent judgment. Bryan wanted desperately to hit something, and Fergus's face was much too convenient.

Bryan's first instinct had been to storm the castle, but wisdom had won out. He'd waited, praying all the while that Kathryn would be safe and that whoever held her would make the mistake of moving her.

With effort, he calmed his anger and relaxed his fists. "Well, if we can capture a mighty Scottish fortress the likes of Perth, then surely we can breach this pile of English stones." Bryan's words suggested far more confidence than he felt.

Just then Thomas returned from the errand Bryan had sent him on. He walked toward them, a bundle of clothing in his hands. At Bryan's raised eyebrow, the man winked.

Fergus demanded, "What are ye two plotting?"

"It seems Thomas has taken holy vows."

With that Thomas shook out the bundle and produced the robe and cowl of a monk. He held the coarse cloth against his body to inspect the fit and Bryan explained their plan to Fergus.

"We will await the evening here in these woods. We cannot get any closer in daylight without being seen. In the meantime, we must prepare ropes and grappling hooks."

"What are ye about, my laird?"

"Thomas will seek entrance to the castle. Even Rodney isn't likely to deny a traveling priest a night's lodging. Then Thomas will offer to hear confessions in return for the hospitality. Hopefully, he can gain access to Kathryn, or at least learn her whereabouts."

"But what of the grappling hooks and ropes?"

"Depending on what he learns, our 'priest' may have to leave the castle by way of them, or allow us entrance." Bryan just hoped this plan would work. "I would prefer to seize the lady outside the castle, but we'll go in if we must."

"Let me go in as the priest," Fergus entreated. "This is all my fault—I should be the one to take the risks."

"While that's true and I appreciate the offer, someone other than Lady Kathryn might recognize you and jeopardize our plan. You've made an impression on Carleton himself."

"But I need to do something."

Bryan put his hand on the man's shoulders. "When we return to Homelea, you will be in charge of Kathryn's protection. Thomas will take most of my men and head to Stirling while I gather the castle and the village folk to take them north."

"Ye would trust me after what I've done?"

Bryan studied him for a moment. "Lady Kathryn can be most persuasive, can she not?"

Fergus nodded and gave a rueful smile.

"I think neither of us is immune to her, Fergus."

"We are only friends, I assure ye, my laird."

"I know that. I also know that you would protect her with your life. And I trust you to see to her safety despite your earlier lapse in judgment. You'll not make that mistake again, will you?"

"Definitely not."

"Good. For now, 'tis Thomas who will go to her."

"Aye, my laird."

Though he'd been furious with both Fergus and Kathryn when he learned she'd been taken, now Bryan's only emotion was fear. Fear that he was too late. A vision of Rodney's hands on Kathryn, of her frightened face, seared through Bryan. He could no longer wait—they must get her out of that castle.

This would be a good time for a miracle, Lord. If you're listening.

AS DUSK APPROACHED, Kathryn heard the bar lifted from the outside of her door. Each time the door had opened these past two days she feared a visit from Rodney, for surely he would soon be here, if what Simon had told her was true. But it was only Peggy with a cleric whose dusty clothing proclaimed him to be a traveler.

"This priest has agreed to hear your confession. Be quick about it."

As the woman left the room, the man closed the door behind her. Kathryn stared at the hooded man.

"Lady Kathryn."

"I did not request a priest."

"Nevertheless, I am here." The hood of his robe covered his face. He pushed the cloth away and it fell to his back. Bright red curls covered his head.

She gasped, "You are no priest. You are Thomas—"

Placing his finger in front of his lips he whispered, "Quiet, my lady." He motioned her to move further from the door and when they stood before the fireplace, he reached for her hand and pressed something cool and metallic into her palm.

Kathryn stared at her hand. A ring. Bryan's ring. She had remarked upon its unusual design that day in the rose garden and she knew it to be his and his alone.

"How do you come to have this ring? How fares its owner?" she pleaded.

"The man who owns this ring and calls ye wife sent me. Bryan wasn't sure ye would recognize me."

"He is well?"

"Aye."

Kathryn's heart leaped. She had feared that Bryan hadn't come for her because of injury, or worse. But he was well. "They hope to lure him into a trap, Thomas. You must warn him."

"My laird is aware of a trap. He sends ye greetings and begs ye to be patient. Ye need not remain here if ye do not wish to."

Not wish to? Of course she wanted to leave. "He will rescue me?"

"If ye will it, my lady. Sir Bryan will not force ye to go. I'm to instruct ye very plainly—ye are free to do as ye choose. And more importantly—I'm to repeat his exact words—'I will make no demands upon you.' Do ye understand his message?"

She nodded. He would risk his life to rescue her but would keep his vow of a chaste marriage. Her decision could be made freely, without fear of consequences.

"Ye must let him know yer desire and he will abide by it."

She was free again to choose. Bryan or Rodney. Scotland or England. She had made this choice once—had anything changed? Rodney, whose presence darkened a room. Bryan, the loyal and honorable knight who would come for her, risk his life for her, if she asked it of him. Would risk his life for a woman who was less than a wife.

"My lady?"

"I'm sorry, what did you say?"

"I haven't much time. Do ye wish to go, or not?"

The choice was easy. "I will return to my husband."

The man didn't smile. "Then I am instructed to take from ye some token, or some special word, to assure my laird of yer decision."

How could Bryan believe she would want to stay here? He obviously didn't trust her and the knowledge pinched. "Won't your word be good enough?"

"No, nor even a note that might be a forgery to trick him. Sir Bryan won't risk the lives of his men to rescue ye unless he is sure of yer desire to return."

She frowned as a painful insight became clear. "Does he think I conspired with Sir Rodney to lure him into such a trap?"

The man didn't flinch or mince his words. "We're at war, m'lady. 'Tis possible."

Kathryn quelled her righteous anger, putting herself in Bryan's place. They had a marriage in name only and a fragile relationship at best. And yet he was nearby, ready to take her back to Homelea.

"But Bryan doesn't really believe it or he wouldn't come for me." The man's face betrayed him. "But you aren't so sure, are you?"

"Let me say it plain, Lady Kathryn. The man is my kin on his mother's side. If ye betray him, the hounds of the devil himself won't keep me from murderin' ye."

Kathryn felt the blood drain from her face.

He gentled his voice. "Now do ye wish to go, give me yer token."

What word or token could she send that he would recognize? Trembling, she reached into the *ciorbholg* at her waist. Would he recognize the combs from her hair? What could she send to convince them—to convince Bryan—that she truly wanted rescue, that she hadn't lured him here?

She dug through the remaining contents of the small bag and unwrapped the protective cloth around a forgotten parcel to find tiny dried flowers, the nosegay of heartsease Bryan had given her as a peace offering.

Smiling in triumph she said, "Take this. Remind my husband of the day he gave it to me and the words we spoke. Tell him . . . tell him his coming here is proof that Adam and I are right. God does care."

The man grinned, a dazzling, boyish grin. "I'll tell him. Is there anything else he should know?"

Knowing that Bryan was undoubtedly worried that Rodney would behave badly, she said, "Please tell him I am well and have not suffered. That Lord Rodney is not in residence."

He seemed to ponder this information, and Kathryn feared he wouldn't take her token to Bryan after all. Then a new thought struck her. "How will the rescue come about? Where and when?"

"Soon. Don't worry yerself, lass. Ye must trust Bryan. He said to keep yer wits about ye and don't hesitate when the moment arrives." He made the sign of the cross. "God be with ye, lady."

She clasped his arm. "Thank you."

When Thomas was gone and her door closed once more, Kathryn knelt on the floor beside her bed to pray. "Please, God. Guide me in the days to come. Let me put my trust in you, for the sake of those I love. And help me guide Bryan to you."

KATHRYN SPENT A RESTLESS NIGHT in constant anticipation of imminent rescue. But dawn arrived and she left her rumpled bed to wash the sleep from her eyes. As she splashed water on her face from the bowl on the table she wondered, would Bryan come today? When and how would he gain entrance to the keep?

Peggy brought porridge, and Kathryn pushed her spoon around the wooden bowl after eating a few spoonfuls. She'd no sooner set it aside than her door burst open to reveal Rodney Carleton. A very angry Rodney Carleton, from the looks of him. And from the damp and muddy condition of his clothes, he had just arrived.

She jumped up and backed away from him so quickly she knocked over the bench she'd been sitting on. "Rodney." She barely squeezed the name past the tightness in her throat at the sight of the last person she wanted to see this morning.

He gave her no time to say more. "Get ready to leave; we ride as soon as I change into dry clothing."

Leave? Today? How would Bryan find her? She couldn't leave. "I will need some time—"

"Don't dawdle, Kathryn. Your husband has not come for you; we shall go to him."

Retreating further, she bumped against the bed. She forced herself to a calmness she certainly didn't feel. "To him?"

"You'll be happy to hear we are going to Homelea."

Kathryn couldn't suppress the gasp of surprise that rose to her lips.

With a gleam in his eye he said, "I have some unfinished business to attend to there."

Isobel. Kathryn grabbed the bedpost for support. "What business?"

"An interesting rumor. It seems your husband may be using Homelea's crossing to ship weapons to Bruce."

"Weapons?" So that was Bryan and Adam's secret. Kathryn sat down on the edge of the bed, her knees weak with the news that Rodney did not know about Isobel after all. "Why do you need to take me along to capture weapons?"

"You may prove valuable as a bargaining tool. He didn't come here, so I will truss you up and dangle you right under his nose."

"What makes you think he'd trade these weapons for a woman he was forced to marry?"

"I'm counting on his noble pride—he won't allow harm to come to his own wife, no matter how he came to marry her. But you needn't fear being forced into his arms, Kathryn. I'm not giving you up—I'll slit his throat and we'll be done with him once and for all."

"You are mad." She didn't doubt that Rodney would kill Bryan if given the chance. But she clung to the hope that God would not allow this evil man to prevail.

Rodney grabbed her cloak from its peg and tossed it to her. "Enough talk. We must leave immediately before they have more of a head start."

"Who has a head start?" What was he talking about? Had Bryan left her instead of mounting a rescue? Had someone kidnapped Isobel as well?

"Never mind, just get moving."

Simon came to the doorway and Rodney spoke to him. "Get her mounted and ready to ride." Then he strode away while Kathryn struggled not to break down in tears.

No, Bryan was nearby. He would not have abandoned her. Was he planning to take her from the castle somehow, or was he watching the road in hopes they would move her? But if so, surely he expected her captors to take her south, not north. Why hadn't she insisted on getting more information from Thomas last night? Now she had no idea if she should try and delay their departure or not.

Trust God. Aye, hadn't she prayed last night to trust God for her deliverance? And he would use Bryan to make it happen. Comforted by the knowledge that all was in God's hands, she walked out the door toward the bailey.

Simon shoved her when she didn't walk fast enough. A heavy morning mist gave promise of rain and a wet, miserable ride. *How fitting,* she thought as she mounted her horse and spread the cloak to cover as much of her as possible.

There was no sign of the "priest," and when she asked about him she was told the man had left at first light. Questions she dared not ask sprang to mind, and once again she feared that by day's end both she and Isobel would be in Rodney's not-so-tender care.

As her horse moved off to follow the others, Kathryn prayed for patience. She must act resigned and not give her captors any reason to suspect that she expected rescue. Still—despite the increasing rain—she kept her head up, discreetly alert to her surroundings just as her priestly visitor had advised. She was gratified to see many of her companions pull their hoods close about them and ride with their heads down to shield themselves from the damp.

They rode across country, avoiding the road. As the morning wore on, she became more and more anxious. Where was Bryan? Why hadn't he come for her already? Something must have gone wrong. He hadn't received her token, or worse yet, didn't believe her sincerity.

He had changed his mind. Kathryn's hopes dwindled and her spirits became as dismal as the cheerless day.

The midday meal was eaten while they rode. Kathryn brushed the crumbs from her cloak as they entered a thickly wooded area where the trees grew straight and tall. To the right was a swiftly moving stream. Kathryn was reminded of a similar stream and a narrow pathway, traveled unwarily three days ago. She sat straighter in the saddle and gathered her reins.

The spot was perfect for an ambush. Did her captors sit straighter in their saddles as well, or was it her imagination? Another few minutes and the opportunity would be lost. With every step of the horse Kathryn willed Bryan to appear. So intent was she on her prayer that she nearly fell from the animal when two dozen screaming, tartan-clad madmen set upon them from all sides. Praying these were Bryan's men and not a band of border raiders, Kathryn hastily halted her horse.

Someone grabbed the bridle, frightening her until she saw the red whortleberry in his bonnet. She recognized the Mackintosh plant badge and the "priest" who'd come to her at Norham. Thomas winked and shouted, "Loch Moy!" and she repeated the war cry in joyous acknowledgment.

At her frantic search amongst the warriors, her companion jerked his head in his leader's direction. She found Black Bryan and when their eyes met, he waved his sword, urging her to move, now. Then he wheeled his horse about and joined the fray, charging straight for Rodney. Their swords engaged just as Bryan's horse stumbled, and the blades glanced off each other.

The rest of the skirmish moved closer to her, and remembering Bryan's warning not to hesitate, Kathryn spurred her horse, driving it to follow the kilted priest-turned-warrior's mount in the opposite direction Bryan had gone. Kathryn allowed herself a backward glance and saw a swirling melee of men and beasts. Clashing swords and bloodcurdling cries sang out as the Scots surrounded her jailers. Saying a prayer for the brave men who fought for her, she whirled away from the skirmish toward freedom. Toward Homelea.

BRYAN DROVE CERIN through the melee toward Rodney Carleton. Bryan's men outnumbered Rodney's by half a dozen, but the English were mounted on horseback while most of Bryan's highlanders were on foot. But the Scots had perfected the art of dragging horsemen from their mounts with the hooks on their lochabar axes. Already half the English stood on the ground fighting hand to hand.

Bryan fought today with his shorter broadsword, knowing he'd need its quickness against a swordsman like Rodney. Bryan watched as Rodney took note of the fleeing riderless horses and then charged at Bryan. The usually sure-footed Cerin stumbled just as Bryan's sword met Rodney's, and the blades slipped to the hilts before Bryan managed to disengage. Bryan maintained his seat, but just barely.

They had no time nor breath for conversation. Rodney pressed his sudden advantage and Bryan barely had time to prepare for the next thrust. Aye, Rodney was formidable with a sword in his hands. Quick and lean where Bryan had strength and stamina. Rodney would have to win quickly or else give the advantage to Bryan.

Bryan parried and thrust, forcing Rodney to remain engaged and not giving him time to rest. The force and number of Bryan's hits against Rodney's blade began to tell. But Rodney's quickness caught Bryan off-guard and Rodney drew first blood, a small cut on Bryan's upper thigh. Smiling in anticipation, Rodney dived under Bryan's next swing and might have cut again had Bryan not signaled Cerin. The warhorse barely missed Rodney's leg as it sank its teeth into the other horse's neck. Rodney's mount squealed in pain and darted backward, nearly unseating Rodney.

With some distance between them, both Rodney and Bryan took a moment to survey the fight. The Scots drove their opponents relentlessly toward the stream bank and a number of the English had begun to retreat, running in the direction their mounts had taken earlier. Rodney yelled to his men to return to the battle and several of them changed course, but most continued to desert the fight.

Bryan knew that men like Rodney's, who fought for pay, were far less loyal than those who fought for a cause. And Bryan's highlanders held true, chasing their foes into the forest.

Seeing the battle was lost, Rodney scowled and saluted with his sword. "We will meet again, Mackintosh," he ground out before three English soldiers joined him and then rode out beside him at his order.

Bryan itched to follow, but his men were otherwise engaged for a critical minute. At last he called off his men, now ready to pursue Carleton, but by then Bryan was more intent on preserving his warriors for Stirling and meeting up with his wife once more. Carleton was right; they would meet again. And Bryan would kill him.

KATHRYN AND THOMAS HEADED NORTH as fast as possible. They didn't stop until the horses were lathered and breathing in great, labored breaths.

As they slowed the poor beasts to a walk, the man said quietly, "Ye were brave back there, lassie." He regarded her thoughtfully. "Perhaps ye'll do."

The compliment caught her off guard. "Ah . . . thank you, Thomas."

They rode northwest. The rain had stopped but the sun did not break through the clouds. Kathryn couldn't discern a trail, but Thomas seemed to know where he was going, so she pulled her head deep inside her hood and allowed her beast to follow. All she cared was that she was leaving England—and Rodney Carleton— far behind.

She tried not to think of how her life would have been if Bryan, Thomas, and the others had not risked their lives to remove her from Rodney's grasp. Or how this latest fight would fuel Rodney's hatred toward Bryan, and her.

Of even greater concern was Isobel. She didn't trust Rodney—he might very well accost the nuns at St. Mary's and steal Isobel away if he learned about the child. Now more than ever she was determined to bring the child under the Black Knight's protection.

After an hour of riding, three of Bryan's soldiers caught up to them. Calling a halt, they stopped at what appeared to be a pre-arranged rendezvous point. While the men busied themselves watering the horses and searching for wood dry enough for a fire, Kathryn watched the rest of her rescuers straggle into the camp in groups of two and three.

"Where is Sir Bryan?" she asked Thomas.

"He'll be along."

Despite her worry for the knight's welfare, her mother's instinct cried out to know her child remained safe. She needed to see for herself that Isobel was all right, that Rodney or his men hadn't gotten to her yet. "Perhaps we should return to Homelea."

"Our orders are to wait for everyone to arrive. There's safety in numbers, my lady."

Though she chafed at the delay, Kathryn stayed busy tending to injuries, pausing in her work to study each of the new arrivals for the one face she was anxious to see. Kathryn feared Bryan had been seriously injured or captured. To keep her mind busy with other thoughts, she checked and rechecked bandages until Thomas gently said, "The lads are fine, my lady. Ye've done a good day's work. Do ye come and rest now."

He led her to a seat by the feeble fire and brought her some bread and cheese. In the distance a horse whinnied and another, closer by, answered. Within a few minutes the last three men rode in. One of them was Bryan, uninjured, from the look of him.

And one of them was Fergus. Fergus? Fergus had taken part in her rescue? Fergus had no business fighting. She ran toward them, unsure whom to go to first. But old habits came easier and Fergus was barely dismounted before she flung herself at him. "What on earth were you doing, fighting like that? You could have been hurt."

Fergus gently took her arms from his neck and stood back. "My lady. 'Tis good to see ye safe."

Bryan walked up to them. Gratitude for his brave rescue forgotten in her fear for Fergus she said, "How could you make him fight when he has such poor vision? That is cruel beyond belief."

Fergus now looked angry. "Kathryn, leave it be."

Bryan's scowl should have warned her but she didn't heed him. Too late she remembered Fergus's comment about being treated like a pet.

"Leave the man alone. He is not a boy to be chastised for doing his duty, nor does he need your permission to follow his conscience." He looked at Fergus. "You did well, today. See to your horse before we ride on."

Fergus nodded in deference and said, "My laird." And without another word he stalked toward the campfire.

She stood dumbfounded, watching his back as he moved away. Slowly she swiveled to face Sir Bryan, belatedly remembering her earlier anxiety for his well-being.

THE SIGHT OF KATHRYN safe among his men made Bryan forget how tired he was. But his eagerness to speak with her had cooled when Kathryn raced to Fergus and hugged him. They had all risked much to take her from Rodney Carleton, and Bryan's disappointment at failing to kill or capture the man cut deep.

He walked to the fire and Kathryn followed. Bryan was aware of Kathryn's puzzled gaze upon him as he asked Thomas, "Has everyone returned?"

"All accounted for, sir, with only minor wounds." He gave a wry smile. "But none fretted over, excepting yerself." He inclined his head in Kathryn's direction.

"Thank you, my friend." So, she had worried about him. He wasn't sure how he felt about that, especially as she'd raced to greet Fergus and she had yet to inquire of Bryan's health.

"Get the men ready to mount up, Thomas. Carleton will come after us, you can be sure, just as soon as he gathers more men. I want to be safely behind the walls at Homelea by dark."

"Aye, my laird."

When Thomas was gone, Bryan took Kathryn's hand and drew her to face him. "Are you all right, Lady Kathryn? Did Rodney . . . hurt you?"

She blushed. "Nay, I am fine. And you?" She looked him over. "You are bleeding, sir."

He looked down at the cut in his trews. "A bit."

She took his hand and tugged at him. "Come, sit here while I tend the wound."

"'Tis but a scratch, my lady."

"Aye, and it needs tending."

Gratified at her obvious concern, he did as she asked, taking a seat and giving her access to wash and bind the cut.

He shifted his weight, uncomfortable with her touch and his own fears. "I'm glad you were spared Rodney's company. I . . . was afraid for you, Kathryn."

Her eyes grew round at his use of her given name. "And I feared for you."

An awkward silence ensued. She didn't chastise him for his breach of etiquette but he would need to hold his emotions in closer check. He said, "I apologize for thinking you might have conspired to lure me into a trap."

She finished tying the bandage and looked him in the eye. "'Tis understandable that you would consider it." She smiled. "Thank you for rescuing me despite your reservations."

He stood up and stepped away from her, but couldn't stop the grin that came to his face. "How could I not when you kept those flowers?"

Her face flushed a becoming shade of pink, and Bryan feared his heart had completely disregarded his head's warnings to remain emotionally detached.

"I'm sorry I disobeyed you. I truly didn't think there was any danger. Not to me, at any rate. I've had much time to think these past days, Sir Bryan. You bade me choose and I chose you because I feared Rodney more than I fear you." She laid a hand on his arm. "That was not very flattering, but 'tis the plain truth."

He said, "Ours is a strange relationship, is it not? Not friends, not lovers. But bound nonetheless until you are safe once and for all from Rodney."

She paced away from him and then back. "Perhaps we should make this a real marriage, my laird."

That was the last thing he'd expected her to say. Regardless of the appeal of her offer, he wasn't sure it was wise. The paleness of her face and nervous twisting of her hands gave proof she was not at ease with her own suggestion. "Why should we do this?"

"So that you may never doubt my loyalty again and so that I

may be assured that Rodney can never claim Homelea through me." She hesitated. "So that in this time of uncertainty we can have one thing that is sure and true."

How he craved the very same things. But that long-kept vow at Carrick could not be so easily set aside, despite his growing affection for her. "I am deeply touched by your offer. But I need time . . . I cannot accept just yet."

"You will consider it?"

"I will."

She stepped close and kissed him on the mouth. He pulled her into his arms and returned the kiss. When it was over, they pulled apart and stared at each other.

She bowed her head and rubbed her hands down her skirt as if to put things back in place. But their relationship could not return to what it was before this kiss. "That was not wise," he said gravely.

When she raised her head she was smiling, a sad little smile. "No, not wise at all."

This couldn't be happening, not now. Not with all that lay at risk at Stirling. Not when he could least afford to cast aside his worries and be . . . a husband. When and if he finally gave his heart to her, he wanted forever, or at least a lifetime, and the odds were against them having it.

Fingers laced as if in prayer she said, "There is something I should have told you, must tell you before we risk another kiss."

A twig snapped and they both jumped. She looked up and Bryan's squire stood nearby. "Sir, the men are ready."

Bryan cleared his throat. "Thank you, Thomas. Have them mount up; we'll be there in a moment."

"Aye, my laird." Thomas walked away and they were alone once more.

"My laird, I must—"

"Hush." Bryan pulled her into his arms, sheltering her head beneath his chin. "When we are safely home, we have much to talk about."

"What I need to tell you can't wait much longer."

He held her at arms' length and looked into her eyes. She seemed anxious and ill at ease. "We will be at Homelea soon. That is, if you can you manage a hard ride?"

With a sigh she said, "I can manage."

"Then let's be off."

ELEVEN

Late afternoon sun washed Homelea with a warm glow as the weary travelers approached. Kathryn couldn't take her eyes from the view. *Home.* A beautiful sight, one she had despaired of seeing again. She made the sign of the cross and recited a silent prayer of thanksgiving for her safe homecoming and for the newly discovered affection between her and her husband.

Bryan rode beside her, and his page held aloft the colors of the Earl of Homelea. A loud cheer arose from the walls as the sentries recognized the pennant and ordered the portcullis raised. The clanging of the gate mixed with the cries of the castle occupants as they rushed to meet Bryan and Kathryn. Soon noise and joyful confusion surrounded them, and she slowed her horse as servants and men at arms alike surged toward her, touching her skirt or the horse's trappings.

"God be praised, my lady, for your safe return."

"Our prayers are answered, Lady Kathryn."

"God bless the earl for returning you to us."

They surged so close, Kathryn was forced to halt her mount for fear of running someone over. Though she appreciated their eager welcome, she was anxious to talk to Bryan. Kathryn dreaded the telling but she would beg if she had to. She was convinced the child was no longer safe at St. Mary's. Bryan dismounted and made his way to her side, stopping several times to accept the thanks and praise of those crowded about him.

He raised his arms to help her get down from her horse. When his hands touched her waist, her people cheered anew, and Kathryn felt her face grow warm. He swung her to the ground and standing close, grinned down at her until her heart began to flutter. All around them her villeins cheered. Evidently they had accepted Bryan as their laird, as she did. Aye, after what he had risked to rescue her, she had been right to offer to make the marriage a true one. Now all that remained was to tell him of Isobel and convince him to raise her.

Her smile faded. How she dreaded the need to confess her lack of virtue to this man. Shame coursed through her and she had second thoughts about her offer, about her growing affection for him. And his slip in using her given name earlier today gave evidence that his feelings were becoming engaged as well. But he would not want a less than virtuous wife—she must resign herself to the very real possibility that they would end their marriage just as they'd agreed. But no matter what they decided about their relationship, someone must go to St. Mary's yet today; tomorrow might be too late.

In the crush of people, she and the knight became separated. Kathryn shook hands and accepted her people's joy at her return until her anxiety overcame courtesy and she pushed through the crowd, searching for Sir Bryan. Finally she saw him standing next to Adam and Anna. She hurried toward them. Anna held someone's squalling toddler over her shoulder. A girl child. "Isobel?" She looked from the child to Anna.

Anna nodded. "Men came to the abbey yesterday asking questions. The nuns feared for her safety, my lady."

Isobel turned, and on seeing Kathryn, put her arms out to be held. Eagerly Kathryn took the child, kissing her and holding her tightly. "Oh, Isobel, Isobel!" Her worst fears were realized. Someone knew about Isobel and might tell Rodney at any time.

Sir Bryan's eyes narrowed in suspicion, moving from Kathryn to the child. "Is this babe the reason for your trip to the abbey?"

"Aye, my laird." She didn't dare meet his gaze.

"Whose babe is she, that you would risk your life?" Sir Bryan demanded.

Laying her hand on the knight's arm she pleaded, "My laird, as you said earlier today, we have much to talk about."

"Aye, that we do."

"Then come. We will eat and I will . . . I will tell you about the child."

He studied her for a moment, then the child, then nodded and strode away.

She reluctantly passed the baby to Anna and motioned her away from Adam. "Where is Nelda?"

As they walked toward the keep, Anna answered, "Her husband was found at the river crossing during the search for you. He's dead. Hit his head on a rock crossing the river."

Kathryn stopped walking. "Oh no. How is Nelda taking the news?"

"She took it hard. Went to her mother in Berwick."

Kathryn looked closely at Isobel. She seemed to be in good health. "Is Isobel weaned then?"

Anna huffed a breath. "She is now. Took to it well enough, don't fret."

Kathryn longed to take Isobel back from Anna's arms and soothe her for this loss. But Kathryn suspected she was more upset than Isobel over Nelda's departure. And Bryan waited for her, for answers.

Kathryn kissed her daughter's cheek. "I'll help you get her ready for bed when I'm done talking with Sir Bryan."

Anna nodded and Kathryn walked away wishing she could stay with Anna and the child instead of dealing with the man who awaited her in the solar. The door was ajar, and a servant carrying food and drink followed her into the room. After setting down the tray, the girl quietly closed the door as she left.

Sir Bryan looked as weary as Kathryn felt, and she wished this meeting could be postponed. She sat across from him, broke off a piece of bread, and offered it to him before saying, "I have reason to believe there may be a spy at Homelea and I fear—"

"There was a spy, Kathryn, but he's dead."

He knew this already? "There was? Do you know who it was?"

"Lachlan the Smith."

"Lachlan?" Her shoulders slumped and she set down the bread without taking any for herself. "The wet nurse's husband."

He frowned. "Wet nurse?"

"Aye, for Isobel."

"Ah, the child in the bailey." His facial features became severe. "Just whose child is she and what is she doing here?"

How to tell him, to plead her case? "If we are ever to have a true marriage there must be honesty between us."

His expression was guarded, but he nodded.

Encouraged she said, "There is more to the story about Rodney's suit for my hand in marriage, the best and the worst part." She paused. "The reason I asked Fergus to take me to the abbey, the reason it was so important, was I needed to see my daughter, Isobel."

He stared at her, clearly puzzled. "Your daughter?"

"Aye."

"Your . . . daughter has been kept at St. Mary's." He stopped as realization struck. "Rodney. You have a child by Rodney Carleton?"

All she could do was nod in agreement. Her throat would not form words, so great was her fear of his reaction, so deep was her shame.

He jumped to his feet, nearly knocking over the table. "Carleton wooed you and got a child on you and didn't marry you?"

The table had pushed into her stomach and she eased it away. "Aye." His face was red with anger. She looked down, hung her head. She should have told him sooner, told him when he proposed a chaste marriage. He'd told her about his vow and she'd kept quiet, thinking to protect Isobel. But the time for secrets was past.

She looked up into dark eyes that were cold as a deep winter night.

"Why didn't you marry him? Or did you? Is that why you agreed to a chaste marriage—you're already married to him?"

"No! Never! I couldn't marry him after what he did to Fergus. I refused him."

She could see by his expression when he remembered the words she'd hoped he would forget.

"As you refused to marry me at first. You told me you would not marry a baseborn knight, and yet you have a child born just the same." Fury and torment twisted his features. Gone was the gentle man who'd kissed her just this afternoon. In his place stood a wounded man. And she'd done this to him. *God forgive me.* She doubted Bryan ever would.

Could she somehow ease the hurt? "You may not believe this now, my laird. But I never, never meant those words. How could I, knowing of Isobel?"

He stared at her and maybe, just maybe he believed her.

"Will you let me tell you all of it?" she asked.

Here was the test. Did he care enough about her—about a possible future together—to listen, to try to understand why she'd said such an awful thing?

He straightened his chair and, to her relief, sat down. "I'm listening."

Relieved, she stood before him. "I was . . . weak, easily tempted. And he was charm itself. I thought he loved me, and I certainly thought I loved him." Slowly, carefully, she explained Rodney's dishonesty, his deception over her father's blessing on their betrothal, and her fall into temptation, leaving nothing out. She owed him the whole truth. Had owed it to him for weeks now.

"When Adam read Bruce's decree that we must marry, I knew I couldn't marry you or anyone else. To do so would have meant admitting to my shameful behavior and revealing Isobel's existence. So to discourage you, I said I wanted to marry someone of my own rank. I am so sorry for any pain that caused you." Tears filled her eyes and she willed herself not to cry.

He nodded, his expression softening somewhat, to her relief.

He said nothing, so she continued. "When you offered a chaste marriage, one that could be dissolved, it seemed an answer to my prayers. Isobel and I would have an able guardian, and I would not have to make this confession or endanger her." Looking at him, knowing that the promise in his kiss might never be fulfilled, the tears fell and she swiped them with the back of her hand.

He stared at her for an uncomfortable length of time before he said, "While I am angry that you didn't tell me this from the start, I think I can understand your reasons. For not telling and for trying to discourage me from the marriage." Bryan blew out his breath, stood and paced away and back. "I'm more angry at Carleton. The dishonorable knave . . . I should have killed him when I had the chance that day in the bailey." He stared at the stone floor for a long moment. "You were the one who was wronged, Kathryn." The knight pushed his fingers through his hair, pulling some of it loose from the leather string that bound it. "Rodney doesn't know of the child?"

"I kept her from him to protect her."

"From her own father? Kathryn, that was unwise."

"He might take her from me or harm her. He is obsessed with controlling Homelea. I fear he may have recently learned of her. Why else did men come to the abbey?" She weakened again, and tears welled in her eyes. She dashed them away, not caring that the knight saw them but not daring to weaken in her resolve to give Isobel Bryan's protection.

She drew a steadying breath before rushing ahead. "I . . . am obviously no longer a maid, my laird. You will have no trouble obtaining an annulment under the circumstances. But until then, I beg you to keep Isobel with us here, at Homelea. Under your protection."

His expression remained unreadable. "I haven't done well in protecting my wife and you ask that I extend my protection, such as it is, to a child?"

"I thought you, of all people, would be inclined to help a kindred spirit. An innocent child, an outcast through no fault of her own."

"Is this why you proposed to make our marriage binding? To soften me toward you for the child's sake?"

"No, you must not believe that!"

"Why not?"

"It isn't true. I truly believe I could come to care for you." *I already—*

"Aye, especially if I take in Rodney's brat."

Kathryn hesitated, not liking his choice of words. Softly she said, "She is here. If you would just protect her—you needn't love her." *Or me.*

She'd hoped that because of his own birth on the wrong side of the blanket, Bryan would be more open to taking Isobel into his care. Surely his good relationship with his own father showed him just how impossible such a bond would be between a man like Rodney and Isobel. Somehow she must convince Sir Bryan to see the child as she did. Not as the child of his hated enemy, but as the child of his heart.

He walked to the window and stared out. "Kathryn, we leave for Stirling as soon as I can manage it. I'm not even sure I can protect you in the middle of a war, let alone a child." His shoulders sagged. "You ask much of me."

She stepped toward him and stopped. "I know I do. But I believe you are up to the task."

He turned to look at her and she wanted to go to him but held back. He shook his head. "You should have told me all of this sooner."

"Aye, I should have. You would not have had to create such a memorable wedding ceremony, for one thing."

He grinned ruefully and shook his head. "Kathryn. What am I to do with you?"

"Nothing has changed, my laird. When the battle at Stirling is over, I can protest the marriage and we will go our separate ways, just as we agreed." But everything had changed for her this afternoon in his arms. Tears threatened with the realization of what she had lost through her lack of honesty.

"Everything has changed. And you must know it."

She hung her head, her heart hurting at the truth he'd spoken. "What are we to do?"

"Let me think on it." He strode out of the room.

BRYAN STALKED TO THE MAIN HALL where a small fire took the chill off the evening. He'd kept his anger under control for the most part during Kathryn's confession. But the more he thought of

Rodney's treatment of her and of her deception, the angrier he became. He took a seat next to Adam. At Adam's raised eyebrow, Bryan produced a murderous scowl and Adam wisely remained silent. Bryan retrieved his dirk from his belt and began to whittle furiously on a piece of wood.

After several minutes Adam commented, "Don't know what you're carving, but it won't amount to much the way you're going at it."

Bryan continued his agitated assault on the wood. Adam tried again. "If you keep that up, we'll be calling on the wee lassie to sew a seam in your hide."

Bryan glared at his foster brother. "If it comes to that, I'll sew it myself."

"Ah, so that's the way of it then," Adam said softly.

Bryan ignored Adam's comment and kept on carving, but with more care. He was hanged if he wanted any more to do with "the wee lassie" this evening. He would stay clear of her until he regained control of his emotions. And figured out just what he was angry about.

Why did he hunger for this woman, whose eyes revealed fear or defiance far more often than they spoke of tender feelings? Why had she returned to him? Because she had feelings for him or because she thought he was her best protection from Rodney? Aye, and the best protection for the child.

Her pretty words about making this a true marriage had been spoken, not for his benefit, but for the child's. Rodney's child, born outside of wedlock just as Bryan had been. Except this poor child hadn't been conceived out of love but in the midst of deceit and betrayal.

He barely registered Adam's movements as the man rose and put more wood on the fire. Bryan stopped carving and stared into the fire. The erratic flames mirrored the chaos of his thoughts. He put his head in his hands. He wanted Kathryn to want him for his own sake, not for the protection he could provide the child. How had he come to this?

He looked up to see Adam watching him closely. Bryan didn't want to share his thoughts. He sliced the knife across the wood, momentarily imagining it was Carleton's white throat. He gouged the wood savagely and nicked his thumb with the knife. "Mother Mary." He shoved the injured finger in his mouth and sucked on the wound.

He'd promised to release Kathryn from the marriage when Scotland was free. Yet the past few days when he'd thought he'd lost her had been horrible. For although he could wield the claymore better than anyone except his king, and he remained undefeated in tournament and battle, the thought of losing Kathryn made him feel weak as a babe. Could he let her go when the time came?

His thoughts drifted back to their kiss. Did she truly have feelings for him as the kiss had indicated? Or had she merely toyed with him to make him more biddable? And what of the fact that she was no longer an untried maid but the mother of a child?

Maybe the best course would be to see her through Stirling and then seek that annulment.

He turned over the piece of wood, examining it as if he could find the answers he sought. He made several savage thrusts, then gradually ceased his attack on the innocent piece of wood. He threw the mangled thing into the fire and put away the dirk.

The nick on his thumb had stopped bleeding, and he rested his elbows on his knees and stared into the fire.

Adam said, "What's vexing you, Bryan?"

Bryan hesitated. "I failed to protect Kathryn from Rodney and nearly lost her. Only now do I truly understand Robert's pain over Elizabeth's capture. Kathryn is besieging my heart but I don't understand her. Nor do I entirely trust her." He looked at Adam. "The child is hers."

Adam drew in a breath. "I feared it might be. And the father?"

"Rodney Carleton. She asks me to take in Carleton's illegitimate child!"

"That is asking a lot," Adam said.

Bryan shook his head. "I want no more people depending on me for their safety."

"I'd trust you with my own loved ones, Bryan. The lady has made a wise choice."

Bryan smiled ruefully. "You're not much help."

Adam rose and laid his hands on Bryan's shoulder. "You'll do the right thing. You always do." He stretched his arms above his head. "Good night, then."

Bryan retrieved another piece of wood and aimlessly carved at it.

Alone before the dying fire, Bryan decided the child could not go back to St. Mary's. Bryan had seen his own father disregard the sacredness of a church, and he doubted Rodney would observe such conventions if they stood in his way. The nuns must have been clever in dissuading him that the child was there. Bryan would have to take on the responsibility for the child's safety. Wasn't it enough he had an unwanted wife to protect?

The dog Maggie laid her shaggy head on his thigh and he set aside the wood to pet her behind the ears. Animals made no demands other than this. Why couldn't people be the same? He could swear the animal sighed in contentment, and he smiled. But the evening's peace was shattered by the wailing of a child quickly hushed. The wailing began again.

He stood and followed the increasingly frantic cries. Although his trips to Adam's home in Moy were infrequent, he'd spent enough time with Adam's little ones to recognize a tired, anxious cry. His instinct was to find the cause for such distress and fix it. He found Kathryn and Anna in the nursery, trying in vain to comfort the toddling child.

Kathryn held the girl to her shoulder, patting the little one's back and saying, "Hush. Hush now." Kathryn looked up in apparent dismay when he entered the room.

"I'm sorry, my laird. 'Tis the strangeness of the surroundings. She'll need a few days to get used to the newness of things." Bryan could remember similar trauma as a young boy. At least he'd been old enough to talk. This little one could only voice her distress by crying, and loudly enough that no one could dispute her unhappiness.

Here, in this unhappy bundle of innocence, was proof of Kathryn's affair with Rodney Carleton. Just as Bryan himself had once been evidence of his parents' illicit love. Robert the Bruce had been prevented by his family from marrying "beneath" him. But Rodney and Kathryn were equals and still she had refused him. Because Rodney had been dishonest and harmed her friend. Out of loyalty, and no doubt a sure sense of self-preservation, she had defied the man who had deceived her.

Bryan grudgingly admired such strength of character and conviction. Some more of his anger dissipated.

Just then the child—Isobel, Kathryn had called her—twisted in Kathryn's arms and faced him. She ceased her cries and stared at him, and he feared the wailing would begin again in earnest. But instead, the child reached out her chubby arms to him. When Kathryn crooned, "Nay, lass," the child squirmed in Kathryn's arms quite forcefully, and fearing the girl would throw herself to the floor, he reached for her.

"I'll take her," he said, surprising himself. But once he had her he didn't know what to do with her. She nestled in his arms and gaped at him in fascination as if he were some creature from a *seanachaidh's* tale. Then it struck him that indeed, she may never have seen a man in her short life at the abbey.

They stared in mutual captivation until she placed a tiny hand on his cheek and rubbed it, pulling her hand back quickly when her skin rasped against his whiskers. She gave a wavering smile and then rubbed her hand on his cheek again. This time the smile lit her face. Adam's youngest had had a similar fascination with his beard, as Bryan recalled. He smiled back.

He touched her wispy blond hair, fairer than Kathryn's and very fine. The child's sturdy little body and trusting eyes spoke to his heart in much the same way as did Cerin and Maggie the hound.

Enchanted with the little mite, he placed his lips on her soft neck and blew air against it, creating a sound he hadn't heard since he'd played with Adam and Adam's cousins years ago. And just as they'd found the noise outrageously funny, Isobel giggled and squirmed. He did it again and peals of laughter filled the room, some of it his own.

With a grin he walked the child about the room, talking in a low voice and now and then blowing upon her skin to the delight of them both.

KATHRYN STARED IN RAPT AMAZEMENT as the fearsome knight made loud, wet noises against her daughter's skin. Both child and man seemed delighted with the effect, and Bryan laughed aloud. Kathryn stood spellbound by the sight and the sound of the huge warrior and the tiny girl laughing together. *Nay, giggling* together.

He walked about the room, carrying Isobel as gently as she'd seen him pet Maggie the dog, and crooning as he'd done with his horse.

Gradually, the exhausted child's head began to nod, and Kathryn walked to him. "Shall I take her?" she whispered.

"No, let her rest." He continued to pace quietly back and forth until Isobel was quite asleep.

At his silent, questioning nod, she showed him to the girl's bed. He gently laid the sleeping child there, then pulled the covers over her. Kathryn watched as he looked upon the tiny sleeping form. Then as if nothing unusual had taken place—as if this were a normal nightly ritual—he looked at Kathryn with his usual mask and said, "Good night, my lady," and strolled from the nursery.

Kathryn sat in a chair by Isobel's bed and gently stroked the wisps of fair hair from her face. Seeing her husband and daughter together had done something strange to her heart. She fell a little in love with the Black Knight as he cradled her sleeping child.

Assured that the babe slept peacefully, she left for her own chamber to prepare for bed. She would return to spend the night in Isobel's room.

In her chamber, Kathryn began to undress in anticipation of washing off the day's dust. But the basin and jug were empty of water. Tired as she was, it was tempting to just ignore the grime and the smell of horse. But she knew she would sleep better if she felt refreshed.

Perturbed with the servant who'd failed to see to this chore, she considered waking the thoughtless girl and making her fetch it. But that would take longer than just doing it herself, so with a sigh, she picked up the jug and headed down the steps. She would have words with her maid in the morning.

Thankful that Anna kept water in the kitchen so she didn't have to trudge all the way to the well, Kathryn went to the large crock, filled the jug and headed back to her room. Halfway across the main hall she heard Isobel crying again and hurried up the steps. Isobel's door was already open—Anna must have heard and come to calm the little one. But it wasn't Anna bending over the bed and picking up the little girl. Bryan, shirt untucked and bootless, held her close as he crooned comforting words. Isobel quieted and snuggled into his strong arms.

Kathryn found herself wishing she could join her daughter in the safety of the knight's embrace.

AS THE CHILD QUIETED, the sweet, innocent smell of her assailed Bryan and he breathed deep of it. For perhaps the first time, he held in his arms the very reason for his chosen profession of arms. To him God had given the gifts of physical strength and courage in battle in order to protect the innocent and the defenseless. Such as Isobel. And Kathryn.

Bryan walked with the child and thought about God's plan for marriage. His mother's lessons came back to him. She'd taught Bryan that man was ordained to seek a wife and to rule his family with God's own love and devotion as his guide. God didn't expect Bryan to be perfect, only to do his will the best he could. By loving as Christ loved.

And by denying his marriage, by not allowing his heart to be engaged, Bryan defied God. And he denied himself the sweetness and the comfort woman was ordained to give to man.

Why hadn't Kathryn told him sooner of the child? But then why should she? When he'd offered her a chaste marriage and the promise to set her free, she had no need to explain her past.

Bryan stared down at Isobel, now sleeping in peace and safety in his arms. *Who will love her if I don't?* Certainly not Rodney Carleton. His only interest would be Isobel's usefulness in controlling Kathryn. And look at how Rodney had injured Fergus in a fit of temper. Thinking of Rodney and his seduction of an innocent maid, Bryan's anger was redirected. Yes, Kathryn's lack of honesty and her words had hurt. But that paled in comparison to what Rodney had done to her. Would still do if given the chance.

Bryan's throat tightened and he prayed a fervent prayer, the first heartfelt prayer he could remember offering in many years. *God, please let us be victorious at Stirling so this little one may live in peace. And if victory is not your will, help me to protect the ones I love.*

KATHRYN WILLED HERSELF TO BE STILL in the doorway, drinking in the picture of the dark knight with his head bent over the golden-haired child in his arms. Isobel had quieted, yet he still held her. His back was to Kathryn, and she could only see the top of the child's head as it lay supported in the crook of his arm. He stared into Isobel's face and gently pushed back the wisps of hair much as she had done earlier.

The jug of water grew heavy, and when she moved into the room to set it down on the stand, he must have heard her, for he turned to face her. She stepped forward, hands outstretched. "I will take her, my laird. You must be tired."

He seemed somewhat reluctant to give Isobel up. "And you also, Kathryn. Will you spend the night here with her?"

"Aye. I only left to fetch some water."

He cleared his throat. "Kathryn." Silence.

"Aye?"

"Perhaps I should lay her down."

Kathryn smiled. "Of course."

His expression held a softness she'd never seen before, and she didn't want to take her gaze from his face. He placed Isobel in her bed once again and pulled the covers over her. Then he took Kathryn's hand and drew her to the doorway.

Looking back at the small shape in the bed he said, "She's a lovable mite."

He looked away, as if the habit of guarding his heart was not easily abandoned, and she hardly knew how to answer him. But what she did know was that watching him this evening with Isobel had shown her clearly that the heart he guarded was full of love. The passions and vulnerability she'd guessed resided in him had made themselves visible. Here was a man worthy of love and loyalty. Her love and loyalty. But would he accept them?

Could they overcome the obstacles in their way—Rodney, her own deception, the looming threat of war?

"You needn't fear for her, Kathryn. I will protect her."

Relief and gratitude filled her. "Thank you, my laird." She could rest easy now because she knew him to be a man of his word.

His mask returned, but seemed much less forbidding.

"Now pray I live long enough to keep that promise."

THE NEXT MORNING Bryan and Thomas sat together breaking their fast. Bryan said, "We will leave for Stirling as soon as I can get the household organized for the trip. We should have been there a week ago."

"Well, ye couldna go without the lassie, nor the supplies, now could ye? Stop fretting. The war will still be waiting for us when we get there."

"I wish I could leave her and the child here." His head spun with all the possible calamities that could befall one or both of them.

"So, yer taking the child too."

197

"Aye. They won't be safe here. I can't spare the men to stay here when they are so badly needed elsewhere."

And still he hadn't told Kathryn of Homelea's imminent destruction. Knowing it couldn't be delayed any longer, Bryan excused himself from Thomas and sent for Kathryn to join him in the solar.

She entered the room with a smile. His decision to protect Isobel evidently pleased her. What he was about to tell her would not.

KATHRYN FELT HER SMILE FADE when she saw Sir Bryan's grim visage. She had hoped that last night's exchange would soften him, but apparently not. Disappointed, she took the chair he indicated and waited for whatever bad news he obviously wanted to tell her.

He stood before the fireplace, hands laced behind his back. "You must know that I carry out my liege laird's wishes, no matter how I may feel about them. I do not disagree with his military tactics or solutions, even now."

Bryan walked to her and stood before her chair, his expression controlled, his eyes filled with what she could only name as regret.

She nodded, afraid to speak.

"My king asks me to do something I have done before without hesitation."

Kathryn was alarmed at his intensity and started to rise, but his hand upon her shoulder stayed her. "My laird, what troubles you?"

"Outside of Lothian, only one stronghold remains in English hands. Stirling."

"Aye, the war goes well. What has this to do with us?" His unswerving gaze and troubled voice only increased her anxiety. And her worry for his well being. His request last night that she

198

pray he would live to keep his promise of protection scared her. Although some of that fear was for her and Isobel, most of it was for him. She found herself becoming rather fond of him and hoped they would create a lasting marriage.

"You know that we must depart for Stirling?"

She came back to the conversation and nodded.

"And you know the fate of castles surrendered to Bruce?"

Of course she did but she repeated it nonetheless. "Once captured, they are razed to the ground."

Bryan gazed steadily at her, acknowledging her words. Slowly the impossible dawned upon Kathryn. She jumped to her feet, nearly bumping into him in her haste. "Nay, my laird. Surely there is no need to destroy this castle. Homelea is yours now." Her distress increased at his implacable expression. "You promised to protect me and mine."

"And so I have. But from the start I told you Homelea belonged to Bruce, to do with as he sees fit." His shoulders sagged, his remorse palpable. "I cannot garrison Homelea with enough men to protect the castle or its people. I have already given the order for preparations to be made—"

"How dare you?" Kathryn gave him no time to finish. "It isn't necessary to raze my home, your home. I will not turn traitor. I won't, I give my word." Tears came easily as anger and anguish merged and she turned her back to him.

"Neither my king nor I think you will betray us, Kathryn."

"How can he ask this of you?" she whispered.

"He doesn't ask, he demands." Bryan's voice softened as he circled to stand in front of her. "Kathryn, you know of the army Edward is assembling. The fight for Stirling Castle will decide Scotland's fate. And ours. We must sacrifice in order to weaken Edward's forces on their march north. We must do all within our power to ensure Scotland's victory and our freedom. Isobel's freedom."

She wiped her tears with the back of her hand. Knowing he was right didn't alleviate her despair. "So that is why you agreed to accept Isobel? Knowing you must give me this news?" A heaviness settled around her heart. "Did you think I would be more forgiving when you tore down my home if you took in the child?"

"No! That had nothing to do with my decision concerning Isobel."

"You should have told me."

"Just as you should have told me about Isobel!"

She had the good grace to look abashed and yet she said, "I trusted you to keep Homelea from harm."

He reached for her and she resisted, but he held fast. "And you can trust me still. The child is safe, is she not?"

Was that pleading she heard in his voice? "Aye, she's safe."

"Please Kathryn, let it go. Do not ruin what we have so painfully gained these past two days."

She'd thought that yielding to Black Bryan had safeguarded her home. Maybe given time she would see this more clearly. He might be right. But his delay in telling her felt like a betrayal, and forgiveness dwelt a long way from her heart. Head bowed, she stepped around him and left the room.

BRYAN STARTED AFTER HER, the warrior in him ready to do battle. He halted in midstride, realizing confrontation was not the answer. He should have told her about Homelea's fate right from the start. But she did not tell him of Isobel! Still . . .

He was at a loss to justify his actions to himself, let alone explain them to an angry, distressed woman. He watched her storm away, the stiffness of her shoulders telling him she would not listen did he try to explain. Bryan returned to the room and sank listlessly onto a bench.

He had razed many castles for Robert, had even known the occupants of some. But he dreaded what must be done this time, because this time his life would be disrupted. *His* home would lie in shambles, along with his marriage. A marriage with which he was fast becoming reconciled despite Kathryn's not telling him of Rodney's child.

Knowing Rodney as he did, it was easy to forgive the innocent girl Kathryn had once been for her transgression. Rodney's fame for deception and treachery was as widespread as his success with the sword. What chance had the lass had with a man such as he?

Hadn't Bryan avoided wedlock all these years to spare himself this kind of turmoil? Yet his weakness for Kathryn had tempted him beyond good judgment. Now, in withholding Robert's order from Kathryn, he had damaged her fledgling trust in him, and he might not have the time to regain it.

He rose to his feet and began to pace the room. Why must he put country and king ahead of his wife? Would it never end, this denial of his needs and desires? When would he be allowed to sit quietly in the sunshine and enjoy life?

And love.

He stopped abruptly, brought up short by such a thought. Since when had his warrior's heart come to desire a quiet spot in the sun? And love? Bryan shook himself. *Love.* The realization that he'd hoped to find affection in his marriage startled him. Had this hope always been there, or had it been born when he first took Kathryn in his arms?

He sat down, resting his hands on his knees. Kathryn, so beautiful, so vibrant and alive. Now they might never have the opportunity to deepen their feelings. His actions, his lack of honor in dealing with her—this is what lay between them. That and the looming battle with England. A battle that would seal the fate of Scotland as well as the fate of his marriage.

A knock on the door interrupted Bryan's musings. Pushing himself to his feet, he set aside the weariness that threatened to overwhelm him and growled, "Come in."

Adam stood in the doorway. "You ruin more than a fortress with this deed, is that not so?"

"Leave it, Adam," he warned. "If this were any other castle, neither of us would question the necessity of destroying it before Edward arrives." He stood, and placed his hand on the other man's shoulder. "I take no joy from carrying out this order. See to the packing and give what comfort you can. I will take care of the rest."

"'Tis you who should give her comfort. She's your wife."

Bryan slammed his hand against the doorpost. "You think it necessary to remind me which of us is her husband?" He looked away, his anger receding as quickly as it had erupted. He bowed his head. "She won't accept my solace nor anything else I offer. Now go, see she is ready to leave by the morrow."

Adam looked at him for a moment as if he had more advice. But all he said was a quiet, "Aye, my laird."

Adam was right. More than stone, wood, and possessions would be done away with the destruction of this castle, and Bryan's heart twisted with the awareness of what Scotland's freedom would cost him.

I should have kept my vow not to marry.

TWELVE

KATHRYN ENTERED HER CHAMBER and slammed the door. The impact caused the wooden bar to fall into place on its own accord, securing the door and insuring her privacy. She stalked to the bed and threw herself on it. The affection she'd thought was growing between them had been naught but a ruse to subdue her. And he claimed she had used their kiss, her offer to make their marriage real, to accomplish the same goal! What kind of man would do such a thing?

Even his agreement to protect Isobel was nothing more than appeasement, knowing he intended to raze Homelea.

He can't be trusted. Not with her home, certainly not with her heart.

In a fit of pique she refused to pack a single thing. He must change his mind. She would wait here for his return from Stirling. He would leave a suitable number of men behind to guard their home. Then they could end this union and be done with each other. A knock on the door startled her, causing her heart to pound. Did he come to her already? She strode to the door as she composed her expression to erase any sign of her recent anger. When she opened the door, Anna entered the room carrying a saddlebag. "I am to help ye pack."

Frowning, Kathryn watched Anna make her way to the trunks where her clothing was stored. "That won't be necessary. We are not leaving, Anna." At the sound of a footstep, Kathryn looked up, and Adam stood in the doorway. Hope filled her. Perhaps he had come to tell her of Sir Bryan's change of heart.

"Gather your belongings and prepare for the journey." His voice was kind, but he was as unyielding as the knight.

Disappointment flooded her. "Why, Adam? Can't you make him see reason?"

"I'm sure Sir Bryan has already explained. He does what he must, my lady. For whatever else you may believe, he is a soldier, bound to his duty and his king."

"But Homelea is his home now," she whispered.

"Aye, and you can be sure this pains him, even if he doesn't show it."

"Why doesn't he show it?" she said, allowing her frustration free rein.

"I cannot say."

"Why do you defend him?"

"Because he is all that stands between you and Rodney Carleton. Because he will risk his life so that you might live under a Scottish government ruled by the king of our choice."

In her heart she knew that Adam was right, that her sacrifice was small compared to the warriors who would face death or a maiming wound. Reluctantly she took the saddlebag from Anna but could not lift a hand to fill it.

Adam pointed to the bag. "Take only what the beasts can carry. All else will be left behind."

"What about the wagons?"

"We must travel quickly, my lady. We'll take no wagons. And we leave at first light." He gave her a remorseful frown. "I'm sorry, but those are my orders. Please excuse me, I have other preparations to oversee."

He bowed and left the doorway. Kathryn and Anna stood stunned as his words took hold. Nothing but what they could fit in a saddlebag . . . the castle was filled with treasures from generations gone by . . . treasures that made it what it was . . . *home.*

Kathryn's voice quivered. "Even Adam has deserted me. How can I leave it all behind? How can he ask it of me?"

Anna shook her head. "I don't know, lass. I suppose we should count our blessings this war hasn't touched us before now. But I don't understand the rush. The English haven't begun to march north yet, have they?"

"I'm sure they have. They must reach Stirling by Midsummer's Day or forfeit the castle."

A deep sadness enveloped her. "Anna, go pack your own things and get Isobel ready. If we must go in the morning, then I will save the most precious of my belongings. I shall stuff these saddlebags full," she said with determination.

The women embraced before Anna left Kathryn standing there, agonizing over what to leave behind. She walked to the corner and opened a trunk. Inside were cherished mementos, reminders of her family, now gone. Gently, she fingered a small, smooth stone. Her sister had given it to her after an argument when she was but five. Jean had died of the flux five winters past. The stone wasn't valuable, but other than a few pieces of her jewelry, it was all Kathryn had of Jean. She placed the stone into a cloth sack along with the necklaces and rings. The sack went into the saddlebag.

Next she fingered a tiny christening gown, lovingly embroidered by her mother. Kathryn and Jean had both worn it, as had Isobel. Kathryn would take it with her in the hope that her other children might wear it one day. *If I ever have another child.* She folded the precious garment and laid it atop the bag of jewelry, pushing aside any thoughts of children and husbands.

Returning to the contents of the chest, Kathryn retrieved a large, silver crucifix on a sturdy chain. The cross was much too heavy for her to wear—it had been worn by the de Lindsay knight who'd accompanied William the Conqueror to England nearly three hundred years earlier. Her father had worn it every day as a symbol of the God he worshipped. Papa had once told her that without his faith, he would never have survived the death of his wife, her mother. She wrapped the cross in a scarf and laid it in the bag, praying that God would strengthen her own faith amidst this upheaval.

Kathryn filled the rest of the saddlebag with clothing. It made a meager pack, and as her tears fell, she raged silently against the man who had taken her love one day and broken her heart the next.

She blew out the candle and crawled into bed. Anger and grief formed a knot in her stomach and her prayers sounded self-pitying to her own ears. God seemed far away. The sleep that finally found her was shallow and plagued with distressing images.

BRYAN SCOWLED AT THE HUDDLED GROUP before him the following morning in Homelea's bailey. They'd broken their fast with a cold meal in a cold main hall and now Kathryn, Anna, and Fergus stood beside their horses, awaiting the order to mount. Fergus held his mother close with one arm and wiped Kathryn's tears with his free hand. Kathryn held Isobel while Anna stood beside her. Bryan heard Fergus murmur, "Hush, lass. All will be well. Perhaps we will return one day. Have hope."

Bryan pivoted from them and inspected the sling the child would ride in. He'd had a crude frame constructed and a cover of oiled cloth procured for protection. To her credit, Kathryn hadn't asked him to take a wagon with goods and supplies, nor packed more than her given saddlebags. She hadn't spoken to him at all, in fact.

Bryan gave the order for them to mount up even as he stifled the urge to shout his frustration. Instead, he held Kathryn's horse as she mounted. "Be safe, wife."

Her features were stony as she asked, "Will you see to the welfare of the nuns at St. Mary's?"

"Aye, they are coming with us."

She looked at him in disbelief. "To Stirling?"

"Aye." He was chagrined himself at the admission. Black Bryan Mackintosh, the man who'd vowed to remain unencumbered until Scotland was free, was headed off to war. With a wife, a child, half a dozen nuns, and a village full of peasants.

She might have thanked him for that small favor, but she steered her horse away, her silence lashing his soul like a well-placed punch.

He watched as Kathryn followed the others away from Homelea and all that was familiar. She did not look back until they neared the curve in the road that would end her sight of the castle. Then he saw her twist about for a last despairing look. When she faced forward once more, her shoulders were hunched over.

He wanted to go to her, take her in his arms and soothe her, but knew she wouldn't allow it. The thought chafed him, and he busied himself with the task at hand, pushing thoughts of Kathryn to someplace less painful.

He divided the men, sending some into the village with orders to make sure all the villagers had left with Adam earlier this morning. They would meet up with Bryan at St. Ninian's kirk near Stirling. A small force, under Bryan's command, remained to burn the huts and cottages and destroy any grain and food left behind as well as any livestock that may have been overlooked. When Edward passed through here, he would find nothing to supply his troops and their beasts.

Bryan set about the destruction of the castle. Although he'd been determined to travel without wagons, he relented, deciding to take just one with several items that would make life easier for Kathryn in camp. It would travel more slowly than he and Cerin, so he would leave a few men to stay with it on its slower journey while he and the rest rode ahead to catch up with Kathryn. It was a small price to pay for Kathryn's comfort. And perhaps the gesture would return him to her good graces.

Then instead of burning everything, he ordered the men to remove the tapestries and household furnishings. The furnishings not going to Stirling were hauled a mile from the castle and buried in the pits he'd had the men dig this past week for this very use, then covered with oiled cloth for protection. He didn't know how long the articles could stay underground and still be usable, but he felt he had to make some effort to preserve them. He had to believe someday they would return to Homelea and live in peace. God willing, Edward would be driven back to England to remain there once and for all.

Bryan watched as his men began the process of tearing down the great castle and the protective curtains of stone surrounding it. His men were more than capable of tearing down the walls without his supervision. Nor did he need to stay while they burned the wooden buildings along the perimeter of the bailey. He mounted Cerin and rode away knowing he'd feel more at ease with Kathryn and the child under his direct protection.

God willing, the Scots would be victorious and Bryan could return and rebuild his home. The village too, could be rebuilt. But for now, Bryan had made sure Scotland's enemies would find no welcome at Homelea.

BY MIDDAY OF THE SECOND DAY of their journey, Kathryn was miserable. Although she was an excellent horsewoman, she was somewhat out of practice and her body protested with the horse's every step. She and Anna took turns carrying Isobel, but even so her back ached from the unaccustomed posture.

A shout went up from the men in the rear of their formation and Fergus gave the order to halt.

"What is it, Fergus?"

"Horses approaching. Until we know if they are friend or foe we must take a defensive position."

But before they could form a circle of protection, word came that the horsemen were Sir Bryan and his men. Within a few minutes her husband rode to where she sat her horse. "Good day, my lady."

"My laird." Though part of her was glad to see him again, part of her was still angry. She really had nothing she wished to say to him. They'd said all there was to say at Homelea. Bryan gave the order for the march to continue. With a curt nod to her he rode to the front of the formation. Kathryn and Fergus rode side by side in silence.

Finally she said, "I'm glad you decided to ride with me. I feel as if I've been deserted."

"Ye are surrounded by friends, Kathryn. Any one of these men would lay down his life to protect ye."

"I don't want them to die for me. I want someone to talk to and to care about me." She knew she must sound a very shrew, but she was feeling out of sorts.

"I suggest ye urge your mare forward and ride with yer husband."

"I don't wish to speak with him." Her voice hardened. "He has destroyed my home and all I hold dear."

Fergus shook his head. "Nay, Kathryn, all ye hold dear travels with ye. Possessions make very poor friends."

"And soldiers make very poor husbands."

"I doubt he took much pleasure in his task." With those cryptic words, he allowed his horse to fall behind, leaving Kathryn to ponder his statement.

She focused her frustration on Bryan. Why hadn't he pleaded with the king to spare her home? If he loved her, he would have disobeyed such a repulsive order. Despite these thoughts, she remembered the regret in his eyes when he'd told her of Homelea's fate. Perhaps Fergus was right in saying the knight had taken little pleasure in carrying out the task. She was being childish in taking the knight to task for doing what must be done.

She watched Sir Bryan now, riding ahead of her. He rode the black stallion well, as if one with the powerful animal. She admired Bryan's long legs and the gentleness of his hands as he guided the horse around obstacles.

Could she ever forgive him? More to the point, could she ever trust him again?

And then she saw clearly—was this how he'd felt when he'd learned about Rodney and Isobel? Betrayed? And yet he'd taken the child into his protection. And not only Isobel, but the nuns and her villagers, too. Would she continue to wallow in self-pity or help him do what must be done to safeguard her loved ones and Homelea's tenants?

The unanswered questions burdened her heart. So did the sight of yet another burned out village and manor home along the roadside. It was the third such they'd passed since leaving Homelea.

Sir Bryan dropped his stallion back to walk beside her. He looked out at the charred buildings and fields. "Are you all right?" he asked, not unkindly.

"Yes, I am fine."

He waved his arm toward the destruction. "'Tis distressing to see, isn't it?"

"Aye," she admitted.

"Even more distressing to be the agent of such ruin."

She stared at him, surprised by this admission. "Then why do it?"

"You know as well as I, Kathryn. We cannot give sustenance to Edward and his army. They must be forced to bring all their supplies with them. It makes them slow and unwieldy and limits the length of their stay in Scotland."

"I'm trying to understand, truly I am. And I can see that mine is not the only sacrifice being made."

"Indeed not." They rode for a few minutes before he said, "When this is done, if I am able, I will return to Homelea with you and help to rebuild it."

"I shall pray for your safekeeping, my laird."

"I welcome your prayers, my lady."

After his admission in her garden about his lack of faith, this statement surprised her, and it must have shown on her face. Before she could reply, he said, "I'm not altogether sure you and Adam are right about God caring how this turns out, but I am hopeful that prayer might make it so."

She smiled at him, unable to remain angry any longer. "Then I shall redouble my efforts on your behalf, my laird."

He dipped his helmeted head in acknowledgment and the barest of smiles graced his harsh features. "If you or the child need to stop, you need only to signal me or one of the men. I know this forced travel must be difficult."

He seemed to be offering another olive branch. "Thank you. We're fine."

Fergus might have been right after all. All she held dear traveled with her, including, it seemed, this difficult man.

THOUGH THE DAY WAS OVERCAST and chilly, Bryan sweated under his chain mail. The accord he'd just witnessed with Kathryn scared him nearly as much as the thought of the upcoming fight with England. If they were going to dissolve this union after the battle, he would need to keep a much closer rein on his emotions.

He avoided Kathryn as much as possible over the rest of the day. Tomorrow they would reach their destination. Kathryn and the others looked as if they'd give most anything to be rid of their horses and just curl up in a warm, soft bed. But there would be no soft bed or warm hearth to welcome them in an army camp.

Bryan spied the great castle at Stirling early the next morning. It sat atop an outcropping of rock over three hundred feet high that rose vertically above the nearly flat surrounding countryside. The village of Stirling stretched along the hillside of the only accessible face of the rock here on the southeast side.

The fortress commanded a view in all directions, and its control of roads and rivers in the area was absolute. The castle dominated the countryside, effectively severing the highlands to the north and the lowlands to the south.

Bryan knew that whoever commanded Stirling commanded Scotland. Edward of England's man, Sir Philip Mowbray, still held the castle. In three days, Edward must arrive with his army or forfeit the strategic fortress to Bruce. In three days a battle would be fought, and Scotland would either be free or defeated for good.

They entered the Torwood, a vast forest with rocky outcroppings that lay across the Roman road they traveled on. When the road left the trees and dipped down into the more open valley of the Bannock Burn, Bryan gave strict orders to stay on the road.

Ever curious, Kathryn asked, "What is the danger, Sir Bryan?"

"Looks can be deceiving, Lady Kathryn. In April, we dug knee-deep pits on either side of the road and fitted them with spikes."

"But I don't see any sign of them."

Patiently he replied, "They've been covered with brushwood and grass to make them difficult to detect. Once discovered they will deter horsemen from trying to use the grassland to advance on Robert's troops."

Kathryn asked no more questions, to Bryan's relief. He was anxious to get her and his other charges past the army camp and into relative safety with the other camp followers. The English were nowhere to be seen, adding to Bryan's unease. Why hadn't they taken up their positions by now as the Scottish army had?

After they forded the swiftly running creek, Bryan led them into the woods of the New Park, a forested royal game preserve. Scotland's army of seven thousand was camped here. Tents and temporary shelters of wood and tree boughs dotted the meager clearings throughout the woods.

They passed through the main camp without incident and skirted around Gilles Hill, behind which the camp followers were sheltered. Pages, grooms, musicians, carpenters, blacksmiths, armor craftsmen, and women to cook and wash for the men all set up camp here in the protection of the small valley behind the hill.

Bryan dismounted and then helped Kathryn from her horse. She walked awkwardly about, no doubt trying to work the stiffness from her muscles. Bryan wanted to get the women settled as quickly as possible so that he could take up his soldier's duties. "Thomas, come here."

Thomas, several years younger than Bryan, aspired to become a knight, as did most squires. He stood nearly as tall as Bryan and flaming red hair curled from under his helm. He had the delicate skin of a redhead and freckles danced across his face. He walked over and bowed. "My laird."

Bryan motioned to Kathryn and she joined him, standing at his side. "Thomas, pitch my tent for the women and show Lady Kathryn how to arrange the inside efficiently. Fly my pennant over the tent and spread the word that any man who approaches these women had better have good reason or be willing to fight me if he does not."

"Aye, my laird." Thomas smiled at her and she dipped her head in recognition.

"I must report to the king. When you have finished here, see to our shelter." Thomas nodded and moved off to begin setting up the tent.

KATHRYN LISTENED as Sir Bryan gave orders to his squire. When Thomas moved off, the knight turned to her, his face lined with tension, and said, "Thomas and I must stay in the camp with the other knights—you will be safe here with Fergus."

"All right."

"I've sent the nuns to St. Ninian's. They'll be safe enough there. The villagers will camp on the other side of this clearing. I'll check on you when I can, but Kathryn, there are more men than women in the camp, and some of the women are the sort who make a living by attending to . . . gatherings such as this. I don't want you or Anna to be mistaken for one of them. Promise me you will not go anywhere without Fergus, not even to fetch water."

Seeing his obvious agitation and concern, she quickly agreed. "I promise." She brushed his arm with her fingers. "What aren't you telling me?"

He pinched the bridge of his nose with his fingers, then said, "I'm tired and there is much to be done. And truthfully, I wish I could have left you behind. Somewhere safer. I need your assurance that you and Anna will not put yourselves or the child in danger by walking through the camp unescorted."

"I will tell them." In a moment of clarity she realized that he was torn between his duty to the king and his duty as a husband, and she sought to reassure him yet again. "Ease your mind, my laird. I understand the importance of obeying you in this."

He took her hand in his and looked into her eyes, eyes that were no longer cold and lacking in emotion. Would that they were, for now his anxiety and the weight of responsibility shone bright. She touched his cheek. "Go with God, Sir Knight."

He surprised her by pulling her to him for a quick hug, and then he left.

Many of Homelea's tenants had come with them and all worked together to create a home of sorts in the woods. Thomas taught them how to set up the camp that would be their home for the foreseeable future.

One day they would return to Homelea, either under Kathryn's auspices as countess, or to serve an English master.

Thirteen

June 22, 1314

BRYAN, ALONG WITH JAMES DOUGLAS and Sir Robert Keith, had taken a small mounted patrol to check on the progress of the English army's march to Stirling. The things they witnessed— the sheer numbers of men and weapons—was enough to over- whelm the most hardened soldier. Bryan shook his head, willing the gloomy thoughts away. Now he and his grim-faced compan- ions rode in silence toward their meeting with King Robert.

For the past seven years, Robert and his little army had success- fully attacked vulnerable targets in quick, well-planned contests. English strength had given way to Scottish cunning and surprise until Bruce controlled all but a few pockets of resistance in the highlands of Scotland.

But Edward of England did not recognize Bruce as the rightful king of Scotland. He came north intent on vanquishing the rebel- lious Scots. Now for the first time since the disastrous Scottish defeat at Methven, the Scots faced their mighty adversary in pitched battle. *God help us.* Only through a miracle or monumental stupidity on the part of the English would the ill-equipped Scotsmen defeat Edward's powerful army.

Bryan allowed a tiny smirk—English stupidity was certainly a possibility. Quickly he squelched such foolishness. *Never under-estimate an enemy.* How many times had Robert told him this?

They reined in the horses at Robert's tent and dismounted wearily. Grooms led the animals away as the men followed Bryan inside where the king and Ceallach awaited them. They exchanged terse greetings and began their report.

Robert's expression hardened as Douglas recounted what they'd seen of the English host. "The English are advancing from Edinburgh in numbers such as none of us have ever seen."

"Give me specifics," the king snapped.

Too tired and discouraged to take offense at Robert's tone, Bryan answered, "We counted over two thousand heavy cavalry, three thousand Welsh archers, and fifteen thousand foot soldiers, my laird."

"Is there no good news?" Robert asked wearily.

Keith answered. "Aye, I don't know why they waited so long to leave Edinburgh, but they've been forced to march twenty-two miles today with only a few brief halts for rest and food. Men and beasts are tired, and they still have nearly ten miles to go to reach Stirling Castle."

"And we stand between them and Stirling." Robert rubbed his forehead. "Twenty thousand of them and seven thousand of us."

No one spoke. Bryan could feel the tension in his companions, whose experience in warfare more than qualified them to assess the situation. And the situation looked bleak. Despite the weapons Ceallach had procured, the English still had superior weaponry. Of special concern was their heavy cavalry—few warriors could withstand the attack of even a single armored knight. And to face the charge of a thousand of them . . . Bryan shuddered at the thought.

Finally, Edward Bruce, the man whose actions had set all this in motion, broke the silence. "The numbers may be deceiving, brother. The body is strong, but the head is weak. Young Edward does not have your strategic abilities, nor is he the warrior his father was. And we've learned that his advisors are arguing among themselves."

"Aye, I'm glad to be facing this whey-faced boy rather than the Hammer of the Scots." Robert appeared thoughtful. "So, the head and the body are poorly connected. We must use that to our advantage. Our troops are disciplined and reasonably well armed, thanks to Ceallach and his companions."

Bryan spoke quietly. "Aye, and our men respect their commanders and their king. We fight for freedom, not riches and glory."

Murmurs of agreement filled the air.

"The men have responded to Ceallach's training, as well," Bruce said. "The English are used to fighting static schiltrons and will not be expecting ours to be mobile. They will no doubt take up a battle position with that false assumption in mind. Then, if we can also use the terrain to our advantage, we may be able to add to their confusion."

Keith responded, "We must find a way to contain the heavy horse. The location of the covered pits will be discovered soon enough and then avoided. Perhaps we should try to push the cavalry onto marshy ground, sir."

The king advised his commanders. "Pray that God favors us with an opportunity to do just that, gentleman. In the meantime, we will keep our knowledge of the English numbers to ourselves. But spread the word that the enemy is advancing in disorder and fatigue. We must keep our men's spirits high. They will need it."

Listening to them, Bryan thought perhaps the odds were more even than he had thought. He allowed himself a brief burst of optimism as Kathryn's face appeared in his mind. *Kathryn, Homelea, and children.* He mentally pushed away such distraction, no matter how pleasant. Best not to become too hopeful.

THE NEXT MORNING Kathryn played with Isobel as Anna struggled to cook with the meager pots and utensils they'd brought with them. Dependable, good-natured Anna didn't grumble, just made do the best she could.

There was more than enough work for both of them, taking care of Isobel, searching for firewood, and cooking for themselves and Fergus. While Anna made porridge and Fergus went to fetch water, Kathryn held Isobel's hands as the child stepped unsteadily around the small clearing in front of their tent. Kathryn had never been able to spend more than a few hours at a time with her and she found she enjoyed this time together with her daughter. Footsteps behind her alerted Kathryn to someone's approach and she looked around to see Fergus running up to their campsite. Water slopped from the pail he carried.

"My lady, come. A wagon has arrived from Homelea with supplies."

"I thought Sir Bryan said he couldn't bring wagons." She remembered too well the meager pack of belongings he'd allowed her to take and that now hung from a rope inside the tent.

"It's just the one, Kathryn. The men who accompanied the wagon told me that Sir Bryan said to bring it to you. But they can't bring it any closer because of the trees."

Wondering what Bryan could have packed for her, Kathryn handed Isobel to Anna and followed Fergus through the trees. There indeed sat one of Homelea's wool wagons piled high with all manner of household items. Kathryn watched as Fergus and the men carried the things to her tent—pillows and blankets, kitchen utensils, a water pitcher, clothing. He'd even sent her trunk of cloth and sewing supplies.

All practical, all things that would simplify life in camp. Just having an extra change of clothing was a pleasure under the circumstances. Of course, she still might have to leave these possessions behind if the Scots lost the battle and she had to flee north to Moy. But as the men unloaded the supplies, she was grateful for Bryan's thoughtfulness, and when they had finished she asked Fergus to take her to him so she could thank him.

They walked in silence to Bryan. She found him sitting before his tent, cleaning his sword while Thomas sat nearby repairing a bridle. Fergus discreetly found a rock to sit on some distance away.

"A word with you, my laird?"

Bryan stared at her a moment. "Thomas, you may finish that later."

Thomas grinned as he laid down the bridle and strode off in the direction of the horses. She felt herself blushing. What did he think of the fact she and her husband didn't share a tent? Did he grin because he thought they wanted time alone?

Thankfully her husband's head was bent over his task, and her face cooled as she pulled Thomas's stool close to the knight and sat down. Straightening her skirts, she said, "A wagon arrived from Homelea."

Although the polishing cloth hesitated for a moment, he made no reply. He seemed to be concentrating on a particular spot, and kept his gaze riveted there. When he didn't answer, she placed her hand upon his forearm, stilling its movement. "Thank you."

He shrugged as if the matter were inconsequential. "'Twas the least I could do." He rose, and placed the sword in its scabbard, then seemed to search for something else to clean. Finally he came and sat in front of her again.

She took his hands in hers, studying his face. His handsome features made her breath catch. She gave herself a mental shake.

"Will we return to Homelea one day?"

He looked down at their hands and said, "I told you I will help you rebuild, God willing."

"Aye. God willing. And when the estate is restored, have you thought of what you'll do? You are the Earl of Homelea—will you take your place as laird?"

He looked at her now, and she marked how he no longer masked his emotions with her. "Being a soldier is all I know, Kathryn. I'm not sure I can be an earl."

"Would you find it boring?"

"I don't think so. But I haven't the skills."

"You could learn."

"Would you teach me?" Now he was grinning and she smiled back. Kathryn felt her resistance giving way to his warm voice. Like the stone walls surrounding the mighty fortresses of Roxborough and Edinburgh, her own defenses were crumbling, and she knew she must let go of her anger over the destruction of Homelea. Her home could be rebuilt, but men—good men like Bryan, Adam, and Thomas—would risk their lives to defend her right to do so.

Truly, if she'd searched for her own husband she couldn't have found one to equal the knight before her. "I would speak with you of our marriage."

BRYAN LOOKED AT HIS WIFE and fought the need to take her in his arms and lose himself. Soon, much too soon, he and his comrades faced death. He didn't want her to be here but could not send her away until the battle was over.

And now, when he needed to focus on the battle and his role in it, now she wanted to discuss the future and their marriage. Mustering all his patience, he answered, "Can't it wait?"

"No, Bryan, it cannot."

His breath caught in his chest. Never before had she used his given name.

Quietly she said, "I am afraid for you." Her voice broke and became a whisper. "A warrior without hope cannot be brave. I would not have you fight tomorrow without knowing that I have come to care for you."

"Kathryn, don't." He stood and turned his back, not trusting himself. He wanted to reach for her and hold her close, but his reason was in an uproar. He had vowed to save his heart from this kind of turmoil, and this woman was slowly breaking down his barriers against her. Could he allow her entrance? He smiled. How could he deny her when she wouldn't go away?

Aye, she'd very nearly tamed the Black Knight, yet he didn't trust himself to speak—feared to let her closer, feared to let her know he cared. Though doing so would ease his heart, 'twould only increase her heartache should he fall in battle.

She stood and followed him, laid her palm against his back. "I am sorry for my anger over Homelea. 'Twas a sacrifice that pales with what you face." She pressed against his shoulder, urging him to turn. But he resisted.

She continued to speak. "You have been a dutiful husband and I have not trusted you, have made you believe yours was the fault for the shortcomings in our marriage. Forgive me," she whispered.

"Truly, Kathryn, there is nothing to forgive." And he meant it. They had both come to this marriage unwillingly and dealt with each other the best they could. There was blame enough to go around.

As the battle for Stirling Castle loomed ever closer, he felt more compelled than ever to guard his affections. He could ill afford to lose his heart on the verge of what could very well be Scotland's final fight against a formidable foe.

Fool. What sort of man denied himself this chance at love when it might be the only one he'd have? He faced her, and looking at her eager and sincere face, wanted to take her into his arms. To hold her close to the heart he was trying so hard to keep from her. Instead, he focused on his promise to keep the marriage chaste. He feared if he did not he might very well break that promise.

"So you no longer find me alarming?"

"I THINK . . . perhaps. . . ." Her heart thudded wildly as she realized the answer was yes, but for far different reasons. Reasons that had less to do with honor and virtue than the twinkle in his eyes when he allowed himself to smile.

In a steadier voice she continued. "No, I don't find you alarming. You've shown me that freedom is priceless, yet it exacts payment from nations as well as individuals. But the rewards are great."

"Aye, 'tis worth dying for, lass."

They stood an arm's length apart, each reluctant to close that distance, to break a promise or cause the other to do so.

Kathryn swallowed, fighting back tears. "'Tis difficult to be a woman—to have my personal freedom dictated to me by whatever man owns my loyalty. I realize that what independence I'll be given will come from my husband."

Bryan studied her, his expression puzzled. "What is it you want of me, lady?"

"You are a man of courage and honor. A man willing to fight for what he believes in; willing to fight to free the land where my children will be born."

A look of alarm crossed his face. "And who will be the father of these children?"

She took a deep breath and plunged ahead anyway. "God willing, you, my laird. I do not wish to dissolve our marriage. I will be your wife and nothing less than that."

They stared at each other, the bond between them palpable. She could see the struggle on his face and knew then that he was as moved by her as she was by him. She saw when he lost the battle within, and when he reached for her she stepped eagerly into his embrace.

He held her gently. "And I would be your husband," he murmured. He bent his head and captured her lips in a soft, questioning kiss. He laced his fingers in her hair, cradling her head with a gentle touch.

The effects of weeks of anxiety and tension melted away, replaced by the wonder of this man who had rescued her and taken in Isobel and asked for nothing in return. Nothing but a kiss.

After several moments Bryan eased away. "Nothing has changed, Kathryn."

"Everything has changed, Bryan. But I understand."

He shook his head and the corners of his mouth tilted up in a rueful grin. "Our marriage will remain chaste—I would not leave you with a fatherless bairn to raise, not with Isobel already on your hip."

"As you wish." She took his hands in hers. "But I want you to know this—from this day on, I take you as my husband. This vow I make of my own free will. I will be your wife until death parts us."

"I once promised you your freedom, Kathryn."

"I release you from that promise."

He looked into her eyes, and though she thought she saw reluctance there, he surprised her. "Then from this day on, I take you as my wife. I make this vow of my own free will, and I will be your husband until death parts us."

They moved into each other's arms and shared a kiss to seal

these vows. Passion and love blossomed, and Kathryn suspected that neither of them would find it easy to forgo their wedding night. But she understood his reasons; not only to protect her but also to keep some distance for his own peace of mind.

When they drew apart, Bryan's grin and uplifted eyebrow let her know her suspicions were correct. "I shall take that kiss as a promise of better things to come."

She felt her face flush.

"But those things must wait, Kathryn. Much as I want you to stay here with me tonight, I must attend to my duties."

"Aye." He must prepare for battle. Though she craved his company, duty called and must be answered. "And I must see to Isobel and the others. Will you be able to join us for the evening meal?"

"I'll try." He kissed her hard and withdrew with obvious reluctance. "Be safe, wife."

As she watched him stride away, she knew that come what may, she'd made the right decision in pledging herself to him. She hoped he felt the same. Now she could only pray that her love, and her Lord, would protect him from harm.

June 23, 1314

RODNEY CARLETON dismounted from his tired horse. The afternoon sun beat down relentlessly, much warmer than usual for this time of year. Gathering and provisioning an army this size had taken longer than Edward had anticipated, and he and his army had left Edinburgh days later than they should have. Thus Rodney and his companions had been forced to march more than twenty miles today with only brief stops for rest and water. Still they were ten miles short of Stirling, and somewhere just the other side of the Torwood, the Scottish army laid in wait.

Tired, dusty, and thirsty, Rodney joined King Edward in the shade of a wide-limbed tree. Sir Robert Clifford and the Earl of Gloucester stood next to the king. The commander of Stirling Castle, Sir Philip Mowbray, joined them.

Squires and pages brought water for the men and their beasts, and Rodney drank deeply before he spoke. "I say, Sir Philip. How did you manage to get past the Scots?"

"By way of a considerable detour." Sir Philip turned to King Edward. "Your Majesty, there is no need to engage in battle with this troublesome rabble. Under the laws of chivalry you have fulfilled your obligation by arriving within three leagues of the castle, and therefore it must remain in your control."

King Edward said, "That may well be true. But I didn't travel all this distance with such an army to turn around and go home. We shall overcome these rebels and march triumphantly through the gates of Stirling. I want Bruce dead."

Sir Philip inclined his head in deference. "Aye, Your Majesty. If you intend to fight, perhaps it would be helpful if I tell you what I have observed of the Scots' preparations."

Rodney and the other commanders listened closely, knowing that their lives depended on having a clear grasp of the battlefield and the deployment of Bruce's troops. After all, Bruce's army had been camped outside of Stirling since April—more than enough time to survey the land and devise a battle plan.

Sir Philip said, "You will not be able to traverse the grassland on either side of the road. The Scots have dug pits there and covered them. And you cannot attack from the western flank as Bruce has barricaded the trails in the New Park."

"What about going around the barricades?"

Mowbray shook his head. "The undergrowth is much too thick for man or beast. The Scottish forces are drawn up in the front of the forest and can retreat north at will."

"Then perhaps my nephew, the Earl of Gloucester, should take the vanguard and advance aggressively against them from the east. That should drive them into the woods where they will be trapped."

"Aye, that will work, especially if you also send a party along the edge of the carse to position themselves north of the Scots and cut off their retreat."

Edward agreed. "Clifford, take six hundred knights along the eastern flatland and make your way north. When you see Gloucester attack, move in for the kill."

The Earl of Hereford spoke up. "My lord, as high constable it is my right to lead the army—therefore I should be the one to lead the vanguard, not the Earl of Gloucester."

"Now see here," Gloucester argued. "I've been training with these men and they are used to my leadership."

"Still, what's right is right and—"

"Gentlemen," Edward bellowed. "You may command the van jointly. Just get it done. If you perform well, this will be a short battle and we can retire to Stirling and Sir Philip's hospitality this evening."

Refreshed by the thought of a quickly won engagement, they began to disperse when Gloucester said, "Your Majesty. May I suggest that should our tactics today not result in defeat of the enemy, we should rest our men and beasts for twenty-four hours before re-engaging the Scots?"

"You may suggest it but I don't think it's warranted. We will crush them, today or tomorrow."

"But—"

"That will be all, Gloucester."

Rodney saw the look on Gloucester's face as he pivoted and retreated from what could only be called a humiliating exchange. They all knew of his quick temper in combat, and Rodney thought Edward had handled the man carelessly. Edward was obviously in an uncharitable mood; Rodney made as if to leave as well.

"Not you," Edward growled, holding Rodney's arm. Fighting his anxiety, Rodney stayed behind while the others left and soon stood alone before his angry king.

"Carleton, you have failed to bring Lady de Lindsay under our rule; failed to trap Bruce or his ill-conceived spawn. And while you did manage to learn about the weapons Bruce bought from who knows where, you failed to intercept them before they reached Stirling."

"Yes, I'm—"

"And you have yet to give me a good excuse for that last failure."

"They—"

"Don't bother. Bring me Mackintosh's head or do not return to London." Edward pivoted on his heel and marched to his waiting horse.

This was all Kathryn's fault. At every turn the woman had managed to thwart Rodney's plans. All of his life people had succumbed to his handsome face and considerable charm. Why hadn't she? Ah, but she would be his, perhaps before this day was over.

Rodney mounted his horse and cantered after Gloucester and Hereford and the English vanguard. He would kill Mackintosh, capture the man's wife and make her his once and for all. With the Scottish rebels defeated, she would come quietly for once.

He caught up to the van as they emerged from the Torwood. Sir Henry de Bohun rode some fifty yards in front of them on his destrier and in full armor. As Rodney rode through a last belt of trees on the north bank of the stream, he saw a lone rider apparently inspecting the Scottish troops that were half hidden behind fortifications on the edge of the New Park.

Rodney strained to make out the man's identity. He rode a small, gray palfrey, and it wasn't until the sunlight gleamed on his helmet that Rodney recognized him. Luck was with the English.

De Bohun must have recognized the rider, too, because he couched his spear and charged.

Fourteen

Kathryn and Anna made bandages from cloth Bryan had sent from Homelea while Fergus went to the main camp for news. When he returned in late afternoon, Kathryn bade him escort her to the creek for water. He was full of excitement about the things he'd learned and listening to him, Kathryn became enthralled. She set her bucket of water down beside the tent and said, "You must take me to where I can observe the battle preparations for myself." When he didn't answer, she pleaded, "Please?"

"Don't know why ye need to know anything more about it. Mind yer healing and leave the fighting to the men," he grumbled.

"Aye. And that I intend to do. But what harm can it be to see where the battle will take place? And perhaps I can recommend a good location for the hospital."

He muttered something that sounded like "confounded female" before saying, "Ye're not going to work in the hospital. Ye're to remain here—Sir Bryan's orders—so that if need be, I can spirit ye north to the Mackintosh stronghold at Moy."

She touched his sleeve. "Soon I will watch loved ones fight. I need to know what is happening, so that if an opportunity to affect the outcome presents itself, I can help."

"Ye'll not be doing any fighting if I want to keep my hide. Bryan will skin me for sure—"

"Tell me what you know," she wheedled.

He huffed his breath then stared her in the eye. "They say the English supply train stretches twenty miles long," he told her.

"Twenty miles? How is that possible?"

"I heard there were one hundred and ten wagons drawn by oxen and another one hundred or so pulled by teams of horses."

Kathryn bowed her head. Only an invincible army would need such a huge quantity of supplies. Her excitement quickly shifted to dread. "When will the fighting begin?"

"Tomorrow, I suspect."

Tomorrow Bryan, Thomas, and Adam would face this foe. Maybe if Fergus could tell her more about how Bruce planned to fight it would ease her mind. "Did you hear of the battle plans? Can you show me the layout of the field?"

"Aye," he said with a sigh. "Come along." They walked to the top of the hill and as they did, Fergus explained, "About three thousand of our men arrived late and will be held in reserve, since they've not been trained. They will remain with ye and the other camp followers here, behind Gillies Hill."

She smiled at Fergus's reminder yet again of Bryan's order. She and Anna would pack in anticipation of a hasty departure as Bryan had ordered. They had even devised a sling for Isobel so that Fergus could carry her on horseback. But she had no intention of sitting in front of her tent waiting for news. She would carry a pouch of medical supplies and help her wounded countrymen as soon as it was safe.

When they reached the top of the rise, Fergus pointed south to where Bruce had placed his troops along the hillside of the New Park. The Scots straddled the ancient Roman road that ran from Edinburgh north to Stirling Castle. That mighty fortress stood on a large cliff to the north of the carseland where the battle would most likely take place.

He pointed toward Stirling. "You see the road there where it dips to the north?"

She nodded.

"Just past the dip is a deep gully and bog. No access there, especially for heavy cavalry. Robert will place his men to the left of the road in that grassy meadow. The meadow on the right ends in a steep bank which drops down into marshland."

"So Edward cannot go around and advance from that direction, either." Kathryn smiled.

"Ye always were quick at yer learnin'," he said approvingly. "And the forest behind us prevents an advance from the west."

"So, the English must proceed up the road and take position to attack from the east."

"Aye, and if they venture too far on either side of the road, they'll find the pits we've dug and filled with impaling sticks."

Kathryn shuddered at the image, glad the English hadn't had time to prepare such a welcome for Bryan and Cerin. "I know nothing of strategy, but it would seem Bruce has prepared well, don't you think?"

"Aye, now all we need is a wee bit of luck."

From their vantage on the hill, Kathryn could see the approach of what appeared to be a few hundred of the vaunted English cavalry as they emerged from the Torwood. Each knight was clad in chain mail covered with a surcoat. The huge horses advanced, their manes and tails and colorful trappings flapping in the breeze. Most of the riders carried a twelve-foot lance and a battle axe. Each knight was surrounded by a squire and several mounted men at arms.

Kathryn imagined a charge by these formidable horsemen could make the bravest man reverse direction and run. How could men afoot possibly withstand such a force?

The horses crossed the meadow that sloped down to the Bannock Burn, whose swift flowing water rippled in the sunlight. Sunlight gleamed off armor. Kathryn knew the shining, heavy metalwork would provide a much better safeguard than Bryan's chain mail and leather hauberk. And many of the other Scots wore less protection than that. Most had shields made of wickerwork, a leather or metal helmet, heavy quilted gambesons on their upper body, and not much else.

The advancing English contracted into a narrow column as they approached the ford of the stream where Kathryn and her group had crossed just yesterday. The first knight to cross the stream was clad in full metal armor and mounted on a powerful horse. His companions remained some distance behind him, slowly navigating the streambed.

A lone rider emerged from the woods on the Scottish side of the stream apparently intent on inspecting the Scottish troops, who were half-hidden in the woodland. With an intake of breath, Kathryn noted the circlet of gold on his helmet and knew it had to be King Robert—alone and unprotected—riding a small, gray palfrey. In his right hand he held a battle-axe, his only other protection the chain mail and hauberk under his surcoat.

The English knight must have recognized Bruce, for he couched his lance and spurred his horse toward the king. Bruce looked up and sat his horse, making no movement whatsoever.

"Run, my laird," Kathryn shouted, to no avail. "Why doesn't he run for the safety of the trees?" But Fergus seemed to be struck speechless by the sight.

Turn the horse around, my laird, quickly. If the other man, better mounted and armed, continued the attack, Bruce would surely be injured or killed and the Scots' cause would be finished before it began.

As she bit a fingernail to the quick, Fergus recovered and answered her question. "He can't back down from a fight. He's won nearly a hundred tournaments—can't very well turn and run in front of men willing to give their lives for him and his cause."

Apparently Bruce had every intention of engaging the knight despite the odds, for he cantered toward the heavily armored Englishman.

Kathryn held her breath, wanting to avert her gaze, yet captivated by the spectacle before her. She watched in horror as Bruce on his small palfrey cantered straight for the thundering war-horse and certain death.

Then, at the last moment, Bruce swerved his nimble horse to one side and stood in his stirrups, chopping down with such force that the head of his axe remained impaled in the knight's helm. The man toppled from his horse and lay unmoving on the ground. Bruce spun his horse about and rode toward his own men, still holding the severed handle. Stunned, Kathryn sank to the ground.

The Scottish forces emerged from the trees, cheering their leader.

The English cavalry now charged the Scottish position, and some of their horses fell squealing into the hidden pits, creating a great deal of confusion. Another wild cry erupted from the Scots as they climbed over their fieldworks and rushed at the now disorganized English cavalry.

Kathryn recognized the Earl of Gloucester—Bruce's cousin—by the crest on his surcoat. She saw his horse stumble, hurling the earl to the ground. His squires rescued him and put him on another horse before they all fled the field.

Bruce waved off his men, sending them back to their lines within the woods and effectively ending the skirmish. The English retreated and Kathryn, shaken by what she'd seen, returned with Fergus to their camp. There they recounted what they'd seen to Anna.

Apparently the first round of this battle went to the outnumbered Scots. The English would no doubt be angry at Bruce's killing of one of their best knights in such a fashion and would want to avenge their honor. Tomorrow Bryan, his squire Thomas, and Adam would face those same Englishmen, and the thought made Kathryn weep.

BRYAN—ALONG WITH BRUCE'S BROTHER EDWARD, Bruce's nephew Thomas Randolph, and the other division commanders— had watched in horror as their king spurred his pony toward the armored English knight. Now Bruce rode toward them, still clutching the severed axe handle and looking at it as if he didn't believe he'd ruined a perfectly good weapon.

They crowded around Robert, railing at him for taking such an unnecessary chance. Bruce shifted away from them and surveying the land, pointed to the east.

"Look there."

A body of English cavalry under Sir Robert Clifford had appeared to the north and east, leaving the cover of the stream bank that had hidden them until now. They were headed toward Randolph's division of five hundred spearmen who guarded the road leading to Stirling. If the English got past Randolph's men, they would take away Bruce's ability to retreat and force him into a fight he wasn't sure he wanted to engage in.

Adam was one of the men under Randolph's command. When

Randolph spurred his horse and raced to join his men, Bryan raced after him. The division needed its commander if it was to be successful. Bryan and Randolph reached the Scots just as Adam saw the approaching cavalry come into view and began to marshal his comrades into a schiltron, a square made up of rows of men, all holding spears and facing outward.

While Adam took up his spear and joined the ranks, Bryan and Randolph rode their horses into the middle of the square before it closed ranks. With their backs to one another they could relay information back and forth. Randolph gave the order for the square to advance. They positioned themselves at the point where the road narrowed and where the English cavalry would have to pass to reach the castle behind the Scots.

Men on foot had no hope against heavy cavalry unless they massed together for strength and protection. The schiltron was the only way to have any chance of success.

The English halted, evidently wanting the schiltron to move closer toward them so the horses could maneuver around it. Bryan cried out to Randolph, and he gave the order to halt. Then one of the English knights charged into the Scots' formation and others followed. Horses, speared by the spikes, fell and hurtled their riders to the ground. The schiltron held and the English losses were for nothing.

The English, unaware that Randolph's spearmen guarded the road, had attacked without being accompanied by archers, the schiltron's greatest enemy. Only arrows shot into the air and then falling into the ranks of spearmen could break down a well-disciplined schiltron, and today, luck was on the side of the Scots. The cavalry was reduced to circling the Scots, heaving their axes and swords and maces in frustration. Every now and then one of the spearmen would lunge from formation and stab a horse so it fell to the ground, leaving its heavily armored rider at the mercy of his enemy.

The sun grew hotter, the dust heavy, but neither side had an advantage. Bryan grew weary, wearier still when he realized this encounter was just the beginning.

Finally the English began to waver and Bryan called to Randolph, "There, an opening." In a stroke of luck or brilliance, Randolph ordered his men forward, driving the schiltron into the opening and splitting the enemy in half. Some of the horsemen fled north to Stirling, others south to the main road. The schiltron had held and thus defeated a more numerous enemy.

Bryan and his comrades watched the English flee, then sat on the ground and took off their helmets. Weary and soaked in sweat, Bryan fanned himself with his helmet. When they'd rested, they marched to Bruce's headquarters where they were heartily congratulated.

Bruce clapped Randolph on the back. "That was a job well done, nephew." He turned to the rest of them and repeated his words of praise. Then he said, "The English cavalry will not take kindly to being defeated by men on foot. They will likely seek to avenge this defeat. You were brave and showed your true mettle today. If you feel you've done enough and wish to retire to your homes, that decision is in your hands."

But to a man they replied, "Send us into battle again, good king, and we shall not fail you."

The king replied, "Then make ready for battle at first light. And God be with you."

SOFT, GOLDEN TRESSES cascaded in curtains all around Bryan, obliterating the men seated around the campfire. . . . With a shake,

Bryan brought his wayward thoughts of Kathryn under control in order to give his full attention to his king.

As the common soldiers left to find their supper and their beds, Bruce called together his chief commanders on the hill overlooking the battleground. Thomas Randolph was considered a brilliant tactician and natural leader. James Douglas, though quiet and gentle by nature, had earned the sobriquet of Black Douglas for his fearless raids into England. Edward Bruce, the king's brother, was an impetuous but brave leader. Those three and Robert himself would command the schiltrons.

Although Bryan had fought with Randolph today, tomorrow he would be with Robert Keith. Sir Robert, keeper of the king's stables, would command Bruce's five hundred light cavalry, with Bryan as his second in command. Keith was a special friend to Bryan because he'd helped him train Cerin. And while he'd been more than willing to assist Randolph today, Bryan would be glad to return to his regular duties with the cavalry.

They awaited Robert's orders, as they'd done so many times in the past. Bryan knew that Robert considered these men as sons. And tomorrow, as their chosen king, he would ask them to lead their men into a battle Bryan feared could not be won. The devil take Edward of England and his greedy nobles!

Bryan took himself to task. No good would come of thoughts such as these, and he banished his pessimism as Bruce addressed his commanders.

"'Twas a good day to be Scottish, eh lads?"

"Aye, my laird."

Randolph said, "We showed our intent today. But you scared us witless with your joust against de Bohun."

"Aye, well, I couldn't back down in front of the men now, could I?"

"'Twould have added a few years to my life if you had," Bryan said, a grin softening the gruffness of his voice.

Sardonic smiles and a few guffaws greeted Bryan's statement while Robert basked in their praise.

Then Douglas voiced his opinion. "Between our sovereign's bravery and Randolph's defeat of Sir Clifford, we have shown our willingness to fight this day."

"Aye, but I fear the English cavalry will rally in their dismay at being defeated by our foot soldiers." Bruce gazed about at the circle of men surrounding him. "Perhaps we've made our point and should retreat. I would protect this army and retire to the country-side to harass the English as we've done in the past."

The king's words startled Bryan, and the others as well, from the cast of their faces. "Sir, if you ever hoped to unite all of Scotland, now is the time. Order us into battle at first light, and we shall not fail you. We shall persevere until Scotland is free."

The voices of his comrades seconded Bryan's declaration. Bryan could tell Bruce was moved by their bravery and determination. Bryan knew it might indeed be wiser to take this outnumbered army and retreat, scorching the earth behind them. Starvation could defeat an army just as easily as weapons. By so doing, Bruce could spare Scotland the annihilation of her young men. And those seated here before him would live to marry and sire more of their kind.

Bruce looked out into the darkness. The jingle of harness and the muffled sounds of men's voices drifted to them on the quiet summer night air. "While our men rest, the English are still bedding down for the night. By the time they have taken battle positions, the dawn will be near."

"They won't be able to unbit their horses either," Keith remarked.

"Aye, man and beast will start the day tired. But more importantly, my scouts have told me the English cavalry are bedding down on the carse, a practical decision. However, that meadow is intersected by streams and is boggy in spots. They'll have little room to maneuver. Since they intend to charge with the cavalry and then send in their infantry on foot, their foot soldiers are behind the horses, between them and the creek."

Bryan was the first to realize the implication. The Bannock Burn and the smaller stream to the north were tidal waters, emptying into the nearby Firth of Forth. "When the tide rises, they will not be able to retreat through the bog that surrounds them."

"Exactly," Bruce said.

"Why would they take up such a position?"

"Because they expect us to remain where we are, to allow them to bring the battle to us. But our schiltrons are not static."

Edward Bruce said, "Then let us move them into better position."

"Patience, brother. Let the English settle first, commit themselves to the carseland." He drew a crude map in the dirt. "Just before dawn, Edward, take your schiltron to the southernmost position. You will engage first and draw the vanguard to you."

Edward nodded.

"Thomas, you'll be left of Edward, and Douglas, you'll be left of him. I shall hold my men in reserve and bring them forward when needed should one of your squares falter. Keith, you and our cavalry must stand by and await my order for your charge."

"It could work, sire," Bryan said quietly. "King Edward and his commanders will expect us to stay close to the woods and our path for retreat."

"Well, that is the accepted course for a small force that is so greatly outnumbered." Bruce smiled. "But since when have I ever followed the accepted course? Now we shall see if Ceallach's training of the men will save the day, for never before have foot soldiers taken the offensive against heavy cavalry."

"Where is Ceallach?" Douglas asked.

"I've sent him to perform a special task. 'Tis best if you know as little as possible about what I've asked him to do."

Bryan was as curious as the rest, but all sat in respectful silence waiting for Bruce to continue.

The silence broke as a guard shouted, "Halt. Who goes there?"

Bryan's companions jumped to their feet at the sentry's cry, forming a protective circle around the king. One by one they sheathed their weapons as the sentry escorted Sir Alexander Seton into the periphery of the fire's glow.

Robert offered a wary welcome to this kinsman who, by a twist of fate, served in the English army. "What brings you here this night, Alex?"

"I come in friendship, my lord, as did my brother, God rest his soul."

"I have need of friends, young Alex. Especially of your caliber and that of your brother. Come join us."

The men returned to their places. Bryan saw tension and distrust on several faces, but Christian Seton had fought and died for the Scots' cause. For that reason Bryan would listen to what Alex had to say.

"What brings you to our camp?" Bruce asked.

"Your Majesty, the English have lost heart and are discouraged after today's skirmishes. 'Twas quite a blow to see a champion of the lists such as de Bohun defeated by a man on a pony, my lord." Alex grinned, and Bryan watched as the men relaxed a bit and leaned forward.

Bruce chuckled. "My comrades were just chastising me for putting myself in such danger."

"Aye, a dangerous but inspired move. The news of your victory and the defeat of Sir Clifford by a parcel of footmen is not sitting well with the rank and file, either."

"Good."

Bryan felt uneasy about young Seton's presence. "What assurance do you offer that you have our interests in mind in bringing such information?"

Alex Seton contemplated the group of warriors. "I pledge my life on pain of being hanged if what I say is not true." He paused. "If you fight tomorrow you will surely win."

Bryan pressed him further. "Why do you come to us, Alex. Who sent you?"

"No one sent me." He sounded angry, but softened his tone when he continued. "I came on my own. I find I cannot take up arms against my fellow Scots. I thought I could," his voice became a whisper, "but I can't."

Bryan backed off, satisfied with Alex's explanation. He could forgive the younger man for being tempted by Edward's promises of wealth far easier than he could have forgiven him for actually fighting against Scotland.

Apparently Bruce felt the same way, since he said, "Then you will remain in my camp as hostage until you can be ransomed."

"I am a willing prisoner, Your Majesty. I will remain in Scotland regardless of the outcome."

"So be it."

As the guard led Alex away to the temporary stockade, Bruce turned to his lieutenants. "What say you? Do we accept this day's victories and live to fight another day, or engage the enemy again tomorrow in hopes of a more resounding victory?"

Without hesitation and nearly in unison they answered, "We fight, my laird."

Bryan detected pride and anguish at war on Robert's face. Eight years of struggle had finally come to this—a small, determined army held the fate of Scotland in its hands. The grassy carse surrounding the Bannock Burn would be stained with blood by this time tomorrow.

"Then God go with you," Bruce prayed.

RODNEY CARLETON, still within the king's immediate retinue but relegated to the fringes, had listened as Edward discussed where to camp for the night. Or what little remained of it.

"The Scots' schiltrons will not come out into the open ground, Your Majesty. They will need to keep their backs protected by the woods. We should take position there, on the carseland, so the cavalry can charge across it and attack."

Edward nodded at the speaker, the Earl of Hereford. "Aye, and place our foot soldiers behind the horses to follow them into the fray once we've broken through the Scottish ranks."

"Just so, my lord."

"See to it."

It had sounded simple enough, Rodney thought as he swore once again when his boot stuck in a bog. The meadow had large patches of hard clay intermixed with soggy patches of bog. They'd had to go into the nearby village and take down doors and beams to cover the boggy areas so that all the horses could find a place to stand.

Now, long after midnight, Rodney and his companions finally found a solid spot on the hard clay of the carse. Here Edward established his command post and they would find what rest they could.

Rodney fastened a bag of grain to his horse's halter even as his own stomach growled. He would save the bread and cheese in his pocket for morning light. When the beast had finished, Rodney removed the feedbag and bridled the horse. They would stand ready for the remainder of the night.

As he leaned against his patient horse and closed his eyes, Rodney wondered where he would find Mackintosh tomorrow. The man rode a better horse than most Scots and Rodney concluded he would be in what passed for the Scottish cavalry unit. By this time tomorrow Black Bryan would be dead, Rodney would return to Edward's favor, and the Countess of Homelea would be a widow and his soon-to-be bride.

FIFTEEN

Bryan strode toward Kathryn's campsite, feeling better than he had a right to. Despite his initial anxiety at having to bring Kathryn along, he found himself glad she was here, especially since she seemed now as ready to take him as a true husband as he was to take her as a true wife. Aye, he'd promised this afternoon to be her husband for as long as he lived. And since his longevity was severely in question—and the thought of lying with Kathryn was all he could think about—he decided that it was his loyal duty to consummate the marriage before battle tomorrow or Robert the Bruce would certainly lose another man.

Despite the late hour, Kathryn sat by the campfire that was some distance from the tent where Anna and the child slept. She raised her head at his approach, and Bryan's heart beat faster at the sight of her.

"I didn't expect to see you this night," she said quietly.

He pulled a large piece of wood close to her and sat down. "We are ready as we can be. Bruce gave us leave to rest and see to our affairs."

Her expression grew solemn at his words, and he felt his own smile fade. She shuddered.

He tipped her chin upward. "What is it?"

"I . . . saw the king today." She grimaced. "I think he killed a man."

"Aye, that he did. How did you see this?"

"Fergus and I watched from the hill. Who was he?"

"'Tis better, easier, when the dead have no name, Kathryn."

"But this was a great knight. He must be of some import. Who was he?"

Perhaps if he satisfied her curiosity it would ease her mind. "Sir Henry de Bohun, the Earl of Hereford's nephew." He heard the intake of her breath. "Why did you watch such a thing?"

"I could not take my eyes from the sight. I feared for Bruce's life."

"So did we all." He stood and paced within the circle of the fire's light, coming to a stop before her. "It will be worse tomorrow, Kathryn. 'Twould be best if you stayed here within the trees and did not watch."

She patted the seat he'd vacated. "Sit and rest yourself." He did as she asked. "You will be there, Bryan. I will watch and pray."

Resigned there was not much he could do to prevent her, he relented. "Aye, then you will. Fergus will stay by you to keep you safe. Promise me you will be safe."

"I promise."

His sigh of relief was louder than he'd meant it to be.

She smiled. "Am I such a trial, my laird? I do not wish to be a trial to you. I only wish to learn to be a good wife, one that God would smile upon. I have never ceased praying for you, Bryan."

She was so lovely. And despite the loss of home, a forced marriage, a kidnapping, still she kept her faith in God. And she prayed for him. It had been many years since anyone had fretted over Black Bryan Mackintosh. "Aye, you are a trial, my lady. You try my resolve to remain distant. I fear that is one battle I've lost for good."

"Is that so?" she tilted her head and looked at him through her eyelashes.

"It is so." And because it was true he dreaded the dawn. "When I think about tomorrow, I fear for you more than for myself."

"And I for you," she whispered. Their words hung heavily between them, and he didn't know how to move past the emotions running through him.

Perhaps sensing his need to retreat to more familiar territory she asked, "Have you eaten?"

"A bit, but I doubt 'twas as good as what you've cooked."

"It's been sitting here awhile but you are welcome to it." She filled a plate for him and while he ate, Kathryn questioned him about his duties. Bryan appreciated the distraction from his worries, from his growing need for her. Otherwise he would surrender to his longing to take her to his tent and lighten his fear in the shelter of her arms. He dragged his thoughts back to Kathryn's last question. From the look on her face, she had repeated it at least once.

"You aren't listening to me," she chided.

He looked down at his hands, afraid to admit what he'd been thinking. Especially since he'd reassured her, assured himself, that they must not risk creating a child in such uncertain times. And yet that very uncertainty, the knowledge that he faced the possibility of death tomorrow drove him to seek the respite to be found with his wife.

"I'm sorry." He lifted his chin toward her tent and grinned. "I had other thoughts on my mind."

She blushed prettily. "That tent is occupied, my laird. Time enough for us when the fight is won."

The miracle of Kathryn's love washed through him. "You were right you know."

"About most things, I'm sure."

He grinned again. "To be sure. But especially when you said that a man shouldn't face death without hope—hope of a life to return to here on earth."

She took his hand and laid her cheek in his palm. "And do you have that hope?"

"Of you? Aye, the words we spoke to each other earlier bind us for all time. God willing, we will return to Homelea and grow old together."

Now it was her turn to grin. "Aye, my laird. There is much to look forward to together."

He quirked an eyebrow.

Her smile dazzled him. "I promise."

He slid closer and she put a restraining hand on his chest. "You still haven't answered my question."

"Which was?"

"What is a schiltron?"

"Where did you hear of that?"

She waved a hand. "Fergus mentioned it this afternoon."

Pushing aside thoughts of her promise of joys to come, he answered, "A schiltron is a square of men, tightly packed together so all face outward with a sharpened stick or pike. Makes them look kind of like a giant hedgehog."

A loosened tendril of her hair caught his attention and he wrapped it around his finger.

She disengaged his finger and pushed the strand behind her ear. "How many men?"

"A thousand, often more." With freedom from his burdens he could now open himself to the gifts of life. One of those gifts was the woman sitting beside him. There were other things he wanted to do besides discuss battle formations. Things to take his mind off of tomorrow. He brushed her jaw line with a thumb, hoping to distract her.

"Are you seducing me, my laird husband?"

"I believe I am." He took hold of her wrist, and the rapidity of her heartbeat told him all he wanted to know.

She rolled her eyes and moved a few inches away. "How does such a configuration fight?"

Mayhap if he satisfied her abominable curiosity he would have more success with his wooing. "Normally, it takes a static position. But Ceallach has taught our men how to move as a unit to fight where needed. Indeed, Randolph's schiltron succeeded in defeating an entire division of English cavalry this afternoon."

"So, both of today's skirmishes were won by our side."

"Aye, it gives us hope."

Their gazes met, and slowly Kathryn rose to her feet and offered her hand. "A warrior must never lose hope, my laird," she whispered.

The invitation he saw in her eyes startled him, causing him to lurch awkwardly to his feet. "Are you sure, Kathryn?" All his old fears came rushing back. "You have Isobel to care for—I don't want to burden you with a fatherless child."

"I would take that chance, Bryan. To give you comfort and to know, if only once, what it means to lie in my husband's arms."

Willingly he followed where she led, to his tent. To bliss. To the secrets only to be learned from a man's wife. She gave herself completely, and humbled him with her gift. Lost in the softness of his wife's body, Bryan pushed aside, for a few brief, blessed hours, the harsh certainties of war.

THE REALITY OF TIME AND PLACE came back to her, and Kathryn clung to Bryan, praying for the strength to let him go and not burden him with her fears. They heard the clink of armor and the noise of men and beasts moving about. The short summer night was nearly over and soon she must release him and return to her own tent.

He pulled away, just far enough so that he could look at her face in the growing light. "Don't worry, lass. I'll take every care to return to you. I have much to look forward to, no?"

Kathryn answered him with a kiss, at once tender and strong.

He accepted the kiss, but too soon he broke away. "Now, if I am to maintain any of my sanity, you must promise to remain on the hilltop with Fergus and the others. You'll be able to see most of the fighting from there, and the English are not likely to advance that far no matter how poorly the battle goes for us."

She could only nod. They stood and dressed, surprisingly at ease with each other.

"When . . . if," he amended, "the tide turns against us, you and Fergus are to make haste to Moy and the safety of my family. I'll not have you taken prisoner. Don't wait for me or try to find me. Leave the wagon behind. Do you understand?"

"Yes," she said, unhappy with his demand, but knowing she must ease his mind.

"You must assure me of your obedience to this request, Kathryn. I cannot fight and protect myself if I'm worried about your safety."

"I will wait for you at Moy," she assured him tearfully.

"Good. I'll come to you or send word as soon as I'm able."

He didn't add, if I'm able, but she sobbed as the thought came to her. He held her close and soothed her until her tears subsided.

He rested his chin on her forehead. "I must go, lass."

She nodded, then pulled a ribbon from her hair and tied it around his sleeve. Tears spilled afresh as she finished the knot. "May my love and the grace of our Heavenly Father protect you, husband."

Bryan's voice sounded thick as he said, "Pray without ceasing, love." Then with a kiss he was gone.

ON MIDSUMMER'S DAY, June twenty-fourth, just after sunrise, Kathryn and Fergus walked to the south slope of Gillies Hill. Today was traditionally the start of the hay harvest. Kathryn wondered how many of her countrymen would live to go home and see to their farms.

Today was also the Feast of St. John the Baptist. In pagan days boys would collect bones and rubbish and burn them, carrying brands about the fields to drive away dragons. Today the English dragon must be driven from Scotland, vanquished in combat.

From where she stood, Kathryn watched the Abbot of Inchaffray give communion to the kneeling men. Bruce called forth those who were to be knighted, and tapped each of them on the shoulder with his sword. Finally the abbot said a blessing. Kathryn and Fergus bowed their heads in prayer as well.

The Scottish army began to assemble into their divisions. The day promised to be bright and sunny as Robert the Bruce, mounted once again on the small, gray palfrey, addressed his army. "Any who are faint of heart may depart at once, with no shame attached."

"We fight or die," the masses shouted.

Kathryn felt the hair rise on her neck upon hearing their words.

Bruce continued, "You could have lived as slaves, but because you long to be free you are with me here. To gain your freedom, you will need to be valiant and strong-hearted. For those who fight manfully I promise to pardon any and all offenses against the Crown. For those who die here today I will cancel all debts to the Crown so your heirs may live in peace and prosperity."

They knelt again to pray for God's deliverance. When they rose Bruce gave the order to advance.

RODNEY WATCHED IN DISBELIEF as the Scottish schiltrons advanced toward the English cavalry. The mood was light amongst Edward's advisors and Edward said, "They will fight? I had thought they'd disappear into the woods."

Rodney said, "'Tis the strangest sight I've ever seen—for such rabble to take on the might of England in battle on hard ground."

When the Scots knelt down before the abbot Edward jested, "Ah, they ask for mercy. We will show no mercy—sound assembly!"

KATHRYN WATCHED BRUCE MAKE HIS WAY to one of the square formations Bryan had talked to her about last night. He'd also told her that he and Cerin would ride with the Scottish cavalry. They were south and to the west and out of sight from where she stood. Many of the camp followers, villagers, and others too poorly armed or trained joined her here where they could watch and wait.

"Our schiltrons are taking up different positions than they had yesterday," she exclaimed.

Fergus observed where she pointed. "Aye, they have," he said in a voice sounding as puzzled as she felt.

"What do you make of it?"

He studied the scene before answering. "You will have heard the noise last night? Must have been the English taking up positions on what solid ground they could find." He grinned. "I don't think they got much sleep."

"But they are now surrounded by the stream on three sides."

"Aye, and that's the reason for the difference in position ye mentioned." Fergus's voice took on a note of glee as he continued. "Instead of waiting for the cavalry to come to him, Robert has penned the heavy horses in an area so small they won't be able to mount a charge."

Kathryn had never seen Fergus so animated. Her own excitement gathered momentum as she grasped the importance of the English position. Now the heavily armored English cavalry would have to negotiate marshy land. And more importantly, the English foot soldiers were trapped between their own cavalry in front and the sharp drop off of the stream behind them. Kathryn smiled. Perhaps the longed-for miracle would occur after all.

The English commanders ordered the cavalry to attack. Without the ability to charge at a run, their effectiveness was greatly reduced. Horses impaled on the Scottish spears fell, dumping their riders to the ground. The riders fought hand to hand with the spearmen, but the schiltrons remained strong as the bodies of horses and men piled up in front of them.

Kathryn searched for and found Bruce's banner. With her heart in her throat, she watched the king's hedgehog-shaped group as it awaited his order to advance.

The morning passed slowly as the English horses, unable to charge, tried without success to break through the Scottish ranks. Trapped behind their own cavalry, very few of the English foot soldiers were able to come forward and engage the Scots. And those that did were even less effective than the calvary against the united Scots.

Kathryn retreated to the shade of a tree in the early afternoon heat. Surely Bryan, Adam, and their companions were growing hungry and weary in the warmth of the day. How much longer? Little progress seemed to be made, and Kathryn wondered if the outcome would end up a stalemate.

She walked back to camp to check on Isobel. Anna was mending under the shade of a tree while the child napped. Kathryn returned to Fergus and the battle and sat with her back propped against a tree. She must have been daydreaming because she came awake at Fergus's shout.

"What is it?" she asked, fearing the worst.

Fergus pointed. "Look, there."

"Oh, no." King Edward's Welsh archers were scrambling up the shallow banks of the Pelstream, a small stream that formed the northern edge of the marshy meadow where the English cavalry lay trapped. The longbow was the schiltron's greatest enemy, for the arrows could be shot high in the air to come down within the ranks. Kathryn's anxiety mounted—the highlanders had only their wickerwork targes to protect them from such an attack.

BRYAN SAT IMPATIENTLY on Cerin as the day progressed. The waiting was the hardest part of being a cavalry officer. Cavalry, especially heavy horses such as the English had, were effective in charging a stationary enemy and breaking his lines so the foot soldiers could gain access.

But only a handful of Scottish knights rode coursers such as Cerin, bigger than the native horses but not so heavy as the English mounts. Bruce simply did not have the funds to equip heavy cavalry. Bryan counted himself lucky to be so well-mounted. Because of their limited numbers and their lack of size and armor, the Scots must wait until such time as they could be sent against English infantry. Or the archers.

Thomas steadied his own horse and asked, "What are we waiting for?"

"The schiltrons are pushing Edward's cavalry back toward the stream. Sooner or later he must find a way to get his archers in place since it's his only hope to break our schiltrons and give his cavalry room to maneuver."

"So we will ride against the archers."

"Aye, I suspect that is what Bruce is saving us for. They will scatter if we attack with strength. But beware, those are Welshmen with longbows. They fire rapidly, and the arrows can penetrate leather and chain mail."

"Then we shall have to ride faster than they can fire." Thomas grinned and they both returned their attention to the battle. Their comrades in the schiltrons must be tiring—how much longer could they hold back Edward's mighty cavalry?

Bryan wrapped Kathryn's ribbon around his finger, remembering her tears as she tied it to his arm this morning. A fierce longing to see her face one last time welled up in him and he fought it. Love warred with duty, and right now duty must win. He and his comrades must win. He prayed that God might give them victory.

"There, my laird. To the north."

Thomas's excited voice pulled Bryan out of his prayer, and he looked where Thomas pointed. Edward had somehow managed to free his archers from the chaos. They were forming on the hard ground on the northern bank of the stream. Bruce would allow most of them to leave the relative safety to be found behind their cavalry. Once his own cavalry charged it would be difficult for them to regroup and make a second strike. Bryan told his men to be vigilant and ride hard when the order came.

The disciplined Welshmen formed ranks and fired a volley of arrows. Many men among the schiltrons fell in death. Bruce signaled to Keith, who gave the order to charge. With a nod to Thomas, Bryan laid his spurs to Cerin's side and they were off. The bowmen managed to release another volley of arrows but were no match for five hundred hard-charging horses.

Bryan drove Cerin straight at a group loading their bows and the archers scattered for cover. Others who stood their ground were simply run down where they stood. Bryan's comrades had similar success and within minutes the Scottish cavalry ended England's most reliable threat to the Scottish troops.

Bryan whirled Cerin about to give chase to any bowmen still determined to fire their weapons. He made a second pass, scattering a small cluster of archers. Grinning with the joy of success, he looked about for Thomas. They would have a grand tale to tell around the campfire tonight.

But the fight wasn't over. A few archers remained and continued to shoot. Thomas's horse went down, an unfortunate victim of a Welsh arrow, sending Thomas crashing to the ground. Thomas stood up unharmed and Bryan raced to his squire and reaching down, dragged him up behind him on Cerin. Thankful for Cerin's size, Bryan put his heels to the horse's sides and they raced away, headed for the safety behind their schiltrons.

But before they were out of range of the Welshmen, Thomas grunted and went slack. Bryan desperately grasped his friend's surcoat while slowing Cerin. But in his attempt to hold on to the man, both of them fell from Cerin's back and into the mud.

BY LATE AFTERNOON the Scots had succeeded in pushing the mighty English horses to the edge of the water behind them. Foot soldiers scrambled down the steep bank and into the swift, deep water, trying not to be trampled by their own cavalry.

Edward of England cried out to his commanders, "We must attempt a charge or all is lost!"

Seeing his chance to return to his king's good graces, Rodney rallied the men under his command and turned toward the Scots. But the sight that greeted him stopped him—and every other Englishman—in his tracks.

Although the last crusade to the Holy Land had ended with the fall of the city of Acre in 1291, there were few men alive who hadn't heard stories of the bravery of the ferocious Templar Knights. Highly disciplined and well-trained, they never retreated in battle. Indeed, they wore a red cross on the front of their white surcoats—none on the back—so that if they weakened and turned back, their comrades would know and would kill them themselves.

Aye, no one who valued his life would take up arms against such men. And six of them, red crosses clearly visible, were charging toward Rodney and Edward of England. The king was so obviously their target that Edward's advisors screamed at him to leave the field.

Rodney would give Edward credit—he was no coward. His king refused to leave, knowing that his desertion of the field would cause his men to flee also. But brave or not, the king must not be captured and the Earl of Pembroke seized the reins of the king's horse and dragged him away. They fought their way through the Scots and headed for Stirling Castle. Rodney beat off several Scots intent on capturing the bridle or trappings of Edward's horse.

Edward's horse was speared, but the valiant animal kept on until they were clear of the fighting. When the horse finally faltered, Edward jumped clear of him and demanded Rodney's horse. All Rodney could say was, "Godspeed, Your Majesty," and hand him the reins.

Rodney found himself walking back to . . . to what? Complete chaos. He still had his sword and he still had Edward's order to find and kill Mackintosh. He headed to where Bruce's flag flew above the melee.

SHOUTS OF "Press on, they fail," reached Kathryn's ears from the Scottish ranks. "Fergus," she shouted. "The English are breaking ranks!"

"Why are they fleeing the battlefield?" Fergus wondered aloud. "Edward himself is fleeing!"

Growing numbers of Scots and English alike were pointing to something behind and to Kathryn's left. She twisted to see what had their attention and nearly fell over her skirt.

Charging down the hill of the New Park were half a dozen mounted knights, each wearing a pure white surcoat emblazoned with a red cross. *Templars.* Templar Knights? Who would be so foolish as to impersonate Templar Knights? If caught, they'd be hanged as heretics, imposters or not. But that didn't stop the English from turning and running in fear as those knights raced their horses down the hill.

The English attack faltered as they began to mill about in confusion. Most of their leaders had fled to protect the king, and the common soldiers were left to fend for themselves.

Fergus cried out in excitement. "Edward is fleeing toward Stirling. He best not take shelter there, or we'll have him, since they are honor-bound to surrender the castle and anyone inside its gates. We've won, Kathryn!"

Kathryn grabbed his arm and pointed to the knights racing down the hill. "Do you see them?"

"Aye, my lady. And so did the English. Look at them run!" He began to dance a jig, but she feared he was overly optimistic.

Suddenly, the camp followers surrounding Kathryn shouted blood-curdling screams and started down the hill, waving pitchforks and whatever makeshift weapons came to hand.

Whether they did so at a signal from Bruce or just in expectation of victory, Kathryn didn't know. But she grabbed the broom someone shoved in her hands, and ran screaming down the hill with Fergus in hot pursuit.

Sixteen

KATHRYN, HER GOOD SENSE RETURNING momentarily, remembered her promise to Bryan, and stopped halfway down the hill while the others ran by her. The English, apparently interpreting the new barrage as reinforcements, began to flee the battlefield in earnest. Soon it would be over, and she would be reunited with Bryan. *Please, God, let him be all right. And the others too.*

Fergus, as out of breath as she was, came to a halt at her side. Together they watched as the desperate English tried to cross the Bannock Burn. From her vantage point, Kathryn could see them become bogged down in the stream's muddy depths. Those in front were crushed by those crowding after them, and before long the bodies of dead and dying men and horses formed a bridge which desperate men stepped upon in their haste to flee.

Kathryn could watch no more. Although those men were enemies who would have gladly killed Bryan or any other Scot, it made her heart sore to see so much death and destruction.

She looked away to where the schiltrons were dispersing as the highlanders tasted victory and gave chase. Here and there lay her countrymen, dead or wounded, among many more of the defeated English. Some of the injured were helped toward the camp, either carried off or leaning on a friend and walking.

Not far from her were several skirmishes between unhorsed

English cavalrymen and the Scottish infantry, but by and large the battle seemed over. She was safe here with Fergus.

Where was Bryan? What had happened to the Scots cavalry after their magnificent charge? What if he was among the wounded? She grabbed hold of Fergus's arm. "I must find Bryan."

"Nay, my lady. We got carried away . . . we shouldn't be here. Come back to the camp and wait for him there."

Ignoring Fergus, she ran down the rest of the hill, searching as she went for the king's banner. Seeing it still unfurled against the sky, her hopes soared. Fergus caught up to her but she pushed aside his hand and struggled toward the flag, sure that Bryan would have gone to Bruce's side now that the fight was nearly won. She would have to face her husband's anger when she found him, but she must know he was safe.

She became separated from Fergus in the crowd of meandering men. Blood stood in pools on the ground. She forced herself to disregard it, picking her way through the mud and past bloodied bodies beyond the need of her meager healing skills.

She stopped to help an injured Scot to his feet. He had a gaping wound on his arm, and Kathryn paused to bind it with material she carried in a pouch at her waist.

"You must go to the main camp and have that cleaned and properly cared for," she admonished, glad there was someone she could aid.

"Aye, lady. God go with ye."

The sights and sounds of the wounded assailed her, and for a moment she considered abandoning her search and going to the makeshift hospital to offer assistance. She would go there, but first she must find Bryan. He had to be over there, where the king's banner flew. The smell of death and blood beset her, but Kathryn pushed on toward the banner once more.

At last she reached the flag, only to find someone had stuck the pole in a hole in a rock, while the king had probably been taken to safety. Oh, saints in heaven, was Bryan with Bruce or here among the bodies strewn about in gruesome postures? She searched in every direction, but didn't find him. Perhaps he'd been wounded and taken to the hospital already.

Staggering from the weight of her skirt, the hem now soaked with mud and blood, Kathryn wiped the sweat from her eyes. A mounted man with the Mackintosh badge on his bonnet rode toward her. With relief, she recognized Fergus.

"Where did you find the horse?" she asked as he dismounted.

"I borrowed it from an Englishman who won't be needin' it." He settled her into the saddle and led the horse toward camp. "There'll be the devil to pay if my laird finds ye down here," he said gruffly.

"Have you seen him? Is he all right?"

"I have no idea where he is, Kathryn."

She held tight to the pommel, taking a deep shuddering breath to calm herself. "We must search for him."

"I will not. I value my life even if ye don't. I'm taking ye back to camp. Ye can wait for him there."

"No, take me to the hospital. He may be wounded."

Fergus seemed to consider her request for a moment as the horse picked its way among human and equine obstacles.

Everywhere, men lay perfectly still or moaned in agony. Horses thrashed in frantic attempts to escape their pain. She tried to shut it out, but just before she closed her eyes she happened to glance down.

She grabbed Fergus's arm. "Stop! Stop Fergus!" She leaped from the horse before the animal halted.

By the time Fergus reached her, she was cradling the head of a youth whose bright red curls were barely distinguishable from the filth and blood smeared in them. Thomas.

Fergus reached out and felt for a pulse. Kathryn searched frantically for wounds.

"He's gone, my lady. Nothing ye can do."

Kathryn wept. She'd come to know him these last few weeks—his freckled face nearly always smiling in amusement at life in general. She drew Thomas's limp body more firmly into her grasp, holding him even as she sat in the mud.

"Fergus, you must search for Bryan. Thomas," she sobbed, "Thomas wouldn't leave Bryan, you know that. I'll stay with him." Her voice broke. "Please, Fergus, quickly."

Fergus gaped at her, obviously thunderstruck as the truth of her words hit him. They both knew that a squire protected his master's back, never left his side. And the loyalty went two ways. Bryan couldn't be far away.

"I can't leave ye, Kat. I can't. 'Tis much too dangerous."

Kathryn rested her forehead on the top of Thomas' head. She must stay with the man until Fergus found Bryan. Then . . . then what? She would either have another man to bury or a husband to love. The sun went behind some clouds, and the day chilled.

Kathryn closed her eyes to the misery around her, closed her ears to the sounds, closed her heart to the pain.

BRYAN FOUND CERIN a short distance from where they'd parted company. Thomas was badly wounded—a Welshman's arrow had found its way through his chain mail and into a lung. He would not live out the day.

If Thomas had not been sitting behind Bryan . . . the arrow would have found him instead. He owed Thomas his life. The least he could do was take him from the battlefield as he'd entered it—

on horseback. Even if it was to simply die in camp rather than on a bloody battlefield.

He captured Cerin's reins and walked back toward Thomas with a heavy heart. Despite the retreat of the English, skirmishes continued across the valley between enemies, and the sights and sounds were unspeakable. But thankfully no one approached him. Bryan had had enough of war for today. For a lifetime.

He neared where he'd left his squire and thought his heart would break at the sight of Kathryn sitting there amidst the carnage. Her eyes were closed and she seemed lost in grief. Thomas must be dead, then. Bryan's throat tightened but he walked on to where Fergus stood watch over them both.

Bryan swallowed his pain and scowled at Fergus. "What is she doing on the battlefield?"

Fergus explained, "We came down the hill with the others and got separated. She was determined to find you. I found her wondering about and we were headed back to the camp when she found . . . Thomas. She willna turn him loose, my laird."

They walked to where she sat, obviously stunned from all she'd seen even before she found Thomas. If only she would have listened to Bryan and stayed on the hill. It was one thing to see battle from a distance; quite another to see it up close. He would take her to task later. Now he needed to get her—get all of them—off the battlefield before some other calamity arose.

"Come, Kathryn." Bryan gently pried her fingers loose, then shifted the man from her lap. Bryan pulled her to her feet and held her.

"Bryan." She trembled. "I thought you were dead, too," she said, clinging fiercely to him.

"Hush, now," he crooned. "I only went to get Cerin to carry Thomas. He died protecting me and I thought to—"

"Holy saints above." She pushed in agitation against Bryan and sensing what was coming, he deftly shifted her to the side and provided support while she emptied her stomach.

WHEN THE RETCHING SUBSIDED, Bryan wiped her brow. "Are you all right?"

She only nodded, not trusting her voice, or her stomach. If Thomas had died protecting Bryan . . . it didn't bear thinking how close she'd come to becoming a widow. She said a fervent prayer for Thomas's soul.

Bryan and Fergus gently wrapped Thomas in his plaid and laid him across Cerin. Even as more tears spilled down her face, Kathryn shifted toward Bryan and drank in the wonderful, sweaty, alive smell of him. She touched his chiseled cheek, his lips, the hair that peeked out from the back of his helmet. She marveled anew at the dark, thick lashes surrounding his brown eyes. She shuddered again at the thought of how near she had come to losing him.

She couldn't take her gaze from him. "You are not wounded?"

"Cuts and bruises, only, beloved."

With a sigh, she pressed her lips to his, keeping her eyes open in order to feast upon the sight of him. His kiss was tender.

Fergus cleared his throat, reminding her they were not alone. And reminding her of the sad task awaiting them.

Bryan pulled away. "We need to leave the field, Kathryn. 'Tisn't safe to be distracted with the enemy so near. You ride the other horse, and Fergus and I will lead them."

Fergus held both horses' reins so that Bryan could stand behind her and help her mount. His hands had barely touched her waist when Fergus cried out, "My laird, beware!"

Bryan spun around and pinned Kathryn behind him. The horse

moved sideways, giving her room to peer around Bryan. There standing before them was Rodney Carleton, sword drawn and ready. She knew Bryan's desire for revenge ran deep, as did Rodney's, and that this fight had been inevitable from that first day in Homelea's bailey.

Quietly, she moved away from Bryan so he could remove the claymore he carried in a scabbard on his back.

NEVER UNDERESTIMATE AN ENEMY. Bruce's words came back to him once more as Bryan thought through his options. Praying that Fergus had remembered to carry the short sword Adam had given him during their lessons, Bryan said, "Kathryn, see to the horses." To his relief she didn't hesitate, walking swiftly to Fergus and taking the reins. Now if she would just stay there and let him concentrate on killing this miserable Englishman.

Bryan reached over his shoulder and withdrew his sword, never taking his gaze off Carleton as he slowly moved away from Kathryn. Fergus moved with him, and Bryan was relieved to see the man indeed held the falchion in his hand. With any luck Fergus had developed some skill with the weapon. Fergus kept Bryan on the side with his bad eye, and seeing that, Bryan's confidence in Adam's training eased his anxiety.

Carleton said, "This is between you and me, Mackintosh. Call off your man."

"You set the rules of engagement when you challenged two armed men, Carleton."

"A one-eyed man isn't much of a challenge, but this isn't his fight. You are the one who has taken everything from me."

"Fergus, stand aside. See to Lady Kathryn." He turned back to Carleton; the ends of their swords nearly touched as Carleton worked his way closer. Bryan slowly sidestepped, trying to put himself between Rodney and Kathryn before engaging Rodney's sword.

They'd been on horseback the last time they met and the advantage had been Bryan's. Now on foot, Rodney's quickness gave him the upper hand. Bryan must wear him down, because strength and stamina were still on his side.

Fergus hadn't moved.

"Fergus, see to my wife!" Fergus hesitated, the need to engage Carleton and seek revenge for his damaged eye written upon his face. And in the moment that Bryan yelled at Fergus, Rodney abruptly lunged. Bryan engaged Rodney's blade and pushed it away. The heavy claymore was longer than Rodney's sword and placed Bryan's body out of range. But Rodney spun away to the right and in a lightning-fast move closed the distance and crashed the broadside of his blade against Bryan's temple.

The helmet rang, protecting Bryan from the worst of the blow but not enough to keep him from sinking to his knees, stunned and disoriented. *Never underestimate an enemy.* The last thing he heard was a ferocious howl from Fergus.

KATHRYN STARED AT BRYAN'S MOTIONLESS BODY and a fierce rage arose in her. Fergus raced into the breach forcing Rodney away from Bryan temporarily. Without thought she raced to her husband and pulled his sword from his lifeless hands. Barely able to hold its weight aloft, she stood guard over Bryan.

Fergus placed himself between her and Rodney and thrust his weapon at the man. They fought and Fergus managed to stay in front of Kathryn. He fought well for several minutes, not giving any ground. But Rodney's skill began to tell as he became more and more aggressive and backed Fergus so close she had to point the blade toward the ground for fear of harming him.

Finally Carleton sliced his sword across Fergus's blade and sent his weapon flying. With a shout of triumph, Carleton rushed toward them. Kathryn lifted her blade once more thinking to defend herself. Fergus sidestepped, lunging for his sword and clearing Rodney's way.

Only then did she realize Rodney's mistake. Unable to halt his forward momentum, he raised his arms and tried to twist out of the way. But he ran right into the point of the sword that Kathryn barely managed to hold upright. He cursed loudly.

If she had been stronger, the blade might have run through his leg, but all it did was cut him. The impact sent her onto her rump and the heavy sword fell to the ground. She grabbed it back up even as she sat there in the dirt and managed to lift it again. Rodney struggled to regain his balance and as he did so, his own sword barely missed Kathryn's trembling arms. She was going to have to put the heavy weapon down.

She heard hoof beats and feared the horses had taken off, frightened by the clashing weapons.

As she lowered the blade, Rodney grinned and stepped toward her, the tip of his sword perilously close to her neck. "Ah," he said, "So the lady comes to her senses. Shall we . . ." He broke off, looking behind her, and cursed under his breath.

"Well, Sir Rodney, you've taken to fighting women have you?" said a familiar and most welcome voice. Adam, sword in hand, stood beside her. It had been his horse she heard. Kathryn breathed a heartfelt prayer of thanksgiving.

"Get the horses, lady."

Though she would have preferred to go to Bryan, she dared not distract Adam from this deadly game. She quickly backed away, went to the horses and picked up the reins, calming them before she turned back to watch the fight.

Adam made no effort to engage Rodney's blade, just circled and backed the other man toward Bryan's inert form where Fergus now kept guard.

But Rodney was too canny for anything so obvious and he moved to the right and away from Bryan. He could now see both men. With a dismissive glance toward Fergus, Rodney turned his attention to Adam. Some kind of signal must have passed between the two Scotsmen, because Adam engaged Rodney's sword and Fergus leaped toward Carleton, burying his short sword to the hilt in Rodney's abdomen. Rodney staggered, a look of astonishment on his face. He toppled to the ground and moaned once before laying still.

Kathryn threw the reins down. She ran to Bryan and knelt beside him, feeling his neck for a pulse and crying with relief when she found it. The blow had simply knocked him unconscious.

Fergus joined her at Bryan's side and Kathryn muttered, "Help me get this helmet off."

They laid him flat and made him comfortable. His face was ashen but his breathing seemed normal.

The blow had sharply dented his helmet and despite all their care, the broken edges scraped Bryan's skin and left a bloody trail along his scalp when they removed it. A huge welt grew on the side of his head. With a stifled oath, Kathryn prayed the hardheadedness she'd so often accused him of would protect him now.

Adam sank down beside her. "If he doesn't come around soon, we'll have to get him on one of the horses and take him to shelter."

"All right. Could you bring me some water, Fergus?"

"I'm not sure I can find any in the creek that isn't tainted, but I'll see what I can do."

She remembered the bridge of bodies and knew he was probably right.

He moved off to do her bidding; Adam stood nearby with the horses.

Kathryn held Bryan's hand, gently rubbing the long, beautiful fingers. Fingers that so skillfully wielded the heavy claymore, now lay unmoving in her hand. Remembering her bridegroom's tender touch, she kissed the callused palm and tried unsuccessfully to hold back her tears.

She'd seen a villager die from a blow to the head. One could never tell with such an injury when or if the patient would awaken.

Hoping somehow he might hear her, she spoke to him. "Please, Bryan. You must wake up."

Fergus brought her some relatively clean, cool water. She pulled a strip from her bandage pouch and dabbed Bryan's brow with it, then wound more around his head to stanch the flow of blood. Fergus and Adam held the horses and watched.

She prayed aloud. "Please, dear Savior. I cannot bear to lose him. I will never love another such as I do this man you've given me." Kathryn held Bryan's hand and laid her cheek in his palm.

Just as she made to raise her head, Bryan's fingers stroked her hair. Afraid she'd imagined it she remained still. The fingers moved again. Her prayers had been answered! She leaned forward to place a kiss on his forehead.

"Bryan," she called softly.

His eyelids fluttered.

"Thank you, Jesus," she whispered. She squeezed Bryan's hand and he weakly returned the pressure. Then she stared into his beautiful dark eyes, and her tears splashed his face.

"You are real, then," he whispered, startling her with his voice as well as the words. Obviously tired from the exertion, Bryan closed his eyes. "'Twas your love that pulled me back, Kathryn. I could feel myself slipping but you wouldn't let go."

Astounded by his words, grateful beyond measure for his recovery, she said, "We'll talk later. Let's get you on a horse and out of this mud."

SEVENTEEN

W ITH SOME SHOVING FROM THE MEN, Bryan managed to mount. He felt dizzy and a bit weak, but thankfully he wasn't seeing double. He was glad for the helmet's protection or he might not have survived such a blow.

The battle was over, the carseland filled with those caring for the wounded or dead, but no one fought any longer. It was over. Scotland was free. But Bryan's heart remained heavy.

He looked at the plaid-draped body lying across Cerin's back and fought back tears. With an effort he pulled his thoughts away from his friend and the unwitting sacrifice he'd made. Bryan's head ached from Rodney's blow, but he was determined to see Thomas properly cared for before going back to camp.

"We'll take him to the kirk in the village. 'Tis most likely where the dead will lay until claimed or buried."

"You should not ride—"

"Kathryn, I appreciate your concern, I truly do. But I must see this done. If you wish to accompany me, you may. But don't try to dissuade me."

No one offered further argument. Kathryn climbed up behind him. Adam and Fergus placed Rodney Carleton across the horse Fergus had found and the four of them made their way to the small church. As they removed Thomas's body from the horse, they learned that Bruce had given orders that the thirty-some English barons and several hundred knights who'd died fighting against him were to be buried honorably and in sanctified ground.

Bryan's first thought on hearing of Bruce's magnanimous gesture was less than charitable where Rodney was concerned. But reason returned and they took Rodney's body and laid it with his countrymen.

Just as they were about to leave, a wagon delivered the body of the Earl of Gloucester. In the tangle of royal bloodlines, he'd been nephew to Edward of England and cousin to Bruce. The earl was taken inside the church where Bruce himself waited to keep vigil over his kinsman.

Asking the others to wait outside, Bryan entered the kirk and found his father sitting pensively beside Gloucester's body. Bryan sat on the bench next to the king and asked, "Is there anything I can do for you, Your Majesty?"

Bruce shook his head. "My cousin fought honorably for his king. 'Tis my duty to honor him and his family for all we've meant to each other despite our political differences."

He faced Bryan and his eyebrows shot up. "Looks like you took quite a blow."

Bryan nodded and winced. "Carleton. Kathryn's man Fergus killed him for it."

"Good." They sat in silence for a few moments. "You should go to your wife, Bryan."

Wife. *Elizabeth!* "My laird. Soon you will be reunited with the queen! Edward must ransom her for one of his captured nobles."

Bruce smiled. "I figure she is worth two or three Englishmen, don't you?"

Bryan chuckled. "That she is."

Bruce cocked his head to look at someone or something behind

Bryan. Bryan turned and saw Kathryn standing in the doorway. He raised his hand in greeting and said, "I'll be there shortly."

Turning back to Bruce he said, "Those Templar Knights were a great surprise to everyone. I suspect that was Ceallach's secret mission you spoke of last night."

"I can only say that Ceallach has an interesting story to tell."

Bryan waited but Bruce said no more. "I'll look forward to hearing it one day." He saw Kathryn again from the corner of his eye. "But just now I'm anxious to have some of the tea Kathryn promised would ease my aching head."

"Go to her, Bryan. Scotland is free and so are you from your vow to safeguard your heart."

Bryan smiled. "I'm afraid I broke that vow some time ago."

Bruce chuckled. "Good. Just don't be in a hurry to make a grandfather of me."

Bryan put a hand on his king's shoulder. "I'll see you tomorrow, my laird." He walked to Kathryn and they went outside and joined the others. Subdued by the day's events, saddened by the loss of Thomas, they arrived at the women's campsite. But despite their sadness at those who were lost, there was much joy in being reunited with those who remained. Anna, holding little Isobel, joined them. Although Bryan was glad to see them, the noise and confusion overwhelmed him.

Kathryn must have seen it for she drew him aside and handed him a cup of tea. "Drink this. It will help."

He did as she said and then rested for a bit. But there was still some difficult business to attend to. When Bryan's headache receded to a manageable level, he called his page to him. They walked some distance away for a private word. He set his hands on the young man's shoulders, ignoring the tracks of tears visible in the dirt on Jamie's face. "You will now be my squire and take on Thomas's duties."

The lad swallowed hard and said, "Aye, my laird."

"You have worked hard to take this position when Thomas should become a knight." He squeezed Jamie's shoulder. "'Tis difficult to gain by another's loss, but we must continue."

Jamie nodded.

"Thomas would understand, Jamie. Now go take care of the horses and bring my tent to this site. We will camp here until we can leave for home."

"Aye, my laird."

Head bowed, Jamie went off to do as he'd been told.

KATHRYN WORRIED ABOUT BRYAN. He'd been moody and distant since their return to the camp and she didn't think it all owed to the injury to his head. After they ate, the men moved and pitched several tents, since Adam and Bryan would now stay in the clearing with the women.

Though evening had come, the long summer daylight lingered. Adam had gone to the main camp for news and when she saw him stride back into camp and head for Bryan, she rose from her chores and joined them.

Adam greeted her but Bryan seemed not to notice her.

After the day Bryan had gone through, she could find patience within her. She sat down by the fire, curious to know what Adam had learned.

Bryan asked, "Do we know where Edward of England is tonight?"

Adam grinned and said, "Nay, but we know where he isn't. Mowbray refused him entrance to Stirling."

Bryan said, "That's unfortunate. I would have liked to add the capture of the king of England to our victories today."

Adam nodded in agreement. "Well, he may be caught yet. Douglas and about sixty of our horsemen are chasing him east toward the coast." Warming to his tale, Adam said excitedly, "We did capture the entire English baggage train."

"All of it?" Kathryn exclaimed. "Fergus told me the English brought over two hundred wagons with them. Whatever will we do with it?"

"Bruce has ordered the goods dispersed to all who fought and any that's left over is to go to the poor." Adam jumped up from his seat. "And believe it or not, the supplies they brought north weren't only for the army. Some of the English nobles brought household goods to furnish the Scottish castles they were sure would be theirs tonight. Can you believe such conceit?"

Kathryn said, "Mayhap I'll find something to take back to decorate Homelea."

Adam chuckled but Bryan scowled. Thinking he had to be tired and perhaps in pain, Kathryn raised her eyebrows and tried to signal Adam. Bless him, he understood and said, "Well, it's been a long, eventful day, brother. You should rest." He inclined his head toward her. "Kathryn, Bryan. Good night."

BRYAN'S HEAD ACHED AND HE LONGED TO SLEEP but there was still much to do. He reached for his sword and a cloth to clean it when Kathryn caught his hand and said, "You look tired, husband."

"I am." He hoped she would simply leave him to his morose thoughts for the night but knowing Kathryn, that was unlikely.

"Why did we spend the evening setting up a new camp? Shouldn't we be preparing to leave?" she asked.

"Anxious as I am to be gone from here, we must stay until the dead are buried, the living paid their wages, and the hostages and prisoners are exchanged. It could take weeks, Kathryn."

She sighed. "That long?"

"I'm afraid so."

She gently took the cleaning cloth from his hand and said, "In that case, could we leave some of the work until tomorrow?" She smiled and he realized she was right.

"Aye, it's been a trying day."

She reached for his hand but he pulled it away. She looked at him in confusion, mirroring his own emotions. He wanted Kathryn more than ever, but knew that he didn't deserve her or her love.

He stood up, careful to move slowly lest his head pound again. "Kathryn, I . . . I need to sleep alone tonight."

He expected her to argue, but she said, "I imagine you do. But I would feel better if you stayed with me so I can check on you through the night. Hard though your head may be, that was quite a blow, and it would ease my mind if you'd allow me to watch over you."

Tell her now.

"You can't still want me for a husband. I will return to Homelea and help you rebuild, but if I learned anything today, it is that I can't stay once that is accomplished."

Surprise and then anger coursed across her expressive face. "What sort of nonsense are you spouting now? Did that blow to your head eliminate what little sense you had?"

"Kathryn—"

"Or perhaps you've forgotten that we spoke words of devotion and commitment. That we bound ourselves to each other in your tent."

"No, I haven't forgotten any of that."

"Good. Because I will not listen to you tell me that you can't be my husband because you weren't able to protect me today."

Did she know him so well that she could read his mind?

She stared at him, eyes blazing. "That's what you're thinking, isn't it?"

She didn't give him a chance to agree or disagree. "Bryan." She softened her tone. "Bryan. Don't you see? You may not always be able to protect me or Isobel."

"That's exactly why—"

Gently she placed her hand over his lips. "You can't protect me from everything, Bryan. But don't you see? God provided for us today—he sent Adam to teach Fergus to fight so that when you couldn't save me, God could. Through Fergus. And Adam."

"That's absurd."

"It is not absurd and you'd know it if you'd simply trust God."

Could it truly be as easy as that? All he needed to do was trust that God would see to their well being? Of all of them? He wanted to believe it. The mere thought of it seemed to lift a sack of stones from between his shoulders. He closed his eyes and raised his face to heaven. Then he opened his eyes and looked at his wife.

He wanted to push her away, push God away and go back to believing that he controlled his life because God didn't care about him. But only a caring God would have looked down on the Scottish army this morning and made sure that justice prevailed. Truly their victory was a miracle of enormous proportion, one not to be ignored. What more would it take for Bryan to believe that God cared about the world he'd created?

"Kathryn, whatever would I do without you?" He pulled her into his arms and held her tight. She struggled to loosen his grip so they could see each other's faces. She spoke again. "Will you doubt God every time he answers a prayer with an answer you don't like or don't understand?"

He shook his head. "Probably. But I am convinced that our

victory today could only have happened through the grace of a benevolent God."

She smiled at him. "I'm glad you feel that way."

"You are amazing, Kathryn. And you are, as always, right."

He could feel the smile that warmed his face as Kathryn's love and God's grace gave him peace. Bryan cradled her face in his hand. "Scotland is free now." With a steady gaze and firm voice he said. "And I am free to give my heart. We can return to Homelea and build a future for Isobel and our children." Bryan wished he could somehow capture the expression on his wife's wonderful face and hold it in his heart forever. Love shone from her eyes and Bryan felt blessed. "I love you, Kathryn."

She kissed his cheek. "As I love you. And I will spend the rest of my life thanking God I yielded my home, and my heart, to Black Bryan Mackintosh."